A CURE FOR GRAVITY

ARTHUR ROSENFELD

A TOM DOHERTY ASSOCIATES BOOK
NEW YORK

For Janelle, for everything

And to Tasman, welcome to the world

This is a work of fiction. All the characters and events portrayed in this book are either products of the author's imagination or are used fictitiously.

A CURE FOR GRAVITY

Copyright © 2000 by Arthur Rosenfeld

A Forge Book
Published by Tom Doherty Associates, LLC
175 Fifth Avenue
New York, NY 10010

www.tor.com

Forge® is a registered trademark of Tom Doherty Associates, LLC.

ISBN: 0-812-56566-5

First edition: September 2000
First mass market edition: July 2001

Printed in the United States of America

0 9 8 7 6 5 4 3 2 1

"[A] charming tale. . . . There's a bravura innocence at the heart of this offbeat novel."   —*Publishers Weekly*

"A touching ghost story that eludes easy comparison to any other book."   —*Booklist*

"A zesty, comic, high-speed American gothic."
      —*Kirkus Reviews*

"*A Cure for Gravity* is the kind of stunning surprise that comes along once a year, if we're lucky. It's like expecting a $90 bicycle for Christmas, and getting a brand new Harley instead. . . . It will be the rare reader who turns the last page without a lump in the throat and a smile on the lips."
      —*Sun-Sentinel*, Ft. Lauderdale, FL

"This wonderful novel doesn't just cure gravity, it cures all matters of heart, mind, and soul. I felt better after reading the title alone, imagine how I felt after reading the whole book."
      —Neil Simon, Pulitzer Prize winning playwright of
      The Odd Couple, Lost in Yonkers, and
      Brighton Beach Memoirs

"Rosenfeld uses the tangle of lives he has created to tell a story that has its mystical moments—but is every bit about the needs of the living. This makes it a love story, of course, and a sweet, telling one at that."
      —*The New York Daily News*

"*A Cure for Gravity* may be seen as mainstream fiction, that just happens to be fast, funny, outrageous, and full of heart."   —*The Mercury News*, San Jose, CA

"*A Cure for Gravity* roars along at the pace of an open-throttled motorcycle."   —*The Tribune*, South Bend, IN

"A novel of surprising imagination and stylistic daring. . . . *A Cure for Gravity* rises to near greatness as a piece of home-grown Magical Realism. Touching, scary, hilarious."
      —*Knight Ridder News Service*

I am deeply indebted, first and foremost, to the Sackler family and Michael Friedman, without whose years of patronage pursuing my dream of writing fiction would have never been possible.

I would also like to thank my good old friend Dennis O'Flaherty, for his unflagging exhortations to excellence. If it's any good, it's because of you, Dennis.

Kudos also to Karla Zounek, my editor at Tor/Forge Books, who had the courage to go where no one had gone before, and to the William Morris Agency's own Matt Bialer, without whom this book would have remained forever in a desk drawer, shedding tears.

ONE

❧

Early that first morning, before the birds shook the dew off their backs, before the street sweepers emerged, before even one footprint appeared on the deck of a sailing boat or one short-order cook took stock of his eggs, even before God thrust his great clammy hands down through the mist and grabbed South Florida in his hot, pulsing grip, Mercury Gant stepped out into the dawn and prepared to abandon his life.

He was a man approaching middle years, and he had seen some things. In particular, he had seen the rhythmic contractions of the chambered nautilus, a spiral-shaped cephalopod which swims by gathering water into its shell in a long inhale and then suddenly expelling it, with great force, so as to shoot like a star through the water. He figured out that life worked more or less the same way the nautilus did, with long periods of energy-gathering quietude followed by periods of massive change. He felt certain that his long inhale was over, and wondered, as he bent to secure the saddlebags on his touring motorcycle, what kind of new life this machine—which held all his remaining material goods, and which supported his very existence on two narrow patches of rubber—would bring him.

He looked the motorcycle over carefully, because he

knew how a great number of miles—the harmonics of tiresong on the tarmac, the repetitive compression and rebound of springs and shock absorbers, his weight shifting in the seat, the toeclicks of the changing gears— could slowly tear a bike apart, loosening things, displacing adjustments, creating a whole constellation of problems which, if not corrected early, might mean nighttime trouble on some lonely shoulder of the road.

He took a deep breath, rubbed his eyes, and performed a couple of toe touches, feeling the sinews stretch back there behind his legs. He twisted his back sharply to get that old, satisfying crack from his spine, and then, ready to continue the job at hand, he walked around the machine, surveying every nut and bolt, testing the tires, the tension, the alignment, the curves. He checked with his finger for wetness around seals, palpated hoses for turgidity, tugged on electrical connections to make sure nothing was loose. He patted the perfect, original paint on the twenty-year-old gas tank—no dings, scratches, or dents—and looked with satisfaction at the aluminum cylinders sticking out of the side.

Feeling the true professional—he had been riding for years—he ran his hands down over his long Australian cattle drover's coat, a garment of dark brown oiled cotton, checking the myriad pockets for the items he'd need handy: the tire gauge, the map, the multitool replete with screwdrivers and pliers, hex wrenches and blades, quarters for tollbooths, wallet, cash, extra key. He examined himself in the bike's side mirror, smiling in an attempt to make his metallic silver eyes sparkle the way they once had. They had been like flying saucers embarrassed by a full sun back when, but these days he couldn't get even a glint out of them. His face was still high-boned and handsome, though, with gray only at the temples and a strong jaw and good teeth, leaving him looking like the army poster boy he had been long ago. He saw a spot on his cheek he'd missed shaving, and rubbed it with his hand. Leave it be, he told himself. One can die chasing perfection.

He donned his earplugs, and his helmet and his gloves, and took one last look at the rented Deerfield Beach walk-up he had occupied for the last six years. He had mopped and swept it, painted and pasted and recarpeted it, not so much to recover the security deposit—he had more than enough money saved up—but to achieve a proper closure, to make a clean break. He had, however, left a cardboard box full of trash sitting in the driveway, the cord from a busted Venetian blind dangling over the edge. The cord bothered him, and he nudged it back in with the tip of his boot, noticing in the process a photograph sticking to the bottom of an empty can of varnish. He peeled the picture off, looked at it with a jump in his throat, and jammed it into his coat.

Wishing he could do the same with his heart, he reset the bike's trip odometer to zero.

———

Click, clack go Umberto Santana's feet on the sidewalk, but sloppily, due to the lifts in his shoes. As sure of what he is about to do as he has ever been of anything, the boy strides resolutely into the Boca Raton Savings Bank and waits quietly in line. When his turn comes, he puts the pistol down on the counter right along with the bag, and beckons.

Ho, says the teller as his face drains of blood. There is training—to keep the thief talking, to press the panic button down low—but the authority of the Beretta, professional sidearm of choice all over the world, scrambles his finger and tongue to deli meats. The teller's a mess. He turns white and whiter awaiting the word.

Money, Umberto commands at last, his finger tight on the trigger. Unlike the teller, he's sticking to the plan. Beat down the Latin accent, talk less than a mouse, hide under the blond wig, trim the line that connects your bleached eyebrows, shave close the light mosaic of stubble on your chin. Fool those bank cameras with the big looping gestures you've been practicing, none of which are really your own, none of which are even characteristically Latin. Speak in deep tones that make you seem older. Have a nose like a Rottweiler and smell fear in advance. Smell impending action too. And behind-the-scenes decisions being made.

Sniff for panic.

Be ready for anything.

Be a hypersensitive creature of crime.

Hundreds, Umberto says in his best false voice, but nothing marked and nothing bound.

The teller makes no move. Umberto racks the slide over the empty magazine, driving a bullet made of air into the waiting chamber.

Be quick or die, he says.

The teller reconnects his brain and fingers and begins filling the bag. Despite his terror, he manages to be amazed by the way the material expands. It's like a gym suit for a damned grizzly bear. How did the thief know they'd be flush with unmarked bills today? The bank's air conditioner roars. Shivering, the teller wishes he'd stayed home.

At the next window, a woman has just seen the gun, and she begins wheezing, a bronchospasmic attack. Her young son presses his head against her chest and hears her buzzing like a chain saw.

Asthma, he nods grimly.

I'm all out of money, the teller informs Umberto.

So get more. You think I got all day here?

The teller moves to the next window, whispers something terse and low to his coworker, and dips into another drawer for hundreds. He comes back with another stack of bills, and then another. As his haul grows, Umberto allows himself a brief, mental exultation. He's doing it! He's changing everything. And it's so easy! He doesn't even sound like himself! Certain that someone has pushed the silent alarm button by now, he urges the teller to get more money from the vault.

Get back here in ninety seconds or I start shooting, he says.

The teller dashes off and returns with an armful, disgorging it into the sack.

One more load, says Umberto, checking his watch, knowing he is cutting it close.

The teller obliges, wondering desperately why help has not yet arrived. Not realizing what's happening, the customers waiting on line, between the ropes, grow restless. There are more than twenty of them, clad to a one in gray uniforms. They are gardeners and maids from the resort a few blocks down, waiting to cash their checks. Umberto is dressed just like they are, even though he does not now and has not ever worked at the resort. It is a good, clever cover, and one that for a time will serve him well.

It's Friday, it's hot, and grand plans abound. Nobody pays attention to the suffocating woman, at least until she drops to her knees, her hands at her throat, her face a blue ocean foaming jellies of spit. Her little boy presses an inhaler to her lips. It doesn't seem to work, maybe because the boy doesn't know how to squeeze it, maybe because the spasm is beyond release. Mommy's not going to make it.

Inside her glass cubicle, the branch manager is on the phone with a yacht broker who is trying to seduce her. She thanks him for the roses on her desk as she fingers their petals and wonders why he chose yellow, which she was raised to believe is the color of condolence.

She looks out. Something is very wrong. There is a pulsing, nearly frozen tableau where a busy bank should be, with people swaying and shifting but no bank business being done. A well-built resort groundskeeper sashays out the door, a bulging bag slung over his shoulder.

The hell? the manager mutters.

The dying woman finally drops to the floor, where she flops right and left like a tiddlywink. This is what has come of personally bringing her son to the bank to start his own savings account rather than doing her banking by phone, as she usually does. The little boy screams out. The manager slams down the phone and rushes over to help. She makes a strong effort with her weight and her hands, pushing and pulsing and even cracking a couple of ribs, all this without knowing that the victim is a United States senator named Vicky Rule, and that the boy's name is Stefan, and that Vicky will be more famous in death than in life, but Stefan, his face all over the papers, will be more famous still.

Finally, sirens converge and officers of the law pour in, powerful automatic weapons at the ready, because recently the Boca Raton City Council has approved the police chief's request for arms that are a match for those of the drug cartels. Umberto's precise whereabouts are of greater interest than an overweight woman on the ground, so by the time the paramedics arrive, Vicky is looking down on the scene from the loft of a gull, feeling no sadness and no pain at all. With a knowing that transcends deep, she grasps that little Stefan will be okay and that she will dance with him again, the next time around, perhaps as his uncle or as his little dog. As she flutters off for a last look at home and husband, Stefan goes into shock. He bats eyelashes like a desert camel's and won't loosen his death grip on his mom's cooling hand. A newspaperman comes in and snaps pictures.

Stubborn Stefan.

Poor Vicky.

Bullhorns. Reassurance. No shots have been fired.

Outside the bank, Umberto runs to a beat-up old Yamaha motorcycle. It is parked behind a clothing store two doors down—such a ratbike nobody would look at it twice. He pulls off his blond wig and sheds his stolen resort uniform, exchanging it for motorcycling leathers which he pulls from a tailpack, which he then fills with the money. He slings a leg over the old beast and fires her up. He has no idea that he will soon be blamed for Vicky Rule's death. He does not even know she has died. He is thinking only of getting away safely.

Inside the bank, tellers are weeping in each other's arms. The manager is somberly handing out yellow roses. As Vicky Rule's corpse is rolled out on a stretcher, Stefan Rule puts up a terrible fight. He claws at the paramedics, he screams and wails. He tears a piece of his hair out, actually unable to imagine life without his mother. In the end, only the manager can comfort him, because she smells like Godiva chocolates and Vicky always smelled like chocolate too.

Umberto is accustomed to drag-racing two-wheeled machines, to burning tires, to fixating on a speck in the distance and bringing it to him instantly, with the throttle. He's used to winning races in Cutler Ridge, and has even been out on the track down in Homestead a few times, but not more than a few, because track time is costly. But this time, leaving the alley, he does no smokeouts, no burnouts, no wheelies, no spins. This time he motors sedately as a butterfly on a nectar trail, leaning one way, then the other, casually warming up the tires in case there is a chase, but mostly listening to the sirens go past him, as the cops look for a blond in a gray work uniform with a sack over his back.

His confidence has been so galvanized by the heist that he doesn't feel the need to ride quickly. He makes a leisurely run down the interstate and ends up in Coconut Grove. He parks his bike, slings the money bag around his neck, and buys himself a smoothie—a mixture of pineapple and mango, papaya, coconut, melon, and lime—not because he can't decide between flavors but because he wants to burn the taste of the tropics deep into his tongue. He knows he's going to have to travel far away, and he wants the memory to last. He shucks and poses for the summer parade of girls going by— doughy girls bubbling out of their jeans; tall, tan, stringy girls too; redheads and blondes, white-skinned and dark. His fingers stray to his bagful of cash.

Look at me, he silently cries. Lissen for a minute, will ju? I've got so much in my pants ju can't imagine. Come ride wit me. Jes' for a couple of hours, okay? Do ju like motorcycles? The wind, it's like a big warm kiss in summer. How 'bout it?

The girl behind the counter taps him on the shoulder, carefully, as if whatever is making him move like he's moving might be contagious.

Here's your smoothie.

Umberto takes it, noticing that she looks vaguely like his lover, a musky, dark, intensely pretty girl with a beauty mark on her cheek, a girl who pushes her panties aside for him but never actually takes them off, there, in the parking lot behind McDonald's. Graciela. He feels a stab at the idea of leaving her, and with that pain, somewhere up in heaven, his star, the pinhole projection of energies that is Umberto Santana, moves suddenly outward on an intercept course with another star. Older, deeper, redder, quieter.

But strong.

———

On the other side of the country, as far from South Florida as one can get, blind Audrey Bishop brings a Port Townsend oyster to her lips and delicately sips the Northwestern brine.

Yum, she says. It tastes like Bartok.

Her Grandma Ruth smiles at the reference to the classical music she always has playing, but the smile doesn't last long. No smile has since the baby came to her, in swaddling clothes, five years ago. Audrey's little head was covered with blond hair then, as now, but not the baby blond that goes away, that can in fact end up any color at all, but the ash-blond of a mature woman, streaked with a premature gray that matched those crazy silver eyes.

I found a pearl, so I ate it, Audrey announces. Can you imagine how many pearls I have inside me by now?

I *can* imagine. You're worth a fortune, you know that?

Audrey beams. Some kind of light comes off her face. Ruth wonders whether it's a love beam straight up to the kid's mother, wherever she is, looking down. She also wonders if she has done the right thing, sending those letters, agreeing to bring shocking change to their little world. She shakes the thought away as if it was a cricket on her shoulder. She's getting old. She can't wade for oysters forever. Her feet stiffen in the chilly water and ache for hours afterward. Sometimes a broken shell cuts her toe and a red river of blood runs away in the water. Don't tell the child. Just keep digging and shuffling, probing and wading.

Ruth's not a complainer.

When your grandfather was alive, he would bake these with fresh spinach, she says. Oysters Rockefeller. A tiny taste of cheese on the top. Gorgonzola.

Outside, a thunderhead builds in a blue sky, the kind of violent blue that comes to the Olympic Peninsula, but only in summer. Ruth watches it coalesce. Audrey takes another oyster up and the juice dribbles down her mouth. Ruth wishes the little girl could see the cloud.

It's going to rain soon, says Audrey. Crash, bang. Trees are going to burn.

Ruth marvels.

Can the child smell the smoke already?

———

The bank has become a nestcone of termites, a big one, tall and hard and brown, the way they grow in tropical scrub, with layer after layer inside, everything mapped out and working according to plan. The FBI is there, and a forensics team. Statements are being taken, and the skills of a sketch artist employed. The bank videotapes are being reviewed, fibers lifted from the carpet where Umberto stood patiently, prints and the tiniest possible flecks of metal from the counter where the loaded pistol lay.

He beckoned? queries the FBI man in charge.

That's right, replies the teller.

With his little finger?

That's what I said.

His pinkie?

Yes!

How odd. And the gun, it was a Beretta?

That's what I told you.

You're familiar with guns?

Never heard of Beretta, if that's what you're asking, but that's what it was. I saw the name on the barrel. You can't forget something aimed at your heart.

Stainless or blue?

Neither. Black.

Black is blue. It's gun talk. Look, what about the man? Was he nervous?

The tape should show you all this. The color of the gun, whether he was nervous or not.

Tell me anyway. Was he nervous?

I was nervous. He seemed like he was taking a walk in the park.

A walk in the park, the FBI man repeated. A woman is dead.

He probably doesn't know that. He was out the door before she expired.

He'll know soon enough. His type likes to watch himself on TV. You say he looked familiar?

I said he was handsome. He looked like Oscar de la Hoya with blond hair.

A dye job?

What am I, a hairdresser? Maybe it was a wig, maybe it was his own hair. I'm not sure.

Did he walk like a fighter or just look like one?

The question puzzles the teller.

How do fighters walk?

Jouncy, like their calf muscles need stretching. Like their heels never quite touch the ground.

FBI agent, Robert "the Eagle" Cooper, was a fighter in college. A Golden Gloves boy. He knows how fighters walk and stalk.

This guy didn't walk on his toes, if that's what you mean. But he was young.

How young?

Twenty-five. The teller shrugged. Less than thirty, for sure.

Thank you, says Cooper. That's all for now.

There is something about the ballsiness of the crime that worries him. Simple and brazen. In his experience the two don't go together. Brazen usually means you've got the thing figured out, you know the odds, the ins, the outs, you've got a plan and a network in place. You don't get brazen if you're just one guy. You get brazen if you're part of a team and have a safety net. Cooper is cold afraid that the guy he's dealing with is just plain lucky, and the lucky ones are the ones who end up in dead files, scot-free, never caught. That cannot happen here—there's a U.S. senator involved.

Seal the place, he tells the cops working under him. Nobody gets in or out until we get a statement from each and every one of these resort workers. One of them might know our man, or even be in on the fun. And somebody get that kid more chocolate before he starts screaming again. It's time to call the father.

One of the hotel maids winks at Cooper, then smiles. She's missing two front teeth.

He sighs. He doesn't feel much like an eagle today.

TWO

❧

Umberto returned home briefly, just to put together what he needed to disappear. His father, Pedro, was there, in front of the TV, a Hatuey beer in his hand.

Hola, he greeted his son.

Adios, Umberto replied.

There was something in the way he said it that made the old man get up out of the chair. This was a man who didn't get up much—who didn't go out.

Ju going to work?

I'm gonna take a long ride, if ju gotta know.

They know about this at the shop? Pedro asked, referring to the motorcycle dealer where Umberto had been working as a mechanic, the kind of mechanic without factory training, the kind of mechanic who changed oil and wrestled the unyielding rubber of brand-new tires onto cold metal rims all day.

Umberto took a long look at his dad, knowing the old man was only asking because he depended on Umberto's paycheck to make the rent and buy his beer and sit in front of the tube, belching and scratching himself.

Sure, he said. Those guys know everything about me.

When ju coming back? Pedro tried to be casual, but he couldn't quite pull it off. There were white flecks at the corners of his mouth, spittle so fine it spored on contact with air.

Umberto didn't answer. Instead he carried the loot bag into his room, locked the door behind him, and spilled the cash out on the bed.

There were mountains of it. He felt elation coming on like a cocaine corkscrew. He wasn't a junkie, but he was still a teenager in Miami. He knew what things felt like, the crack of the whip, the melting of snow. None of that compared to this. With trembling fingers he set to counting.

Pedro knocked on the door.

Ju can't just go off, he shouted. I won't let ju.

It was a show of false bravado, and they both knew it. It had been a long time since the old man had used his belt or his fists. Umberto was bigger and stronger, and although he wasn't a bad son—in many ways he was a very good one, considering the burden his father had become—he wasn't about to take any guff, not when he was paying the bills with knuckles skinned flat as ocean snapper. Still, there was one thing about his father that commanded his attention, and that was the old man's intimate relationship with the *orishas*, the gods and goddesses of Caribbean Santeria. The old man brought offerings and muttered prayers and sang songs to them, to *Oshún*—who seemed to answer—for money and to *Obatalá*—on whom the jury was still out—to protect his soul.

Yeah, yeah.

Open the door! Pedro hammered.

Oye! Chill out, will ju? This isn't Cuba and ju are not Castro.

Umberto wanted to finish the count. He was beginning to get the idea that he'd gotten more than he'd bargained for. The piles were so tight and thick—banks could squeeze money together, that much was for sure—that even a little one held maybe a couple of hundred bills.

Twenty thousand bucks. And there were piles and piles and piles.

More thuds on the door. Only the soft eye of the fist for the old man, regular thuds, like a metronome designed to annoy.

Umberto made a quick job of dumping the loot into the laundry bag he hung on the back of the door before opening it.

Will ju leave me alone? he demanded.

I don't want ju to go. Ju are only seventeen. Ju need to stay around.

I don't need to do anything, okay? I'm going to see the country. I'm young. It's summertime.

What about ju job?

I don't gotta worry about my job right now, okay? Business is slow. It's too hot to ride bikes.

Don't go too far on that thing. It's dangerous.

I built it myself, okay? Put it together outta the box. It's perfect.

There's crazies out there. Drinkers.

Like ju? Umberto inquired.

Pedro's eyes narrowed. He wheezed, tapped his stomach, considered his son. Later, after Umberto was lost, and much later, after Umberto was found again, Pedro would review the boy's life, floating the memory in bottle after bottle of the watery Cuban brew. Umberto painting with his fingers, Umberto on his bicycle, Umberto in the arms of his mother, when she was still young and fresh and satisfied with her life, her hair dark and long and clinging moistly, beautifully, to her forehead. Umberto, in flagrante, trembling with fear at the sight of his father's balled hands, the young white girl with the nose ring and tatoos wriggling out from under him and dashing off like a chastened albino squirrel.

But right then, the old man was thinking only of the money and of how long he could last alone. He backed out of the room, afraid, and Umberto hauled the soft saddlebags from under the bed and began packing. He wasn't an experienced traveler, so at first he couldn't fit everything in. Then he asked himself whether he really needed three pairs of bluejeans—one tapered, one boot-cut, one slimfit—and whether some of the underwear couldn't stay home.

Laundromats.

He pared down. He knew he wouldn't hit cold weather, but he knew he'd hit rain. Out with the cotton, in with the nylon. The rain suit, the Playtex living gloves, the soft shoes. Stuff. Zip. Sit on it to make it flat. He had to ask himself why he hadn't done this before. Why he hadn't had the bike all ready to roll. Why he had stopped home at all. He supposed that last was like knocking wood. That and maybe he wanted one last look at what his old man had become and at the life he was leaving behind.

The money fit into the expanded tailpack, with the exception of one large stack of bills. He took a long sniff of that one, the sweet smell of ink, and shoved it into his pants, up front, by his navel, wondering if the Highway Patrol ran with dog noses out the window, on the high-speed sniff, on the prowl, looking for him. He speculated that he might be taken for a drug runner with all that cash.

But where is the Halliburton case?

Where are the duds?

The Porsche?

The girl on his arm?

The fiery burn in his veins?

He closed his bedroom door quietly, draped in his goods, and walked past where his father was sitting. He pulled out the wad of bills and tossed it. Pedro caught it in midair, like he'd been expecting it, and brushed through it with his thumb, casually, like it was nothing to him. Like he held twenty large every day.

Buy Mama something nice, said Umberto bitterly as he went out to his motorcycle. And then have another beer.

The ride across the Everglades devours Gant's coat.
There are wings on his cheeks and harsh prayers in his
teeth. There are gadflies and dragons and mozzies and
gnats. The sun comes up behind him, and a second,
pearlescent layer of insect chum affixes itself to his face
shield, filtering the gathering light into a rainbow too
beautiful to smear, creating a psychedelic trip across Alligator Alley, with its vast skies and its methane pockets
and waves of schlieren rising off the giant grassy swamp.
Gant fights flying bits of truck tire from overnight long-
haul men and glances with mild interest at the low reptile
predators by the side of the road.

Those teeth!

The bike hums along happily in the breeze. Buttoned
up he may be, but Gant gets a wasp sting at the base of
his throat. For a time it hurts him to swallow. Egrets fly
in from the beach, great blue herons, higher up than
they're wont to be, modern pterosaurs riding the El Niño
wind in from the Gulf of Mexico. Gant's arms and
shoulders are sore. His wrists throb. It's too hot and too
windy to escape Florida completely today, and part of
him is glad. He's headed for the other coast, clear across
the state from Deerfield, and wants a proper, contempla-
tive good-bye to the state, replete with something bitter-
sweet and alcoholic, something to taste a sunset by.

While Umberto robs the bank, Gant finds the sandy
shoal they call Captiva, an island clear out on the Gulf,
on what used to be clean water, where silent snook
cruise the shallows beneath the Sanibel bridge and where
manatees the size of paddling cattle still peek out of
tributaries for a taste of the salty from a bath of the
sweet. Amid Bentleys and Benzes and hideaway homes,
Gant motors sedately out as far as he can go, and finds
a little motel with a white picket fence, therein to sleep
off the heat.

Later, a short walk takes him to open water. He

watches waves come in from Tampico. He mixes his own drink on the sand, an Ezra Brooks bourbon with a strong squeeze of lime, and sips good-bye to the sun. He doesn't even think about calling the Northwest.

It is still too soon.

———

A United States senator dead and $340,000 missing. Agent Eagle Cooper, the raptor who can't see his man. Not even on the videotape, on which he has been counting and which has turned out to be a sorry mess. Grainy, with people moving like organic pogo sticks, their legs merged together. Lack of detail. A head here, a blurry arm there. White shirts. Dark skirts. The condition finally traced to an accumulation of dust on the lens, the result of the ozone from the air conditioner duct right in front of the camera.

Charged particles drawn to glass. Umberto no more than a sober mover with blond hair and a deliberate pace, one sidelong look at the camera revealing big dark glasses and a collar pulled high.

The interviews with the resort employees helped even less. Most of them didn't speak English, and no matter the language, there was no talk of the thief. How could people be so dull and so blind as to notice neither a bank robbery in progress nor poor dying Vicky Rule as she clutched her throat and flapped her wings and gasped for air and blued down?

The Fort Lauderdale Federal Building's climate-control system was on the blink, and the bank robbery case file was stuck to Cooper's blotter. It was so hot inside that the BATF gunchasers on the top floor fried eggs on their sill. Cooper hit his desk in discomfort and frustration, bringing sweat droplets into the air. He ran through some possibilities in his mind. The perpetrator was a blond. The perpetrator was a brunette pretending to be a blond. The perpetrator was blond a pretending to be a brunette pretending to be blond. And there were other decisions. What if he were a she? The teller was adamant, but another witness said he walked delicately and that he swung his hips. Big woman? Transsexual? Cross-dresser? Drag queen? This was South Florida, after all. Cooper's previous assignment, Greenwich, Connecticut, would have presented fewer variables.

And the money. How did the bastard know the bank was moving cash in for a private client who had decided to liquidate stock holdings for an antique car auction? Clean cash, too. Who withdrew this kind of cash anymore? Drug dealers, that's who. Russian mafia. The Cali Cartel. Maybe the car collector had engaged this cool thief to run a scam on his own FDIC-insured funds. Sweet, Cooper thought, shaking his head, but also pretty far-fetched. More likely, the perp had just been lucky.

He tapped an almost useless 8×10 blowup made from the videotape. The tip of his pen made a little x on Umberto's groin, gouging deep into the paper, flaking off the emulsion.

Not *that* lucky, he said out loud, thinking of Vicky Rule, thinking of that little boy's face on the front page of the morning paper, thinking of the high stink he'd had to wave off from his boss.

I'm going to get you, Blondie.

———

Umberto covered the same hot strip as Gant did, a few hours behind him but at greater velocity. To the fleeing felon, Alligator Alley was an obstacle to be conquered—leaving the state was his primary concern—and he did so bent low over the gas tank of his shiny black cruise missile Triumph, the fairing cheating a hole in the air so pure and so round that, unlike Gant, only the very top of his helmet suffered insect hits. The rusty old Yamaha and its telltale license plate were history. Umberto had shredded the plate with metal shears, filed the frame and engine numbers, and thrown the painted parts into a

Dumpster. The Triumph was a virgin, bought just for the flight, the bees knees for speed. It reminded him of Batman's bat cycle—he was a great fan of comic books and superheroes—and made him feel like the caped crusader himself.

Behind him, the fabric fringes of the bag of money flapped angrily in the wind, but only when he violated the cocoon of stillness by stretching an arm or a leg. The rest of the time the money was as safe and secure as a kangaroo's joey because Umberto used a sophisticated radar detector which also watched for laser. He blazed on toward Naples. For a solid mile his tires kissed Gant's very own tracks. He didn't stop for the wind, which had eased up anyway, and he didn't stop for the sunset. He was New Orleans bound. He thought of Bourbon Street and of bars. He thought of vampires with thin black goatees and wooden canes, and of chicory coffee and hookers on balconies and side streets and parasols and rednecks wrestling guitars. He thought of the wrought iron gates to the cemeteries he'd seen in travel brochures. He rode on, and just after midnight he tucked into a truckstop motel outside of Bayou La Batre. He pushed the bike into the room and used the money for a headfall.

Sweet dreams, Umberto.

You karma cheater, you.

————

At the edge of the Appalachicola Forest, the sky sets to drooling on Gant. He pulls into a diner that was once a Chinese restaurant. Obviously, chow mein didn't fly up here by Tallahassee, as a two-egg breakfast special is now advertised in the window. He drives his bike up under the eave of the pagoda; scalloped wood, painted red and trimmed in gold. He can almost hear the cymbals crashing. He can almost see steppe horsemen collide.

Gong.

Inside it's frigid with conditioned air. The windows

are fogged; the tables empty. Newspaper tidings of the Rules are strewn about; Stefan and Vicky and bereaved husband Tim. There's a tasteless photo of Vicky's feet on the stretcher, caught in the glass doors of the bank. There's another of Stefan's tear-streaked face. The editorial page is full of angry speculation into what kind of a society we've become. So is the *Miami Herald*. These are the headlines:

Senator Dies While Bored Crowd Looks On
Wherefore Art Thou, FBI?
Video Security/False Security
Child Watches Mother's Last Gasp

The waitress comes up. She too has seen the world at war, and she has even seen Lindbergh fly. The fancy motorcycle on the other side of the window doesn't impress her.

What'll it be?

An order of wheat toast, please.

We've only got white, she announces with a defiant look.

Make it white, then.

To drink?

Tea.

We've only got Lipton. Nothing fancy. Not here.

Make it Lipton.

Eggs?

No thank you. He taps his heart. Cholesterol.

We've got Eggbeaters.

Here?

This gets a small smile.

He agrees to an omelette.

Terrible thing. She nods at the paper.

The bank robbery or the senator dying?

Both, I guess. That poor little boy. They'll get the thief in the end. They'll hang him high.

Not his fault about the senator.

She gets a certain set to her hips. There's no arguing with her.

No robbery, no gun. No gun, no asthma attack.

He planned a robbery, not a murder. Planned it well, too. Three hundred and forty thousand in cash.

A shake of the head. A smoothing of the ketchup-stained apron.

He'll get what he deserves.

You think?

Most people do, in the end.

I hope you're right, mutters Gant.

But she's already gone.

Tables to wipe, glasses to clean, napkins to fold.

Cold coffee to toss.

&ot;

Ruth Bishop stared resolutely at the unraveling road, afraid that if she looked away for even a moment she might lose track of her life and get lost, like time itself often did, here among the tall, dark, sour trees of the Olympic Peninsula. She made a turn and was rewarded with a peek through the tall evergreens at the cold, flat water of Discovery Bay. Some fishermen, customers of her downtown shoe store, had told her that whales had appeared, inexplicably, out of season.

I'd like to see those whales, Audrey said.

How did you know I was thinking of whales?

These strange telepathies were growing more frequent, which scared her sometimes. Ruth didn't realize that the whole world works on telepathy, and that anyway Audrey was only receiving what Ruth herself put out.

I just knew.

Well, shall we go look for them?

Audrey sat up excitedly, her little back ramrod straight.

Now?

Smiling, Ruth took a dirt turnoff down to the bay. It

was a back road she hadn't used in years. Maybe nobody had, the way the brambles sang against the side of the bus. Things were changing in Port Townsend, Washington—more yuppies, fewer rebels—but the enclave remained a great place to hide. She liked the town bumper sticker:

We're All Here Because We're Not All There

Two rocks struck the underside of the bus in sharp succession. *Knock knock.*

Come in! cried Audrey.

She liked to play with her grandmother, pretend she was out of it when in fact she knew precisely what was going on. She knew they were driving on dirt. She'd heard the sound of gravel when they first left sealed road.

They drove just a little bit out onto the beach. It was more rocks than sand, with a thick black layer of tangled seaweed down by the water. Ruth parked and unhooked the kayak. The tie-downs were rusted and it took some work, but at length Ruth got it to slide down off the bus. The little boat had been up there for nearly two years, since the fishing boat belonging to her husband, Hiram, had been found, empty, nudged gently up on some shoals, with no body, no blood, no signs of a struggle, no note.

She lifted Audrey into the front seat.

You remember how?

Of course, Gramma! You worry too much!

Ruth pushed them off with a run and hopped in without wetting her feet. She'd been good at this once. Really good. So good she could use a thin little Inuit paddle with barely a blade to speak of and barely a ripple made under steam. An Eskimo roller, she was, too, before her blood grew too thin to take the cold.

Make a grenade of the hips.

Quick, draw in the breath.

Face the numbing cold, pull on the shaft, pop up like a sputtering geyser.

Ruth aimed the kayak straight out from shore. She figured the worst that could happen was that she and Audrey would have a bit of sea air. The best, well, maybe Audrey would get to hear a whale blow, way off in the distance. Ears like that child had, she could hear the sun come up over Coeur d'Alene.

Whales can tell if we're afraid, Audrey announced.

Really? How?

They can hear our hearts with sonar.

Did you learn that in school?

No, Grandpa told me.

A fog blew in, half mist, half drizzle, and pressed the sea so flat a horsefly could skate across it. Ruth wasn't worried. She was a fisherman's widow. She'd been in far worse. Audrey turned back with sightless eyes. She licked the rain from her lips.

Salty, she said.

And then it happened. So fast, Ruth hadn't the chance to utter even one sound. The huge black flank, the hovering tail, the flash of white chin, the beady eye.

Pffaaaa! The orca drenched them with the spew from its lungs.

Whale! cried Audrey, knowing, because to her ears he was as bombastic as Beethoven.

She leaned over to put her hand in the water.

No! cried her grandmother, envisioning gleaming white teeth.

The kayak rocked on the whale's headwave, but all that happened was that the huge flat head touched the little tiny hand for a brief instant, gently, before pulling back and down, invisible again.

Mommy! Audrey cried out, vibrating with pleasure.

Ruth could barely breathe. She tasted her own bile and coughed.

Gramma? Are you all right?

No answer.

Gramma?

I'm fine.

Mommy sent that whale to me, you know.

Your mother is dead ashes, and even when she was alive she hated anything bigger and stronger than she was, Ruth thought, but she didn't say it.

Shakily, she headed for shore.

———

Umberto Santana motored down Bourbon Street like a conquering Moor. His elbows were locked in push-up position, holding his chest up off the tank and the bars, and he hid inside his bright red helmet, his face shield dark, the mega-motor rumbling quietly beneath him. Moths clinging to the dark side of streetlights along the avenue charted his progress with a trembling in their wispy wings. A former football star, his belly now hanging low over his belt, pointed at Umberto's machine and crushed a beer can against his forehead in appreciation. Only fools and drunks were out on New Orleans streets in June. The hot, thick air was a curtain, and the play didn't start until long after sundown.

Umberto rode down to the bank of the Mississippi River and parked his bike by Audubon Park, chaining it carefully while pigeons clattered down. He slung the money bag around his neck and walked to Cafe du Monde, generating a line of sweat down his back which tickled him lightly as it ran.

Like a woman's fingernail.

Like Graciela's tongue.

Two thirty-five-year-old secretaries shared a plate of beignets and watched him appreciatively. Dark and handsome, thought one. Fit and beautiful, thought the other. He saw them staring, and he stopped.

Okay if I sit down?

They glanced at each other and touched knees excitedly beneath the table when he pulled out a chair, looping the strap of the money bag around his ankle and casually drawing it tight.

It's hot, one of the women said. My name is Betty.

She was chemically blonde, with dark roots and gaps between her teeth, but her body was ripe and her blouse wide open to show a lightly crinkled, aging cleavage.

That hole in the ozone layer. That sun.

A waiter came by, and the second woman, Lisle, suggested lemonade. She was brunette, lithe, pretty, nervous. Her skin was white and her neck bore red splotches. She had a habit of stretching her hands over her head, forcing her breasts upward against her white blouse. Umberto decided he liked her and ordered the lemonade.

You ladies aren't from New Orleans, are you?

He can beat the latino accent if he really, really tries.

Pittsburgh, lied Betty.

Chicago, Lisle said at the same time.

Why would you lie to me? Umberto inquired. Afraid I'm going to follow you home?

Would you? Lisle responded impulsively.

Everybody began laughing. Betty offered Umberto a beignet. He'd never had one before, but he didn't want them to know that. Seeing his hesitation, Lisle picked up the greasy pastry and held it to his lips. He touched the powdered sugar with his tongue, licking her deep purple fingernails on purpose, grazing her flesh with his teeth when he took a bite, making her shudder.

Love is hard to find, he said softly, but nothing else matters.

Lisle knew it was a line, but it melted her anyway. She licked her fingers and shuddered.

What about money? asked Betty.

Except money. Umberto smiled.

The sun dropped ever so slightly in the sky, but the temperature went up, trapped in the cocoon of high pressure over the Southeast. The humidity rose too, from the river. Lisle fanned herself with her napkin.

I simply must get out of this heat, she said.

Umberto signaled the waiter, and when he came over, pressed a hundred-dollar bill into his hand.

Bring me the check, he said. And some chocolate sauce to go.

Moments later he was walking behind the girls, mesmerized by the curves of their bare legs and the swing of their hips. They knew he was watching and tried not to sweat, but it was hotter than a baboon's breath, and by the time they got to their place, a gabled, balconied, pink-painted bed-and-breakfast joint off Napoleon, they were all dripping like swimmers. An elderly Canadian couple watched them walk up the stairs, Umberto's hands on two skirtlincs, three sets of footsteps clacking in unison on thinly carpeted boards.

They undressed him and put his muddy boots carefully by the door. Such precision! Such restraint! The room had a claw-foot bathtub, and they put him in it. They were excited by how young his body looked, a bit worried, too, but their lust won out. Betty shampooed him and Lisle followed the soap lines down. Umberto kept his eyes closed and thought of Graciela. When he was clean, the secretaries joined him in the tub. The hand shower became Umberto's weapon, fleshy mountains and valleys his prey. He sprayed them down, soaped them up, licked and caressed and bent them over as they all swallowed each other's histories, rocking the tub from where it had stood, impassively, for eighty-one years, having seen a thing or two.

Afterward, they huddled together, half asleep, sloshing a little to adjust here and there, adding cool water and spilling it onto the floor. On the ceiling below, in an empty room, the dark water stain grew in a ragged circle around a chandelier. Finally, the drops let go and fell to the bed, soaking the comforter.

Drip. Drop.

I'm a superhero, but my father is a drunk and my

mother is a whore, Umberto wanted to tell them.

But he didn't.

_____

The heat nauseates Gant. At Mobile, he's already stopping for ice. He puts it in his helmet, drops it down his pants, his shirt, his boots, his gloves. He fills his mouth with it, and pours the melt-off over the BMW bike's jutting, hot cylinders. He leaves the coast route in desperation, unable to bear even one more traffic light. The trip has temporarily lost its pilgrimage feel. Gant's not an explorer anymore, not a voyeur, not a tourist. He's a survivor, plain and simple, and the relentless heat rising from the concrete is his foe. On the interstate, he plonks along, his bike's engine pinging from low octane.

When he reaches New Orleans, he heads for the French Quarter, thinking only of beer. He picks the first dark cavern, named for a pirate, and slumps down in a chair, under a fan. The bartender silently brings him a cold one. He presses the bottle to his forehead, then downs the pint in one gulp.

What's a good place to stay? he asks.

End of the block, turn right on Napoleon. Three doors down. Kinda touristy, but clean.

Gant saddles up with painful reluctance, but reaches the inn quickly. He pays in advance for the room, lays his stuff out, wipes the grime off his bags, takes a shower and heads for the bed.

What's this wet spot?

Annoyed, he pads down the stairs in his shorts. The proprietress takes in his fine gray eyes, his trim belly and strong shoulders, the sprinkling of gray hairs on his chest, and she smiles.

How can I help you, Mr. Gant?

There's a leak in the ceiling. The bed's gotten all wet.

The woman's surprised. She's never heard this one before. She says she'll take care of it. Gant goes back up to his room and sits in front of the air conditioner, fighting the pit in his stomach that has come to mean Caroline. To torture himself more, he takes her picture from his pocket. Five years have passed since he saw her last. He should have just left the damn picture behind. Now the emulsion has stuck to the coat's liner and Caroline's right shoulder is missing. He tries to find it in the pocket, thinking maybe he can glue it back somehow, but the project is ridiculous and for some reason brings tears. He can't patch anything anymore; it's way past time for that. He jams the photo into the seam of the air conditioner's front panel and watches it flutter in the breeze. If he squints his eye just right, it looks like Caroline is moving.

Upstairs, the innkeeper knocks hard on the door. Umberto wakes first, and thinks at once of the money. It's safe there, under the bed. He opens the door, wrapped in a towel. Beyond him, the sluggish women struggle for cover. The water has turned cold and the romance is gone. The innkeeper takes one look at him and turns red.

Who the hell are you?

A friend. He smiles.

Let me see the bathtub!

Not now.

Yes, now. She pushes the door open. Betty and Lisle are angry, tangled, ashamed. The innkeeper surveys the soaked floorboards.

Everybody out, she says. Right this minute.

Half an hour later, all three of them are gone and Gant is slumped over the back of the chair.

He doesn't even hear them on the stairs.

THREE

❧

Tim Rule made his fortune by building row after row
of affordable, good-quality tract houses amid the stench
and the heat of the Everglades. It was his curse that a
wetland filled with algae, 'gator teeth, water moccasins
and rats, sawgrass, Indian bones and the shards of a
crashed commercial airliner had become his own personal Treasure Island. To maintain the image Vicky's
political career taught him he required—that of a concerned developer responsive to his public's interests—
he was forced to live in the swamp himself. To deaden
the pain, he built a palatial estate: acres of black screen,
a tennis court, a swimming pool half indoors and half
out. The Rule home had to cover the bases for visiting
princes, builders, bankers and pols, and as such was designed to please every possible palate. It was replete with
fake Grecian urns, real Japanese pottery, wild Mexican
sculpture, Roy Lichtenstein prints, Peter Maxes, War-
hols, Libermans, even a Goya.

What had once been a refuge for ideas, games and
plans was now Rule's fortress of solitude, especially as
distraught young Stefan lay sedated in his vast upstairs
room and the help, a live-in Brazilian couple, all legal
and benefitted, had retired for the night.

Tim was alone.

He had his work, of course, and his mistress—mistresses, to be fair, for there was a new one he had been cultivating on the day of terror at the bank, a young redhead who worked at a South Beach boutique. Yet nothing had prepared him for the terribly unexpected fact that now—with Vicky gone—her asthma and her ambition and her parties and her fat all seemed small grievances. He was shocked into breathlessness by the realization that he loved her, and that he missed her, and that he would never, ever see her again.

He poured himself a long Balvenie and inhaled the loam. Then another. Then another. Finally, he went out to his office, sat down at his rolltop desk and unlocked the secret drawer wherein he stored his shiny magnum wheelgun. Contemplating revenge, he picked up the phone and dialed his lawyer, at home, at night.

Are you all right? asked Ron Bernstein.

The lawyer had been expecting the call. Rule didn't only build houses, he cracked the whip of influence too, and Bernstein was the sharp leather tip.

I want him, Rule said, spinning the well-oiled cylinder. And I don't want to listen to any talk of his not being responsible, not knowing she had asthma. I want this to come out my way. He killed her, and I want him.

You'll have him.

I want him to fry. I'll turn this town upside down until they fry him.

I know, I know, Bernstein soothed, and I spoke with the FBI today.

This long, the bastard could be anywhere.

Nah. These guys aren't smart enough to flee. Bernstein tried to be casual. They stay around for a few days, trying to hold their secret inside, and then the gloating starts and pretty soon they're at it again, no plan, just to repeat the thrill. That's when they get caught. You can be sure he's still in South Florida. We'll be meeting him soon enough.

Yesterday won't be soon enough, Tim Rule growled.

He dumped the bullets into his moist and angry palm and pulled the trigger over and over again.

Click click click.

———

Umberto countered the southward flow of the Red River, keeping to two-lane blacktop. He rode north through Louisiana, past Morganza and Batchelor and Mansura and Boyce. The Triumph purred, not seeming to mind the heat. Each push down on the shift lever, each slight squeeze of the clutch, every blast of the horn, flash of the lights, twist of the wrist, everything worked with silky perfection.

The Brits.

He brought six cars and a pickup to their knees. He rounded bend after bend, devouring dales and hills that had once taken pilgrims weeks to traverse, countryside which had taken slaves years to cotton. When he wasn't plotting the best line through a turn, his thoughts were drifting to Lisle, but never to Betty—whom he'd felt was a hard, selfish woman with little love in her heart—and not that day to Graciela, because it hurt him too much to think of her.

He entered a blind curve fast, leaned the bike over, felt the weight of the tailpack full of cash press against his right kidney. His radar detector screamed.

Cop car.

Behind the tree.

Natchitoches Parish Sheriff.

Umberto glanced down at the map in the clear pocket atop the bag on his tank. He could run for the interstate, but not faster than a radio. He could lose himself in the back roads, but the cop knew them better.

A race was a poor bet.

Umberto had been good in school—there had even been mention of college—but he sensed it was because he talked a good line, not because he knew a damn thing at all. He easily figured where to get answers, where to crib notes, dig up information, plagiarize points of view. He didn't realize that the capacity to solve problems was what his teachers were looking for in the first place— that they loved the way he thought on his feet and the way he talked.

His gift for the gab. Bet on it. Hide that detector in his tank bag. Put on the turn signal. Pull over.

He stood on the shoulder. Mosquitoes alit. The bike's engine ticked. Sweat trickled down his armpits. Don't think of the money, he said to himself. Maybe this bastard's got ESP. Also, don't look at the bag. Act casual. Be cool. If he was looking for you, the gun would already be out.

He heard the cackle of a radio and the creak of the patrol car door. Sheriff Abraham Tunney got out. He was big and black and used to people telling him no. No, you can't finish school with those marks—he graduated. No, you're not tall enough to play basketball— he was state champion. No, you won't get a date with white girl Harriet—he married her. No, I wasn't speeding—he made the bust on radar. No, I didn't steal this car—he had the tags on his hot sheet. No, I didn't do those things to my ex-girlfriend—he had the hair samples in a clean, glycine envelope.

No, I didn't rob a bank in Boca Raton.

Red lights, Umberto observed with more poise than any other seventeen-year-old in the world could muster when faced with a cop and in the intimate company of a stolen fortune. Most places these days they're blue.

See a lot of flashing lights, do you? Sheriff Tunney inquired. There were great, dark blotches under his armpits and the handle of his autopistol glistened with moisture. Summer in Louisiana. Umberto was glad he had taken the empty Beretta apart and left it in pieces in five different canals. He was glad his license was clean.

Jes' when they go past.

Pretty nice bike for a young guy like you.

I work bikes, that's why.

And where do you do that?

Fort Lauderdale.

Stick to the truth. At least close to the truth.

So is this a customer's bike?

Tunney knew from his radio that the machine was registered to one Umberto Santana, age seventeen, of Cutler Ridge. He was just fishing. He just wanted to see what he could see.

No, Officer, this beauty's mine.

Bike shop pays well, huh?

Umberto smiled and told the absolute truth again.

Cost me a year of work. Skinned knuckles too, and some bruises.

Pretty fast, I guess.

It's smooth, Officer. Ju know, I jes' move along with the day.

Abraham Tunney cleaned his mirrored sunglasses with his sleeve. Umberto saw a world in those moist, blinking cop eyes. Sawed-off-shotgun wars with the Klan, an albino son who couldn't go out in fair weather, a wife who wasn't the cook Abraham wished she were and who didn't look as good as she used to.

Moving along is exactly what you were doing.

Jes' enjoying the machine.

To the tune of eighty-five miles per hour in a fifty-mile-per-hour zone.

Ju kiddin' me?

There are tractors on these roads, night and day, Tunney said grimly.

I didn' know that, sir.

Cows and horses too. Children coming home from school, even though I'll give you it's early for that right now.

It's so damn hot out here, I was jes' trying to get somewhere.

Where might that be?

Natchitoches. That how you say it?

That's right. But what about after Natchitoches?

Maybe east to the beach and back home. Like I said, I'm jes' out riding. I didn' mean anything bad.

Tunney grunted.

It's Saturday. I haul you in now, we'll both have to wait for the judge. That wouldn't be any good, the air conditioning's down in the courthouse.

Maybe we can work somethin' out?

Tunney didn't like the sound of that so much. Too glib. Too dismissive. Too much a veiled bribe.

Now what's that supposed to mean? he asked slowly.

Umberto felt his mistake right away. Everything was in the next word, and the one after that.

Jes' that I slow down for the schoolkids, ride careful.

Tunney took a step toward the bike. He looked at the wheels, the way the tires rubbed high on the rim. Lots of leaning. Little gobs of melted rubber. He looked for scrapes on the footpegs and found them. He looked for crash evidence, bad paint down low, bondo—even though the damn thing was brand-new—any signs of a spill. Nothing. So the kid was skillful. And lucky.

This isn't South Florida, he said. Paramedics are more than five minutes away.

I realize that, sir.

Looking at the soft luggage, Tunney imagined the kid's kit spread all over the road: underwear, condoms, shaving cream—though there isn't much of a beard— the road rash on the body, the fibers from the helmet. The shiny white glisten of bone.

I don't want to be scraping you up off the road, he said.

I don' want that either, Sheriff.

I've got deputies, Tunney lied. They're all over the place. Beat the limit by five and they'll be on you like flies.

I know they will. I believe that. Really. But they won't have to. No sir. They won't even notice me, I'll be so quiet and so good.

Tunney dragged it out. He put his hand on the saddlebags, gave a push and a squeeze. Umberto's adrenals opened into his blood. He began to entertain combat fantasies, to stare at Tunney's gun. The sheriff moved toward the tailpack.

Ju don't mind, I'd like to get going, Umberto declared. The breeze is the only thing I've got for the heat. No air conditioner for me, you know?

Tunney nodded.

Keep in mind I'll be watching you, he said with great calm.

Ju a hard man to forget. Umberto grinned.

Tunney allowed himself to return the smile and retreated to his car without getting to the money.

Ju don't know me, *meng*, Umberto muttered quietly into his helmet.

Not as I really am.

———

Blind Audrey Bishop lies in her bed at night, in a house made of strong logs, deep in the forest. Even though it's hot everywhere else in the country, here in the Northwest the nights are cold enough to need the heat that's piped into the floor by the system her grandfather built with his own hands, laying every duct, figuring the square footage, the amount of air needing to be forced, the output of the furnace. Sometimes, like tonight, she lies under the duvet, the down pulled clear up to her nose, and lets one leg hang out, lets her foot touch the floor, feels the heat on her sole.

Ruth has attached stars to the ceiling, creating a paste-on luminescent galaxy over the bed. She has never quite accepted Audrey's blindness. Now, in the dark, Audrey talks to her mother.

Are you maybe coming back for my birthday? It's in two weeks, you know. Just in case you forgot.

———

I'm going to be six.

———

Where have you *been* all this time?

—

Grampa went fishing and he never came back. Gramma says *he's* dead too. I was the last person he hugged. I brought him his sandwiches on the boat. It was a very windy day. Salt was in the air. Now there's just Gramma and me. Doesn't that sound lonely?

—

Doesn't it?

—

I would be less lonely if I had a brother or a sister, you know that, Mommy? I keep asking Gramma if I have one somewhere and she gives me a funny look, kind of sad, and says no. Do I? Could you surprise me for my birthday maybe and bring me one?

—

Could you?

—

I touched a whale today. I thought you might have made him come up from down deep. Tomorrow we're having a sale at the store. Not just sandals, but shoes for people who really need to protect their toes. We went and put up a sign at the marina and at the post office and at the mill. I talked to some of the secretaries and told them to come too. I think they will. To save money. Women are smarter than men, aren't they? Gramma says they are. Could you make sure she gets a lot of money?

—

Outside, a fox slides stealthily through the brush. Audrey hears it and holds her breath. A salamander wriggles down deeper into the soil beneath a lush fern. Audrey hears that too. A squirrel dashes through dead leaves, afraid to be afield so late. The moon yawns yellow overhead. A bird rustles its wings, a sound which makes Audrey's eyelids heavy. Inside, her foot still on the warm floor, she fights off sleep just long enough to ask one more question.

Since we're on the subject of men, she whispers, why don't I have a dad?

———

Graciela Perez adjusts her brown McDonald's server's skirt so that the button faces front and center. She rings the doorbell. She has never been to Umberto's house—they've kept their affair secret and dark—and she is nervous because a bad pimple has come up overnight, right on the tip of her nose, and because her hair is flat and sticky from the frying grease and the grill. She figures Umberto must be sick, since the service manager at the bike shop said he hadn't shown up in days. That, or he'd had to stay at home and help his old man dry out again.

She presses the doorbell one more time.

Briiiiiiing.

It is taking a long time for anyone to answer the door. She waits. She knocks.

Where in the world could that boy be? Racing? Tripping? He doesn't do that. He's clean. That's what she likes about him. That and the flattering lies he tells her and the way he keeps his dreams to himself, though not so well that she can't tell he has them. Dreams make women love a man, it's fantasies that are the problem.

The door swings inward without warning, and the smell of beer wafts out. This must be the old man. *Dios mío,* but he needs a bath and a shave.

I'm here for Umberto, she says.

Pedro Santana stares at her. In the background, a baseball game comes over the television. The bases are loaded.

Come in, he says as the television explodes with noise.

He bunts it! Can you believe it, ladies and gentlemen? Look at this field come alive!

Graciela steps into the house. There isn't much light in the room, just the TV and an electric candle, but it's bright enough to see a huge female cockroach scuttle for a dusting of chips by the vinyl recliner in front of the television. Graciela knows from her work at McDonald's that roaches carry thousands of babies inside. She feels a thrill. She might have Umberto's baby inside her too. Her period is late. This is what she has come to tell him.

Umberto! she calls out, watching Pedro carefully.

Yes, there is something of the boy in him, or something of him in the boy, a certain straightness of back. And they have the same chin, like the prow of a boat parting water. She imagines that when he was younger, he would have been handsome, but now, at forty, his stubble is gray and his arms sag and there is a brewery tucked under his shirt.

He stares at her with a look she knows too well.

He's not here, says Pedro. Ju want a drink?

She shakes her head.

He takes a step forward. Wavering.

She takes a step back.

Ju sure?

I'm sure. I have to go now.

He positions himself between her and the door, cagily, like a wild dog or a wolf.

Who are ju?

His girlfriend, Graciela.

Never heard of ju.

That stings, because it is probably true, the tight-lipped bastard.

Pedro closes in. He has noticed her thighs, which she knows is bad news because they are the part of her all men notice, the swell she keeps hidden below the counter when she takes orders. These thighs of hers have a certain muscular, bulging roundness at the front, like she's seen on tall blond models who play volleyball on the beach. But her look is natural, with her since birth, not gained. She had never done a thing in the sand, except one time with Umberto when they were both a little drunk and a summer wind was whipping the stars around.

Pedro touches her lightly on both arms, steering her toward the recliner.

No, she says, but he seems so sad she doesn't stop him from kneeling before her, on the filthy carpet, making the chips go crunch and the cockroach skedaddle. He reaches for her legs with a sigh.

Umberto's gone, he says. He's not coming back. It's jes' me and it's jes ju.

Fly ball! It's up, it's over center field. He goes for it! Oh no! It slips out of his hand. Could this be it, sports fans? Could this be the turnaround we've been waiting for?

Suddenly there is a noise at the door, and a volley of Spanish cursing rolls in. Pedro leaps to his feet.

Borracho! comes a voice like a human cattle prod. What are you doing!

Graciela is afraid. She knows who it must be—the low-cut blouse, the skirt too short, the eyelashes, the boots, the perfume, enough mascara to draw a message to Mars.

Consuela! Umberto's father babbles. What are ju doing here?

Graciela is up now, smoothing her clothes.

Consuela turns knife-eyes her way.

You dare? In my own house?

She takes a gun from her purse, a little pearl-handled .25, which to Graciela looks like a cannon.

I came for Umberto, the girl stutters.

Umberto's gone, you little bitch. Don't you know that? Everybody knows that.

She raises the gun higher.

Put that thing away, Pedro mutters. Nothing happened.

Graciela can see the old whore is crazy. There is no balance in the eyes, nothing to power the extensor muscles of the first finger, nothing to keep that trigger from moving back.

Terrified, Graciela starts to talk.

I missed my period, she says.

Pedro sucks in air like a Hoover. The gun wavers in Consuela's hand.

It's Umberto's. It has to be. I haven't been with anyone else. Could you help me find him, please? He doesn't know.

Consuela fires a round into the sofa.

Bang!

And then another, and another.

Bang! Bang!

Pedro rolls around on the floor, dodging bullets he's sure are aimed at him. The gravid cockroach hides under the recliner. Graciela stares at Umberto's mother with big soft brown eyes, and she makes an observation.

You're worried about him too, aren't you?

———

Clouds gathered like councilmen over the Oklahoma panhandle, moving in from the flat red bluffs of New Mexico. Gant rode straight into them, his Australian greatcoat trailing behind him like a wizard's waving wand. The BMW ate up mile after mile of gently sloping highway, the gain in altitude almost imperceptible, as the road rose parallel to the Old Santa Fe Trail. Heading west out of Enid, Gant zigged and zagged, choosing a farm road here, a state route there, trying to ease the boredom, get brief breaks from the gathering wind, and relieve the monotonous view of oil derricks and tractors, cow pies and scrub. He rejoiced in the brute sensations of the ride, his buttocks and thighs sticking to the hot seat, the low-frequency vibration in his hands, the omnipotent sense of flying coupled with the joy that comes from breaking free of material shackles. No surfboard out here, no closet, no lightbulbs to change—save maybe a faulty turn signal—no dishes that need washing, no IRS forms to complete, no rented apartment to suck down your paycheck.

He rode past Meno, Cedardale, Curtis and Fort Supply. The state gathered up its garter as it was squeezed between Kansas to the north and Texas down below. On the map the panhandle looked manageable, but the distances were deceptive. The wind and the upgrade took their toll on the engine's efficiency, and for the first time in his life Gant ran out of gas. At first he thought it was an electrical failure, but when he put the machine up on its center stand and walked forward to check the lights, he saw there was still juice in the battery and that everything glowed as it should. He tried the starter a few times and it whined and the engine turned over but refused to ignite. He removed a spark plug and tested for arcing and when he saw and smelled the bright blue light he knew for sure it was the fuel. He tipped the bike far to the right and then far to the left again, listening for sloshing—impossible the way the wind rustled the grass—and trying to see the level through the hole in the top of the tank. Finally resigned, he turned the machine into the wind, so it wouldn't blow over, and stuck out his thumb.

It was hot, but the dry desert air was less punishing than the heaviness of the South. After an hour of waiting, Gant lay down in the grass by the side of the road. With his eyes closed and the sun warming his coat, his legs straight out and his arms out too, he considered his preoccupation with equilibrium—why else would one travel on two wheels?—and thought about the miles he had covered as a soldier, sales rep, skipper.

Limo driver.

———

Michael Hamilton, Caroline's husband, comes out from behind the gate. He leads the little boy, Xavier, to the car, holding him by the hand. He's a handsome man, Hamilton is, fit and tan in his Lacoste tennis shirt. His arms and chest are swollen with the kind of muscle that comes from lifting weights at the gym, not from lifting luggage into a yawning trunk, and his face—covered by skin that isn't old but isn't young either—shows no trace of a double chin. His eyes are clear, and his hair is gray, but only at the temples. He's tall and blond and he's got a heavy, gold, Swiss watch on his wrist and a striped belt and green trousers and Top-Siders, no socks. He might be one of the guards at Buckingham Palace, out of black-and-red uniform, of course, and without the ridiculous hat; a big brawny man, but with a degree from Princeton and lots of money and everything going his way.

Ha.

The boy looks just like him, except he's no more than eight or nine. He's going to be really tall, Gant can tell that, and he's towheaded, like his father. But after Gant catches his first glimpse of Caroline, he decides the boy is going to darken up.

In the limo's sideview mirror, she is just a concatenation of light rays skewed by convex glass: legs bent the wrong way, skirt shown too wide, face behind bug glasses and mass of hair tied back. Even so, she opens Gant as surely as a sous-chef shucks a clam.

We're running late, Hamilton says as he stuffs Xavier into the backseat. I'll make it worth your while if you get us to the airport in time for the flight.

I'll do my best, sir.

Forget your best, just get me to the airport quickly. The luggage is waiting by the front door. And don't forget my wife's skis. I don't want to have to listen to it if we get to the mountain without them.

Gant gets a quick glance from Caroline, and the contact, even through her shades, is enough to root him to the spot. The energy! Those lips! The barest hint of a smile. The body. My God. Viewed straight on, her angles take his breath away.

Hamilton sticks his head out the car window.

Excuse me. I believe I said we were in a rush.

Gant breaks Caroline's spell and dashes for the bags. He loads them. They leave. A little later, in the car, there is talk of Telluride and the Rockies.

The Alps are higher, says the boy.

The Rockies are high enough, says Hamilton.

Same hotel suite as last year? Caroline interrupts.

Exactly the same.

I thought so. Can't we ever do something new? Push the envelope a little bit?

Quit your bitching for just five minutes, will you?

Daddy, asks the boy, are you going to spend the whole time getting massages and lying in the sauna like you did last year?

Of course he is, Caroline says bitterly. That's what your father does.

In response, Hamilton opens a newspaper and tunes them out. Gant glances at the mirror just in time to see Caroline take off her bug glasses and gaze out the window. Hazel. Her eyes are hazel. He wonders what it is about him and what is it about her that makes him so idiotically joyous just to have seen those eyes. Can an infatuation happen so quickly? In just one instant? He wonders so hard he drives into the adjoining lane, nearly sideswiping a pickup truck.

For Chrissake watch the road, Hamilton snaps. It's the airport I'm after, not the morgue.

Yes sir, he says, checking the mirror. Caroline is watching him, a satisfied smile on her face. There she is in the car with two men and a boy.

Her harem.

Blaaaaaap!

Gant awakened in the cornfield to the sound of a horn. A battered old pickup, primed in soil-colored rust, pulled to the side of the road beside him. A lean man in a ten-gallon hat with scarecrow legs and his belt tucked tight got out.

You all right, mister?

Just out of gas.

Snort. Sniff. A spit of tobacco, a nod.

Happens out here. The rise kind of creeps up on you.

And the wind, adds Gant.

That too.

Gant made to get up and discovered he was covered with locusts. They leapt off as he rose, but not quickly, sticking to the oiled cotton of his coat as if they were feeding on it.

You happen to have any in your truck?

Some, I reckon.

Just a gallon or two's all I need, enough to get me to the next town.

The farmer grinned, showing holes in his upper jaw where there should have been teeth.

You're heading west, right?

That's right.

I've got tractor fuel in the back, nothing fancy. I could fill yer tank up for you.

I would appreciate that, said Gant, brushing off the last of the locusts.

Can't say as I've ever seen the bugs take to a man like that.

Happens to me down south too. With the mosquitoes. Must be my warm heart.

Sure must. Here, the locusts get thick when there's a tornado nearby. You'd best be finding shelter, from what they're saying on the radio.

I'll keep that in mind.

Gonna rain too. We need it. Been drier than a witch's tit.

The gas gurgled and splashed. Gant's tank came full. He dug for a ten spot, considered a twenty. The farmer waved him off.

Forget it.

Please, said Gant.

You'd do the same for me, right?

As a matter of fact, I would.

The farmer smiled, took out his Old Salem, stuffed a wad into his cheek and regarded Gant with squinty eyes.

You out of Florida, then?

That's right.

Long ride.

I needed the time to think. I'm between some things.

You're smart to know it, the farmer spit. There's lots of folks set out for the future without considering where they've been. Then they get lost, see? Start wailing and kicking and crying a good game. Stress, they call it. Poor planning's what it really is.

Nodding, Gant buttoned up his coat, put his helmet back on, turned the throttle a few times, lit the engine.

German? asked the farmer.

Right again.

Good bike?

The best, to my way of thinking. These things go on forever.

That's something. It really is.

The two men looked at each other for a long moment, and then the farmer got back in his truck and drove away, leaving the tire dust to settle on Gant, who promptly set off into the wind. It wasn't five minutes later, just shy of Forgan and after Mocane, that he saw Caroline walking along the road. Striding west in the afternoon sun, her hair shining, her gait purposeful and long, she wore a cocktail dress Gant had seen before, white, to set off the long, thick, almost purple cascade of her hair.

Gant's mouth turned to cotton and he twisted the throttle. The bike leapt forward. He grew close enough to see her high heels.

Not the shoes for out here. Through his helmet and over the engine, Gant could hear them click and clack on the tarmac as she moved, not floating like an apparition should but walking like a real human being.

Impossible.

He drew closer. Close enough to see her high cheekbones and sloe eyes. Her tall forehead and aquiline nose. Those arms, fit and strong, like a small man's. Those endless legs.

Caroline?

His hands tightened like claws on the bars as he guided his machine over. Damn if he didn't get close enough to touch the mole on her shoulder and smell her Christian Dior. Sputtering, fighting the driveline lash, shifting it down, pulling in the clutch, he came to a stop.

Caroline! he cried.

But suddenly she wasn't there. On the horizon, a twister grew darkly, spinning up sand.

Where was he going to hide?

In his mirrors, Gant saw another rider approaching.

The wind began to howl.

FOUR

❧

Mr. Emerson? called out Special Agent Eagle Cooper.

He waited a moment, and when there was no response, passed underneath the rubber bottom edge of the garage door, noting the slotted holes for heavy padlocks and the strong braces on the door's inside surface. It made him uneasy to penetrate this guy's inner sanctum, which smelled faintly of gasoline and old leather. He half-expected there to be machine guns or poison darts protecting the gleaming gullwing Mercedes Benz, the Phantom II Rolls-Royce, the immaculate Ferrari Daytona, the rough E-type Jaguar convertible, the Shelby Cobra with the chromed roll bar and not a scratch on the bumper, the low-slung early Morgan, the high-wheeled Bugatti.

Hello? he bellowed, figuring that with the door open, somebody had to be home. This was a good Boca Raton neighborhood, but Cooper was a cop. He knew anything could happen anywhere.

Who is it? a muffled female voice responded.

Cooper squeezed past the grille of the Rolls, brushed against the chest-high headlights the size of pizza pans, and followed the arched, sloping fender around to the front quarter panel, wherefrom protruded a pair of small feet. A woman rolled herself out and stared up at him, grease on her cheek, a Snap-on wrench in her hand.

Overalls.

Cooper had a weakness for overalls. Facial smears too, due—although he would never admit it—to a crush on his first grade art teacher, a young woman who perpetually wore OshKosh and always had a smile for Eagle on her paint-streaked face. Even at six years old he knew that if he had been twelve years older he would have hunted her down like a wild deer.

Special Agent Eagle Cooper, FBI. I'm looking for Mr. Emerson.

Mr. Emerson is deceased. I'm his daughter, Suzanne.

Cooper stared at the woman's pale blue eyes, her lightly freckled skin, her thick blond hair, and saw his whole case flying out the window. She rose gracefully to her feet and put out her hand. Cooper could make out the edge of her hips, luscious; her breasts, heavy; her waist, trim. He showed his ID.

Is this about the bank robbery? Because if it is, I've already talked to the police and told them everything I know. I liquidated some shares of a mutual fund and asked for the money in cash so that I could drive a hard bargain at a car auction in California. The thief got lucky, I guess.

Cooper nodded, looked around.

So these vehicles are yours?

Her hand traced the chocolate fender of the Phantom.

I'm a stockbroker, Mr. Cooper. I have my own trading firm. Vintage cars are a family passion. Things were built to last forever back then. The shock absorbers on this Rolls, for example—which my father bought new—use regular motor oil as dampening fluid. When the ride gets rough, say after eighty or ninety thousand miles, you just drain the oil, replace the seals, and fill them up again. Good for another ten years. That's what I was doing, and I'd as soon get to it. I'm due back at the office in an hour.

Cooper pulled a couple of photographs from his vest

pocket, the blowups from the bank camera. Grainy, not worth much, but all he had.

He handed them to Suzanne.

Do you recognize this man?

She took the pictures, shuffled them, looked carefully.

Not much of a picture, so I can't be one hundred percent sure, but he doesn't look familiar. Is there some reason I should pay special attention to his crotch?

Damn if Cooper hadn't forgotten the red *x* he scratched on the photo with his pen.

Bureau business, he blustered, the blood rising to his face. Technical stuff—has to do with his weapon.

Weapon. That must be a law enforcement term. Suzanne smiled.

Embarrassed, Cooper slid the photo back into his pocket.

What bank employees knew you asked for cash, Ms. Emerson?

I only deal with the vice president.

Did you tell anyone else?

A couple of trusted friends who were also going to the auction. Because of the robbery, I was only armed with a checkbook and couldn't quite make the deal I wanted on an Auburn speedster. I've been after the car for years. Quite disappointing.

Cooper nodded and, not quite ready to leave, wandered over to the Mercedes sports car.

May I?

Sure. Just don't scratch the leather with your gun.

Cooper slid in and examined the old-style round gauges and the instruments and controls. Suzanne joined him. He tried not to stare at the way she filled out her denim.

How do you know so much about cars?

My passions get all my attention.

Cooper felt a little frisson along his spine.

I love this smell, he said. It's comforting, like old pajamas.

She stared at him in surprise. Men didn't surprise her too often anymore, even if they popped in with diamond earrings or radical views of the Dow. She took in his large frame, his small nose, big lips, dainty ears. He wasn't handsome, she decided, but he had character. She wiped the grease smudge from the Rolls-Royce undercarriage off her cheek and tucked an errant wisp of blond hair back behind her ear.

I love the smell too. These are the original seats. My father brought this car back from Cuba in 1962. It was good for a hundred and fifty miles an hour back then.

That's something, said Cooper.

They must teach you to drive fast in FBI school, Agent Cooper.

Call me Eagle.

Okay. She smiled. It's funny. I've never met anyone named for a bird before. But I suppose if you *are* going to be named for a bird, an eagle is the bird to be named for. It wouldn't do to be called kingfisher, shag or crow.

You're a piece of work, Ms. Emerson.

Call me Suzanne. And since you're wondering, I'm thirty-eight and single.

Thank you, Cooper said awkwardly.

She smiled at his clumsiness, and for a few moments they both stared straight ahead, over the dash and through the windshield.

Eagle, she said at last, mostly because she was tired of waiting. Will you have dinner with me?

Me? Dinner with you?

That's what I asked.

Sure, he said quickly.

Thanks. She smiled again. I think that sounds great.

Cooper grabbed hold of the cueball-white shift knob and leaned into her eyes.

Vroom, he said, feeling like a raptor once more.

————

Umberto's attention has not been distracted by an apparition from his sad, painful past, and so he sees the tornado before Gant does. The deathcloud is so huge and so horrifying and so close that all he can do is take a long blink at speed and hope that when he opens his eyes again his wheels will still be on the road and the black funnel on the horizon will turn out to be some pathological mote in his eye.

Gant is struck not by terror but by melancholy. He's still thinking about Caroline, and he is still wondering whether the carpet of locusts from which he arose might be a harbinger of some phenomenon entirely different from the one posited by the farmer. Maybe he is still under a cover of darkness. Maybe he has yet to emerge. He calculates his gas mileage and range and wonders whether this strange wind is going to strand him again in the face of a long uphill climb.

At the speck of a town that is Optima, in the middle of Texas County, far from any substantial habitation, the twister touches down with a roar. The two motorcyclists come abreast of each other on the road, Gant with his black helmet and his crazy coat flapping, Umberto hunkered down, his hand on the cash behind him.

Gant points at a silo in the distance, figuring they are better off in a castle of grain than in the middle of an unforgiving oil field, and they both twist their throttles. Gant's bike pulls like a tractor against the time and space that is Oklahoma. Umberto's starship simply rockets ahead. They are both within range of the sweet boozy smell of the corn fermenting at the bottom of the silo when they are assailed by speeding grasses.

Whip.

And by spiraling stones.

Whack.

They are struck on their protective gear, without much effect, but also on vulnerable spots like knees and fingers, and on their wrists, too, and the backs of their necks. Gant cringes down into his coat as something flies by him, a piece of an oil rig, giant girders suspended in the air for a moment, cured of gravity. Umberto feels his front wheel going light and struggles to keep his bike pointed at the silo door.

The roar is tremendous now, as is the wind, but the unexpected thing is the darkness. Gant loses sight of the silo. He can't even see Umberto. He squeezes the brake lever, trying to stop the whole world, and there comes a fearsome whiff of manure and a great sucking noise, and suddenly he's not on the ground anymore, and neither is the boy. They catch a glimpse of each other as they rise into the air on motorcycles turned to magic carpets.

Float.

Spin.

Gant gets the dry heaves from an excess of adrenaline. Umberto feels his bladder go. A plastic panel flies off the Honda, and a saddlebag follows suit. Gant's tankbag is shredded. His map hovers before him, shows him the great expanse of the United States, and then evaporates into atoms. A barn cat zooms by, claws out like a cartoon character, mouth wide open, eyes bulging, fur erect.

Meow.

Gant isn't sure how high they are, but he knows it's much too far to fall. Umberto's money bag suddenly pops off his bike and without thinking at all, he leaps out of the saddle, grabs it, and clutches it to his chest.

The world turns from black to yellow.

Kernels and cobs whirl about.

It's snowing corn.

They're over the silo. The roof has been ripped off, and it floats by. Gant twists his throttle once, just to convince himself that he still has control over his engine, a small and meaningless move, to be sure, but somehow reassuring.

Images whizz by, and Gant can't be sure that they're not real. He is convinced that he has entered a realm where the imagined and the concrete intertwine. As if with the eyes of a hawk, he sees himself and Caroline in a rented skiff, snuggled up against a sandbar off Marco Island, making frantic love at the stern. He sees the boat wag gently from side to side.

Splish.

Splash.

And suddenly, Umberto is there, flying solo, hand outstretched. Gant grabs him, and with a monumental effort twists him around so that he lands on the back of the BMW. Terrified, Umberto latches on. Gant tries to pry him loose so he can breathe.

The twin horsemen fall.

The change in gravity comes suddenly, as they are now out of the whirling hands of the dervish.

Sir Isaac's rules.

Everything around them plummets at the same pace. The great, shiny, circular silo, fully fifteen stories tall, has been emasculated by the twister, but not so emasculated that there still aren't retaining walls at the bottom. Not so emasculated that there isn't a grand pillow of corn into which Umberto's Triumph falls, rubber side down, only to disappear under the kernels. Not so emasculated that the same embrace of maize doesn't reach up to meet the Triumph, the BMW, Umberto and Gant.

And the money.

They drop through progressively denser layers of corn, those at the bottom dank and fermenting and thick with settled moisture. Their fall from three hundred feet is cushioned so that they feel barely a scratch, although it is hard to breathe for the corn dust and hard to move for the cobs. Reflexively, Gant guns the engine—the corn would set to flame if it weren't so moist—and the rear tire spins and sprays everything that touches it until, like a giant blower, it clears enough for the riders to see an air hole, and beyond it the gradually restored light of day.

Without a word, they turn the bike around and half ride, half push it out through the hole in the silo and into the sunshine. All around them, stunned sparrows lie fluttering on the field, little wings twitching, little beaks opening and closing, free of the vacuum of low pressure, oxygen finally restored. Gant begins setting them on their feet.

Leave 'em, says Umberto. They're just birds.

Doesn't cost me anything to help, Gant replies.

The boy disappears into the silo and comes back out pushing his machine. He sets it on the center stand and goes hunting for his saddlebag and the missing fairing panel. He finds the panel perhaps a hundred feet away, and the saddlebag twenty feet past that. He walks back slowly, still not sure of the ground.

Gant is still righting sparrows.

Pissed my pants, *meng*, Umberto mutters. I never done that before.

You've never flown without an airplane before either, says Gant. Forgive yourself.

Umberto nods. He's still in a trance. He reaffixes the panel and the bag, takes out a clean set of clothes and strips himself naked right there in the field.

Ju saved me, he says, struggling into clean jeans.

I doubt that.

Ju showed me this building. Ju pulled me in.

Gant waves the whole thing away. He's uncomfortable with compliments. He's a quiet, self-critical man, someone who always thinks he should do better, do more, particularly for others. He has a strangely utopian view of things, almost fantastical, like Don Quixote, which renders him extremely vulnerable to the way the world can be and the way people treat him, lie to him, use him. But sometimes, like the old knight at the windmill, he can be tough as hell.

How come ju wear the freaky coat, *meng*? Umberto pursues. Ju look like maybe ju could be Batman.

Personally, I'd rather be a warlock, says Gant. Or a wizard.

Ju better not rely on magic, *meng*. Not in this world.

Magic got us through that twister.

That wasn't magic, that was luck. Don't ju know that? I used to know more than I know now. Gant smiles.

Umberto reattaches his money bag, stretching the bungees, getting everything straight. He hits the starter. The bike whines but won't catch.

Tornadoes make low pressure, says Gant, massaging the chest of a sparrow hawk he fears will stay dead. Low pressure makes vapor lock. Try opening the gas cap, then closing it again.

Umberto, the mechanic, does as he is told.

Pop.

Whoosh.

Gas starts flowing again. The Triumph ignites.

Where ju headed? inquires Umberto as all the sparrows suddenly leap for the sky.

FIVE

❦

Audrey Bishop stood at the prow of the Seattle ferry like a bowsprit, her hands out in the wet wind as if to part the gleaming waters of Puget Sound. It was a rare bright day in the cloudy city, and the cars, the people, the riveted decks of the ferryboat, even the bubbling kelp, seemed to drink in the sun like wine.

Ruth rested inside the microbus, a crackly recording of Slim Harpo's blues on the boom box in the backseat. The visor was down to shield her eyes from the sun, and she could see her face in the mirror.

Wrinkles.

She rubbed her eyes, looked out at Audrey standing in the breeze, the little girl's hands clasped tight around the big steel chain that ran across the car deck to keep things in place. She wondered for a moment how the cold links felt in those small hands, whether Audrey's remaining senses, to compensate for her blindness, were deeper, keener, different, the way the doctor had said they might be. Ruth had gotten used to pondering the miracle that was her granddaughter day and night, and although she knew she had done the right thing for the girl, she worried about herself. What if Audrey were taken from her, moved clear away to another state? She knew that wasn't the plan, but things change. People change. With Hiram gone she had naught but Audrey and a shop full of shoes.

The ferrymaster sounded the deep Klaxon horn and the passengers began to stream back to their cars. The downtown landing approached, the big black rubber bumpers opening like a giant maw hungry for the ship. The sun was high over the Space Needle, which seemed like nothing so much as a giant finger pointing enthusiastically upward, just in case every last soul hadn't noticed it wasn't raining.

Ruth collected Audrey and led her by the hand back to the bus.

Bump.

The ferry touched ground. They drove in silence up the hill toward the medical center.

This is a stupid waste of money, Audrey announced.

Ruth turned down the music.

Your health is never a waste of money.

But I'm never going to see. I'm blind forever. The doctor's just going to tell me that again, Audrey declared, blinking a tear back and looking stubbornly out the window.

Ruth winced at the frustration in Audrey's voice. God knew the little girl had plenty to be bitter about, blind and motherless, her future uncertain. Still, it wasn't like her to sound so negative.

Ruth turned into the medical center parking lot. She was just as glad Audrey couldn't see the place, all dark red brick and imposing, not a happy building at all. She turned off the engine and gave Audrey a one-armed squeeze.

The only thing that's forever is love, and I love you, she said.

They followed the maze of elevators and corridors to Dr. Pearson's office. Pearson, a neurologist, had cared for Audrey all the way through. There had been others, of course—the second opinion, She's blind; the third opinion, She's going to stay blind; the fourth opinion,

Get used to the fact that she's permanently blind—but none had been as kind as Pearson.

The preliminary examination Audrey received while awaiting the doctor was perfunctory. A gum-chewing, punker nurse, bedecked in body piercings and tattoos, put some drops in the little girl's eyes while chewing gum loudly—*smack, smack*—and spraying Audrey with a fine mist of saliva. At length, Pearson came into the examination room. Tall, graying at the temples, showing only a happy tie with bubble gum–colored balloons under his white coat, he wore a spicy cologne to help his blind patients know him. He pressed Ruth's hand in greeting, told Audrey she looked beautiful, and took a peek at the child's optic nerve with a penlight. Then, without warning, he pulled a realistic-looking water pistol from his pocket and pointed it at her nose.

She ducked.

Ruth came out of her chair.

What's wrong with me? demanded Audrey, apparently unaware anything odd had happened. I'm going to be six, you know. You can tell me about myself. Really.

Pearson smiled sadly.

You are suffering from something called cortical blindness. This means that the problem with your vision isn't in your eyes—you have very pretty eyes, by the way, young lady—but with your brain; specifically with what's called your occipital lobe, near the base of your skull.

What's wrong with my brain?

It won't process visual information. It doesn't know you're seeing.

Why not?

Probably because of a bump on the your head when you were very little.

Ruth winced, praying the doctor was wrong. She couldn't bear to think what it suggested.

When will I get better?

Pearson sat down on the edge of the examination table and took Audrey's hand.

The brain is a funny part of the body, Audrey. We don't understand it very well. What matters most is that you don't worry too much about seeing. The world is full of sounds and feelings.

Smells, too, Audrey interjected. You are just a bunch of peppered peaches to me.

She loves music most, Ruth said anxiously. She wanted the doctor to see that Audrey had passion. She wanted the doctor to recognize her rich life.

Audrey nodded. On the other side of the wall, a colony of ants marched single file across the countertop in the staff pantry, their destination a box of Fig Newtons.

Pitter patter.

Audrey heard their feet. The Triumphal March from Verdi's *Aida*.

An army! she cried.

———

Bound irrevocably, aerially, together, the riders plunged into New Mexico at moonrise, engines singing. They took on fuel at Clayton and negotiated the twisting Don Carlos Hills as if they were salt flats. At one point, Gant pulled over and turned off his key and Umberto followed suit. They watched the stars with interest until Gant began to howl. After a moment, coyotes started howling back from far away, their voices echoing through the canyons.

Ju one fucking strange dude, said the boy.

I just don't want to think about the past anymore, said Gant.

And singing with dogs will help?

Not dogs. Coyotes.

What's that?

Coyotes? Wiley Coyote? Chaser of roadrunners? Stealer of babies? Eater of rabbits? Coyote's a Spanish word, for God's sake.

I'm not Spanish. I'm Cuban American.

Okay, okay. Never mind.

Umberto squinted at the map in the starlight.

Listen, *meng*. How 'bout we ride to Santa Fe and get a fancy room and drink expensive champagne? I gotta thank ju for saving my life.

Gant knew that Santa Fe meant a dip south, and he hesitated.

Really, I didn't save you, he said at length. You would have landed in the corn anyway. You were just lucky.

Only the really heavy stuff fell straight down, jes' in case ju didn't notice, and ju and me together on your bike—we were heavy.

Gant spread his hands. Umberto looked out over the desert.

So much space, the boy said. Finally, I think I left the gods behind.

What gods?

The gods of Santeria I grew up around in Miami. They're not desert gods, they're tied to the ocean. They were always looking over my shoulder anyway, so good fucking riddance.

I don't believe in gods, Gant said thoughtfully. But I do believe in magic. As a force underpinning everything, holding it all together.

Umberto nodded, processing things.

My name's Umberto Santana, he said at last.

I'm Mercury Gant.

I might have figured ju'd have some crazy name, the way ju howl at wild dogs.

My first foster father sold aluminum siding. Gant smiled. Mercury was the name of his favorite brand. Strong as steel, he used to say. Lasts forever. Doesn't scratch, doesn't dent, doesn't scar.

Umberto gazed out over the hills, thinking not only about the strange and shiny liquid his dentist—a drinking crony of Pedro's—had used to fill his cavities, but of how much his eyes could relax looking so far away into the night, out here where the ground went up and down and the stars dipped down to meet it and there were no muffled shots in the distance and nobody's blood was boiling from the wet heat, and Cuba and Castro and hatred and frustration seemed problems as far away as those tiny stars up there.

Sorry, *meng*, but ju look like maybe ju got a couple of scars. I bet the kids must have made some fun wit' you, huh? Anyway, how about it? Ju gonna ride with me to Santa Fe?

Sure, Gant decided right then and there. I'll do that.

They rolled on through Gladstone, Mills, Grasslands and Roy, taking the mountain road to Wagon Mound, crossing the canyon of the Canadian River. They fueled up when they crossed the interstate, finding that they still had plenty of energy, and pressed west toward Guadalupita and Mora as the promise of dawn turned the horizon pale. The sun finally appeared in the tight mountain turns of the Santa Fe National Forest, making the pines glow. The smell of piñon filled Umberto's helmet, delighting him with how foreign it was, and how fresh. It made him think that maybe he was free at last, that he really would be able to start again. When the sun actually showed itself for the first time over the ragged treetops, he thought of Graciela.

She lit up sometimes too.

And she smelled wonderful.

Maybe when he got where he was going, wherever that was, he could send for her.

The heat built quickly, turning the day into a scorcher. When they finally rolled into Santa Fe, they were grimy, tornado-whipped, sweaty, and pale from the dust of the road. Also, they were an odd couple, their relationship unclear to both of them and to the world. No hotel would have them.

Convention in town. Sorry.
We've been booked for months.
Might I recommend a hostel?

There are several good campgrounds on the edge of town.

Finally they pulled into a big, impersonal chain hotel near the city's center. It was the kind of place Gant might have serviced in his limo. It was the kind of place of which Umberto had always dreamed, with pale marble floors and Indian paintings of gaunt men on starving horses and beleaguered women wandering with poles.

I'm sorry, gentlemen, our rooms start at three hundred and fifty dollars, and we're completely full tonight.

Gant felt a wave of fatigue wash over him.

Don't you have anything at all? We've been riding all night.

I'm afraid not.

Umberto surreptitiously pulled a hundred-dollar bill out of his tailpack and tucked it into the dark-suited manager's breast pocket.

The best room, he whispered. And the best champagne. Deeply chilled.

Snap snap went the fingers, and suddenly bellmen were scurrying everywhere, like squirrels, and the riders found themselves in a penthouse suite: two big rooms, two queen beds, a john the size of Pedro Santana's living room.

Deeply chilled? Gant repeated as he closed the door behind them.

Like a James Bond movie. Umberto grinned.

Gant flopped down on the bed, rejoicing in the sweet release of the muscles in his lower back, muscles that had held him up and over the handlebars for what seemed like years. The boy took a shower and emerged wrapped in a white terry cloth robe emblazoned with the hotel's marque.

I've got pins and needles in my hands, he announced.

Just the engine vibes, Gant reassured him. It will pass.

Louis Roederer champagne arrived, on a rolling cart covered with white linen, protruding from a silver bucket, cradled by fine crushed ice.

This is damn nice of you, but are you sure you can afford this place?

Sure I'm sure, *meng*. I'm Umberto Santana.

We flew, Gant mused. Damned if we didn't actually fly.

He worked the cork and they drank the bottle down like pop and Umberto picked up the phone and ordered another.

You're some crazy kid. Gant laughed.

Ju should have seen jourself, spinning around on that shitpile of jours. Umberto giggled.

You should have seen yourself leap into midair for that tailpack. How many hundreds you got in there?

There was a pause. Umberto stared silently down at his stomach. If Gant had been sober, he would have stopped there, but he wasn't, and he didn't.

What did you do, rob a bank?

Ju talk too much, *meng*.

Ah. But I ride that old Beemer pretty well, huh?

Ju sure do, Umberto replied instantly. He wanted the moment to pass. He regretted saying what he had. Ju been riding a long time, huh?

Started younger than you, Gant confirmed.

What kinda work ju do?

Right now I'm just traveling.

How about before ju left?

Sales.

Siding, like ju dad?

No. Tires.

Before that?

You got a lot of questions for a guy who doesn't want me to talk.

Yeah, well. So what did ju do?

Fishing boat charters.

How about right away? Ju know, like your first job?

Right away, I was in the army. After that, I was a limo driver. What about you?

Motorcycle wrench.

Good to know. You got a girlfriend at home?

Yeah, I got a girlfriend.

How come you didn't bring her along?

I work alone.

You love her?

There ju go again, Umberto said, trying to rise out of the cushioned wicker chair that held him, but failing.

Relax, tornado boy. We're just together as an accident of wind.

With that, Gant stumbled off to bed.

Umberto fell asleep right there in the chair.

Do not disturb.

————

The pink hotel in Boca Raton's was a landmark: a golf course, a beach club, tennis courts, several restaurants, a fitness and pool club, and a convention center. There was a new tower and an old wing, and a custom wooden cabin chrysler that plowed the flat waters of the Boca inlet to bring guests to the ocean. Special Agent Cooper was interested in exactly none of these amenities. All that concerned him was the employment records of the astonishing number of people who maintained the grounds and kept the rooms clean.

The task was appalling, partly because his boss, Special Agent in Charge Nancy Fortier, a woman with the political nose of a prison bloodhound, had set him at the huge number of files solo as punishment for not making quicker progress in apprehending the man responsible for the death of Vicky Rule. She was feeling the pressure of Timothy Rule, who wanted the thief flogged, keel-hauled, maimed and finally murdered, whether he had seen what was happening with Vicky or not.

Cooper rubbed his tired eyes and looking out through the small office window onto the regal row of palm trees that led to the guard station and the front gate. Guard station, he snorted. To keep the Rolexes, BMWs, diamond bracelets and Jaguars safe. The Shining Path Guerrillas could land a helicopter on the back forty and everybody would be too busy doing their nails and watching their tees even to notice. Cooper had already used the Bureau computer to crossmatch for criminal records. He had come up with nothing more than a woman on probation for shoplifting diapers and a grizzled ex-con who had given up boosting cars in favor of Jesus and was now leading the hotel choir in the Christmas parade. All that was left was to check for suspicious deposits to bank accounts—as if the thief would take the money from one bank and put it in another—and to go carefully through the files of the able-bodied young men on the grounds staff. Outwardly he was examining papers, but inwardly he was waiting for his muse, a Sherlockian homunculus who resided on his shoulder, shoved rapiers of investigative insight through his temples, producing the kind of quick and early results, and promotions, that common wisdom held came only from police busywork.

The butler did it.

Is there a silent business partner?

Any offshore insurance policies?

Check the victim's last stock trade.

Ask the wife if she purchased the poisoned condoms herself.

Look for loose floorboards under the bed.

Search for another screen name.

Were those the suspected killer's usual brand of socks?

Cooper wondered whether his unpredictable muse might possibly be playing both sides, like a rogue arms dealer, or whether he had a cousin, a criminal munchkin Moriarty who whispered in the ear of successful thieves.

Pssst. Rob a bank.

Hey! Use a gun.

Trust me. Just walk out slow and easy.

Such mysticism helped him explain why he hadn't even a tiny concrete lead, and helped him avoid facing the other possible reason for his lack of insight.

Suzanne.

He'd been thinking about her all day. He was in the grips of a ridiculous romantic fantasy. He had been swept completely off his feet. He never thought about what it would be like to grow old with a woman, to care for her when she was sick, to touch her hand underneath a restaurant table or share a coffee with her in the kitchen or Sunday strawberries in bed. Maybe that was because the girls he generally dated were Bureau employees, secretaries or clerks too close to law enforcement to offer him the caring and balance he craved. Suzanne, on the other hand, was obviously smart, forthright, eager and attractive, and he sensed a potential depth to her which he hadn't found in others. It didn't hurt that she had money, but it wasn't particularly important to him either. If it had been, he could have followed his father into real estate, or used his own law school contacts to join a criminal defense practice in Miami. No, Suzanne had a sparkle, a positivity, a light which he knew would shine right through the dark curtains around his soul.

So, at 6:30 that evening, he closed up the employment records and went to the marble-tiled men's room. He washed the ink off his fingers and the day off his face, combed his hair, straightened his tie, and went to the hotel bar to wait for her. When she didn't show up on time, he ordered vodka with juice of the fresh-squeezed pink grapefruit—Cooper loved citrus fruits—and when, after half an hour, she still hadn't shown up, he had another. He'd been working so hard on the case all day that he had eaten almost nothing, and he found himself drunk enough to feel his heartbeat in his hands.

After an hour, she walked in and he lurched slightly when he stood to greet her.

Devil in a Blue Dress, he hummed.

Oh no, she said to herself. Not a lush with a gun. What *was* I thinking?

She made herself smile while she explained that she'd been held up by an overactive Dow Jones, but he could read the concern in her eyes and see that she felt stupid for having worn the neon low-cut with the push-up bra, and for having worked so hard with her makeup, and she remained standing, the better to make good her escape.

Take it easy on me, he said with boyishly reassuring charm. I was so nervous about seeing you today that I couldn't eat a thing and you're an hour late and I had two drinks. It wouldn't have hit me so bad except I rarely touch booze. I'll be okay after we have some dinner.

Okay. So what are you drinking? she asked gamely, her relief palpable.

He held the cocktail to her lips so she could have a sip.

Yum, she declared. I love grapefruit.

Big points for you, he said. And you look fabulous. But tell me, why did you cover your freckles with makeup? I love your freckles.

Something went moist as sweetbread inside her and she had to fight the urge to kiss him then and there. Instead, she ordered the same drink for herself, and when she finished it they moved to the dining room, where they had a leisurely meal of pasta, shrimp, fava beans and duck washed down with Merlot. Afterward, they rode the old wooden boat back and forth to the beach club, pressed together in the hot summer air, at the stern, where the breeze was best, and where the glow of the little red running light made life seem as exotic as a Moroccan bazaar. Their lips met for the first time on the way back, and she put her hand on his gun because it intensified her pleasure.

Safety's on, he mumbled into her mouth. Just in case going you're trying to shoot me. I wouldn't mind, like this, with you, except that it would deprive me of what's in store for us together.

Her hand crept down between his legs, and the boat captain, who had glanced back at them, turned away, embarrassed. The air was filled with brine and diesel, which she liked very much, and her perfume, something rich and lemony, worked wonders on the wickedness center in Cooper's brain.

I've got a room, she murmured.

So do I, he said.

Mine's better. She smiled.

And so it was, a penthouse suite with a balcony they used for lovemaking with a view of Boca, and to the north, the twinkling lights of Palm Beach. During the hours they stayed connected, sharing secrets and lies and fears and quirks, Cooper never once thought of Umberto Santana or Victoria Rule, but once, in the middle of the night, still on the balcony, he awoke to the whirring sound of what in his dreams was the bank's video camera, but which turned out to be a mosquito.

Suzanne's leg was heavy on his chest.

Heavy in a good way.

SIX

❧

I spent all my cash at the salon, says Caroline. Do you mind coming in for a minute while I get some?

A sailboat floats by on the Intracoastal Waterway, its mast visible behind the house. Gant parks the white stretch Lincoln by the imposing black gate, and Caroline punches in the security code. Mesmerized by the swell of her hips against her tight pantsuit, he follows her up the walkway, between the sweet-smelling ginger plants and the birds of paradise and the roses.

I keep money in the kitchen. She smiles, unlocking the front door.

Cookie jar?

How did you know? You've been watching me, haven't you?

You bet he has, but right now he takes in a view of the spiral staircase and the overstuffed furniture, forgettable artwork in rococo picture frames, zebra-skin rug and Tiffany lamps. He takes in the sparkling swimming pool and the Jet Skis and the yacht. He takes in the money. Somewhere, Gato Barbieri is playing "Europa." He follows Caroline through the swinging door to the kitchen, imagining maids in black dresses and white aprons and butlers in white coats shouldering silver trays bearing Pimms Cups and Canadian Club.

He bumps right into her, because she is frozen in the doorway; her hand is at her mouth.

The boy.

The man.

The blood.

———

Wake up! Umberto shouts, jostling Gant's shoulder.

Wuh?

Some kind of nightmare, *meng*. Hey, I'm glad I'm not ju. Ju screaming like ju on bad acid.

Gant focuses his eyes. The boy's hair is washed, his face is shaven, his cheeks bright, his hips jaunty.

What time is it?

6:30

Gant's tongue is thorny and he's got a head like Saturn's rings. He groans and falls back against the pillow, covering his eyes.

Thanks for not stealing my money, by the way, says Umberto. He's only half joking.

Thank *you* for turning my world into pea soup.

Hey, that was four hundred bucks' worth of champagne.

That makes all the difference. Gant sighs. It really does.

I paid the bill, okay? So let's ride.

Temples pounding, Gant trundles off to the shower, wondering whether he really wants company. This motorcycle ride is a transition for him. It's his way of giving himself time to adjust. He knows that's why he hasn't taken an airplane across the country. He decides it wouldn't be bad to have the kid along.

You ever seen a ghost, Umberto? he calls out.

I've seen guys on speed and crank and heroin. They're weren't ghosts yet, but they were getting there.

This wasn't the answer Gant was after, and he turns his attention to washing himself. His challenge is to devise a new cleansing ritual right then and there. Changing something basic about himself each day is part of his plan to break up the old Mercury like a clogged drain. He takes a washcloth, something no self-respecting ex–Special Forces man would do, and lathers it heavily with the perfumed hotel soap. Then he scrubs himself until he is as pink as a flamingo and shows abraded high spots on his cheeks. That should do it. Now he smells like a French whore.

At the same time, Umberto is outside the hotel, polishing the bikes, intrigued by the way the BMW's cylinders jut out, wondering why Gant hasn't erased them when leaning over in turns, marveling at the sheer funk of the machine, the industrial, agricultural simplicity of it, puzzling on what kind of a man would ride such a contraption and sleep through the chance to steal so much dough.

They're on the road within the hour. Umberto is buzzing on coffee he brewed himself in the room, and it takes Gant, normally a rider capable of smooth, effortless speed, all his concentration to keep up. He comes close to a couple of cars and curbs, mistakes born of his vicious hangover, and is more relieved than anything when Umberto pulls over to fill up in Los Alamos.

Biological weapons.

Atomic bombs.

Parks and flowers.

An all-American city.

Let's take this dirt road to Cuba. The boy grins, pointing gamely at a little red squiggle on the map. I know these bikes are heavy, but we're tornado tamers, *meng*. We can do it, right?

Gant nods wearily. The kid does have a certain infectious charm.

They take the required detour from the main road, and within half an hour they are on an unpaved mountain pass. All about them are white fences bearing Department of Defense insignias. Military installations strike Gant as incongruous, up here in the wilderness, but Umberto seems not to notice. He's of a different generation. His is a world of smart bombs and video war and satellites that can read postage stamps. It *does* occur to the boy that perhaps he's being tracked, not by ghosts in their midst but by cop satellites, by NASA. He shrugs off the feeling. If they wanted him, they'd have him by now. They don't even know he exists. They don't care.

He had no idea of Tim Rule's obsession, nor of his power.

The riding pair climbs higher. The high plateau turns to pine forest and the sun is warm on their helmets, the backs of their hands, the tops of their legs. Crest. Rocky road. The downside. Rio de Las Vacas. The whole Arroyo del Agua spreads out before them, bounded by the San Juan Range to the north and the Jemez Mountains to the east. Gant pulls over and takes off his helmet.

Cattle, he declares. This scrubland was once a green valley, I can promise you that. Ranchers sacrificed it for the sake of a side of beef. Look at it now, dried and parched. If we didn't have such a taste for burgers, the world would be a better place.

Forget burgers, the boy cries. Think filet mignon!

On the outside, Umberto is glib, but inside he's wishing he could share his new wealth with Graciela, wishing she could have tasted the previous night's champagne. His reverie is interrupted by the sound of a logging truck barreling down the hill. It's a big black rig, an old Peterbilt with a hood like an Alsatian's nose and tires in shreds from the stones. *Rumble.* Diesel smoke like dragon's breath. *Puff.* The riders move a bit farther off the roadway. Umberto keeps his eye on his money. Gant keeps his eye on the approaching grille.

Morning time. Miller time.

The trucker is drunk. To him, the bikes look like fair game. He swerves to the right, and his front wheel, fully as tall as the middle of Gant's chest, sideswipes the BMW's left saddlebag. The blow knocks the bike clean over, and Umberto, standing between the bikes, is made a flesh sandwich. *Crunch.* His fall brings the fast Triumph down. A piece of the fairing rips off, taking a mirror and a corner of windshield too. The handlebars of Gant's machine pin Umberto's leg against the Triumph's muffler, and like an iron burning a dress shirt right through to the board, the chromed steel evaporates his jeans and starts in on the flesh of his leg, hair first, then epidermis, dermis, fascia, connective tissue. Umberto screams and wriggles, trying to pull his leg away but succeeding only in sliding it against the muffler, stretching out the burn.

The trailer passes in the same line as the cab, spitting gravel at Gant's raised hands. One of the pieces lodges in his forehead, right at the hairline. Another cracks the corner of his lip. He tastes the road, the oily residue of the rock, and then there is only a rumbling in the ground under his feet, a great dust cloud from the monster. Umberto rocks on the ground like a wounded armadillo. Gant wrestles his bike upright, shuts off the gasoline, pulls out his emergency kit.

Bite on this, he orders, handing Umberto a folded-up leather riding glove. He snips the boy's bluejeans at the cuff and yanks the fabric back, pulling long strings of cotton out of the raw flesh. Umberto is stoic, but the iodine bath that comes next gets him twitching and digging his heel into the ground so hard he almost makes it through to China. When Gant smears antibiotic salve over the burn, Umberto's eyes roll back in his head. When Gant finally applies gauze to the wounded flesh, Umberto moans into the dirty glove and bangs his fist hard on the footpeg.

Sorry, mutters Gant. It's deep. I've cleaned it, but you need to rest here for a while. He picks up a baseball-sized stone, tucks it into his shirt, starts his bike and heads off, raising a rooster tail of dust behind him. It doesn't take him long to catch up with the truck, sliding through the turns, holding the throttle wide open on the straights like a dirt track demon. The shaft-driven BMW is immune to the rigors of the road, and its plush suspension soaks up the rises and dips. Gant closes in from the right side, trying to stay stealthy, but the driver sees the motorcycle headlight, and thinking that more fun is in the offing, swerves first to one side and then to the other, blocking the road. Gant dodges the mudflap at the rear right of the truck, then drafts the wake and slingshots forward until he is next to the cab.

He's just a kid! he screams at the driver, standing up on the pegs. His whole life's in front of him! What the hell were you thinking?

The driver raises his middle finger and wrenches the wheel murderously to the left. Gant evades the truck with a flick of his hips, then hurls the stone, which passes through the open window, strikes the driver's elbow, then bounces onto his face.

Mask of pain.

Open mouth.

Dangling tooth.

Eyes of surprise.

Gant twists the throttle and shoots ahead so the swinging trailer doesn't clean the trees with his hide, then steers off the road to a safe spot by a boulder. *Pssss.* Airbrakes. The trucker slows, stops the rig across the road so Gant can't get back to Umberto. The door to the cab opens. Gant's heart pounds. He's thinking shotgun. He's thinking it all might end right there. Suddenly, from far down the road, he hears engines, tires, horns. Cursing, the trucker slams the door, gives Gant a look of pure hatred, and roars off. A caravan of white Department of Defense vans comes into view as Gant turns around. There are men in coats and ties inside, and they gesture for him to stop, but he doesn't, not until he is back at Umberto's side.

The boy is standing. The Triumph too.

Guys in the van helped me out, he says.

Gant nods.

Where did ju go?

Something I needed to do.

Umberto waits for more, but that's all there is.

We need to fix ju face, he says at last.

Gant checks his look in his side mirror. The cut above his brow has clotted, leaving an angry streak of dried blood, and his lip looks raw. He cleans himself with the first aid kit.

Above them, in a tree, a woodpecker finds bugs.

Everything is so quiet.

————

Graciela sits on the commode, protected on either side by metal partition walls. From above, not much can be seen but her glorious crown of black hair, a sweet-smelling forest which once benefited from Umberto's nuzzling the way a real forest benefits from a fire, but which now lies flat and lonely because the boy is gone. She is there for some minutes, while outside, in the kitchen, French fries sizzle and burgers hiss and chicken gets dry in the middle. Graciella doesn't usually work mornings, but today she's pulling double duty. Her shift hasn't quite started though, and she is relieving herself for the first time that day, to catch the nocturnal hormones, in accordance with the pregnancy test instructions. Through the bathroom wall, she hears fat Shirley take a drive-thru order for an Egg McMuffin. She guesses that Shirley eats two meals for every one she sells.

Graciela wonders whether she will have a fat baby. She fears fat. She will do anything to avoid it, not just because she knows Umberto has a taste for slender but because she has dreams of becoming a movie star. In truth, she has the looks for it, but will have to work even harder than she has been to drop her strong Cuban accent, at least if she wants to work in Hollywood. She will also have to exercise, an activity she abhors.

The small, white, plastic test tray has a plus sign and a minus sign in it. One of these will soon flush pink with news. Graciela waits, the tray on the floor in front of her, her elbows on her bare knees. She knows she's pregnant—her sore nipples and missed period are the clues—but she wants to make one hundred percent sure. She wants to have the test to show Umberto when he comes back. She wonders where he could be, what could have made him leave so suddenly and without warning, and she wonders if he knows that in her heart of hearts she has always been holding out for someone else, someone who could waltz into her life and change it. It's not true love she's looking for, she already feels that for Umberto, but rather a male instrument of transformation, a film director or a photographer or a rich man who will put her up and show her off and take her where she will be seen by the right people. This is why she always works the front counter instead of cooking in the back—a work schedule for which she must pay by using her fingers and lips on the manager, alone, at night, after everyone else has gone home. Even so, it's worth it for her. She is certain that just the right man will someday come in and order a Big Mac.

She wonders if her child will have its father's terribly handsome eyes or his beautiful hands, which she knows are prettier than her own. She makes a genetic rundown of what she and Umberto Santana should contribute:

Hair—his is good but hers is better.

Eyes—hers are pretty but his are more exotic.

Nose—hers is perfection, as are her cheekbones.

Arms—hers are good but his are better.

Legs—hers once caused a traffic accident in Coconut Grove.

Butt—well, maybe *that* was what caused the accident.

Feet—his are better; she doesn't like her long toes.

Shoulders—they are both blessed.

Chest—their kid, boy or girl, will be lucky to have hers. It's all about shape and it's all about proportion. She knows this from women's magazines.

Charm and luck and magic—those things must all be Umberto's.

If it's a boy, Graciela will have to worry about gangs. Just yesterday a teenage boy was shot in the head while watching television by the window in his mother's living room while she was cooking dinner. Prime time goodbye. If it's a girl, she'll have to worry that she doesn't get pregnant too early or that she'll be more successful and prettier than her mother, something that would bring Graciela a mixture of pride and pain. At eighteen, the idea of not reaching her dreams makes Graciela grip her own knees so tightly she'll have small bruises later.

She wanted to do the pregnancy test with Umberto's arms around her in some fancy hotel, maybe one of the high rises on Biscayne Bay, overlooking the water, like in *Miami Vice*. She thinks about how things will be when Umberto comes back, how maybe he'll get a better job, maybe start his own business, a motorcycle shop or a gas station, a speedymart, even something romantic like a Cuban restaurant on Calle Ocho.

She thinks of them in a home near Mercy Hospital, someplace on the water, in the fancy part of Coconut Grove, a yacht in the background, white and grand and proud, with antennas and blacked-out windows. She thinks of fluffing up feather pillows. She thinks of strutting out to the boat, paparazzi cameramen lying in wait for her. She thinks of sunning in a string bikini while they interview her for *Entertainment Tonight*, her little baby playing on the deck with a rope around her waist so she won't fall overboard.

The test finished, the sign appears, down there on the dirty floor.

Plus.

———

The pair came in fast as falcons, having covered the ground from Nageezi, Bloomfield, Aztec and Cedar Hill in record time. They paused to take in the great spectacle of the Animas River basin, and then drove straight into town for gas. They filled up and wiped down and Umberto bought a fresh pair of jeans and some gauze for his bandage. They stopped at a diner for breakfast, and Gant ate like the Hound of the Baskervilles.

Ju a pig, *meng*. Ju know that? Umberto smiled. Just like that piece of shit bike ju ride. What's with you and that thing anyway?

Gant gave back something between a smile and a wince, because of the cut on his lip.

Classic, simple machine, he replied. You can fix it anywhere, anytime. The design's been around since 1923, and the construction's first cabin. I like things that last.

And I like shit that changes, the boy cried. I want every day to be a different adventure. I don't want to die wishing for shit I never got.

Wait until you're older. Gant smiled gently. Probably you'll worry about dying knowing you could have made the world a better place for the people around you but didn't.

Umberto heaped three teaspoons of sugar into his coffee.

Yeah, yeah. So where ju headed, Mercury?

West Coast.

Vacation?

More to check out if I like it, see if I want to stay.

Umberto nodded, scanned the local newspaper he'd picked up. He never used to look at the paper, but he was looking at it now. He didn't want cops climbing up his ass without a little warning.

Ju ever been up on a balloon? he asked Gant, pointing at a picture of the brightly colored craft they'd seen on the way in.

Don't love heights, said Gant, thinking of a certain jump he'd taken in Nam, thinking of his tangled parachute and the forest canopy that saved him.

How about the circus? That's in town too.

How about we keep riding?

The circus is cool, *meng*. We can shoot for a teddy bear at the penny arcade.

I'm not big on freak shows.

Personally, I see a freak, I thank God it's them not me.

Yeah, said Gant. You can do that. But what then? They're still there, looking out at you. That's got to do something to your heart.

Ju walk away, *meng*. There's no point dwelling on shit like that. It's not like ju can do anything for them, besides maybe give 'em a dollar.

There's always something you can do. You just have to care enough to do it.

Okay, okay. How about monsters? They got those at the circus too.

I'm burned out on monsters. Gant sighed.

Ju take your comic books too seriously. Umberto grinned. Jes' listen to this deal, okay? Ju go with me to the circus, I keep ju company on the road for a while. Can't lose, right?

As long as we don't stay all day, Gant grumbled. His face was hurting him now, and the miles ahead seemed suddenly insurmountable.

They rode on full stomachs to the local fairground and parked in the soft dirt, by candy cane tents rising up out of the high desert. They braced their side stands with flattened beer cans so their bikes—which had lately seen their fill of undignified poses—would stay upright. Inside the big top, they watched bears ride bicycles and they watched monkeys trip clowns. Cowhands, the majority of the audience, hooted and cheered for a beautiful acrobat. Umberto ripped chunks of cotton candy off a white paper cone and pointed up at her with a red sticky finger.

Check *her* out!

You check her out, Gant replied. I'll watch the tigers.

They came bounding into the ring, their pungent aroma shooting up the tent pole like a jetstream. The trainer followed, the Liberace of cat tamers. The tigers, white ones, made a circle like a wagon train, tongue to tail. *Crack*, went the whip. Faster circled the cats.

You been married?

Never, Gant replied.

But you've got some sweetheart hiding out west, don't you?

The tigers set to jumping through flaming hoops, and Gant's answer was lost in the roar of the crowd.

Later, at the arcade, Umberto set himself up with fifty dollars' worth of tickets at the shooting gallery and fired at the rotating windmills and the flying ducks, and the pop-up beavers and the chimney witch. Gant watched with arms akimbo as the boy missed and missed and missed.

Ever shoot a real gun?

Nah.

Right. Now listen up. Push out with one hand and pull back with the other, that will steady the barrel. Now pretend you're a tank and the rifle's the turret. Swivel left and right, swivel up and down. Use your whole body, but keep that gun locked into your hand.

Umberto complied, and the results were instantaneous. Bells started ringing, and before long he won a stuffed beagle. A crowd gathered around them, which made Umberto nervous, so he gave the dog to a little red-headed boy and announced it was time to go.

That was when the fortune-teller got Gant by the arm.

He wasn't a typical-looking seer, not thick and dark and Transylvanian, but thin and nervous and cigarette-smoking and vain. He tucked a loose lock of stringy brown hair out of his face often, trying to maintain it behind first one ear and then another, to no avail at all. He was sallow and soft and he looked longingly at Umberto, not with desire but with envy. He had always wanted to be handsome, and he had always wanted to be tall.

And lucky.

And rich.

And free.

Come to my booth, he said. Work's slow. I'll tell you the future for free.

Umberto nudged Gant. Let's go, he said. Let's ride.

No cards, no crystal ball. I'll work purely with energy. You got spirits attached to you. I can see that from here.

Gant felt a rush of confusion. Fortune-tellers and spirits attached. What was he doing here, in the middle of the country, at a circus, with a thief? Time paused for a millisecond as the impulse to ride off met the impulse to relieve himself of the burdens he was carrying. If someone could really exorcise his demons . . . well, he'd do anything.

Don't believe this voodoo shit, *meng*, Umberto urged.

But Gant was already on his way to the mystic's tent, moving the way people do when they find themselves in front of the refrigerator without remembering how they got there. The tent was a shady affair with AstroTurf on the floor, the smell of stale coffee in the air, an old TV with rabbit ear antennas, and a folding card table beside an overstuffed chair into which the fortune-teller pressed Gant firmly while Umberto looked on from the door, seeing a spark of electricity—nothing more than a small drizzle of electrons—jump from the fortune-teller's hand to Gant's forehead.

In or out, the fortune-teller snapped.

Reluctantly, Umberto slid in.

Relax, the fortune-teller commanded. Breathe in, breathe out. In, out. You are sinking into a warm tropical sea. Deeper and deeper. Deeper and deeper.

Gant closed his eyes and his breath migrated to his belly.

Tell me your name.

Mercury.

Entities are riding your soul like a horse, Mercury.

Entities, Umberto muttered, rolling his eyes.

A lock of loose hair fell forward over the fortune-teller's nose, but he didn't push it out of the way. He was concerned with other things.

They are souls who lost their way to Heaven, he explained calmly. When a soul gets lost, it panics, and attaches itself to the first safe haven, a house, a tree, a person.

Gant felt weak-willed and frail, like he couldn't move if he tried. His soles sank into the AstroTurf, his sit-bones touched springs in the chair.

Who's on me? he whispered.

Soul attached to Mercury, speak your name, the fortune-teller intoned.

Pretty girl acrobat, give me a blow job, Umberto mimicked his tone.

Xavier, Gant's lips moved.

And when did you attach yourself to Mercury, Xavier?

The moment he stepped into my house.

Do you remember that moment, Mercury?

Yes.

Oh, come on! cried Umberto.

Why did you attach to Mercury, Xavier?

Because he was sad. It was Gant's voice, but not really, and it sure wasn't Gant speaking.

And you liked that about him?

It felt comfortable.

Because you were sad too?

Very sad.

Why were you so sad, Xavier?

Mercury knows.

Do you know, Mercury?

Gant let out a convulsive sob.

Hey! Ju stop making him cry! Umberto exclaimed.

How have you affected Mercury since you've been with him, Xavier?

There's a long silence.

Xavier?

I've made him sadder.

But one of the reasons you were drawn to Mercury is that he was kind. Am I right, Xavier?

Kind. Yes.

Well, we're going to give you the opportunity to do something kind for Mercury. Clinging to Mercury isn't the place for you, you know that, don't you? I'd like to call a spirit guide, someone who knows and loves Xavier, somebody to take him up to the light, to the spirit plane where he belongs. Will somebody come down for Xavier?

Somebody's coming. The voice and the being behind the voice were Gant this time.

It would be me if I could get that acrobat down here. I'd come all over the place. Jesus, Mercury, why do ju listen to this shit? Ju some kind of idiot? He got ju in some kind of a trance, or what?

Umberto did not understand the burden Gant carried. He could not know how badly Gant wanted his memories to be wiped away.

It's his father, Michael, Gant whispered, and his arms are open.

Xavier! Your father's here. He's happy to see you, said the fortune-teller.

They're holding hands! Gant said.

You're going to miss him, aren't you, Mercury?

Yes.

That's fine. Don't worry. Now, I call upon the other entity inside Mercury. Come forward.

There was no response.

Come on now, you can't hide from me, the fortune-teller declared.

Still nothing.

Tell us your name.

Gant began to perspire. His breathing became fast and shallow.

You don't stop fuckin' with my friend's head, I'm gonna bust up your shit right now, Umberto threatened.

Tell us your name! the fortune-teller insisted.

Gant groaned and thrashed in the chair.

Fuck this, Umberto said, taking a step forward.

The fortune-teller held up his hand, violently, strongly, but it didn't stop Umberto, who was not comfortable with things he didn't understand. Deep down he feared that if there were really entities and spirits, he himself might be in dire straits. He put his hands on Gant's arm.

No! the fortune-teller hissed. She'll never let go if you wake him now.

Umberto paid no attention. He set to shaking Gant like a rag doll.

Oh, said Gant, coming out of it slowly, his eyelids fluttering.

Ju okay, *meng*?

I'm so small, Gant replied. So alone.

You turned into some dude named Xavier.

She's still stuck on you, the fortune-teller declared. I could have done something, but your friend insisted on waking you up.

Don't listen to him, Mercury.

I couldn't get her off, the fortune-teller bemoaned.

Suddenly Gant was up.

Suddenly Gant was running.

Caroline! he screamed.

Tears hitting the ground, he was to his bike before Umberto could catch him. He yanked on his helmet and took off with a roar, sending dirt everywhere.

Because he had to tie down the money, and because Gant rode so fast, the boy didn't catch up until they were halfway to Cortez, just south of a town called Mayday.

SEVEN

❧

Tim Rule strode through the FBI offices as if his legs were canes and his arms were cannons. Little Stefan had to run to keep up.

I'm here to see Special Agent Cooper, Rule told the receptionist. Already he'd gone through a metal detector and a frisking—his big gold watch—and he was in no mood for objections.

Is he expecting you?

Just tell him it's Timothy Rule.

In less than two minutes, Eagle appeared. He had on his best happy face, but that didn't wash with Rule, who had made his first million slumlording in South Miami–Dade, enforcing rental payments with hired gunslingers and thugs, and his hundredth million outmaneuvering Big Sugar in the Everglades land deal which allowed the biggest and most lucrative development in South Florida's history.

You look happy. I gather that means you've caught our man, said Rule, following Cooper to his office.

I'm working on it.

Rule was a terrible snob, and as he looked around the bare little room he thought to himself that no man with so little taste, no man working in such a sterile environment, could possibly produce results. It didn't occur to him that Eagle's real work took place on the street and at the computer, nor did he have any idea of the agent's fascination with Umberto Santana and his dedication to the collar.

The average bank robber makes three grand for his trouble, said Cooper, closing the door behind him.

You think I'm interested in the bank robbery? thundered Rule. I'm not interested in the bank robbery, Agent Cooper, I'm interested in the man who killed my wife.

Maybe your son should wait outside, Cooper suggested.

In response, little Stefan picked up a red-and-white model Corvette Stingray from Cooper's desk and spun the wheels with his hands.

V-8 power, he declared.

The child had the skin of a poltergeist, thought Cooper. Little blue veins running up and down from neck to eyelids, his carotid pulse showing how hard he was taking his mother's death and how much he needed good hugging, supportive counseling, special attention, special food.

You can play with that if you want, Cooper said gently, but be careful not to break it.

Forget the toy, snapped Rule. You find the killer, I'll buy you a real Corvette.

Are you attempting to bribe me, sir?

I'm attempting to get some serious action on a murder investigation, Mr. Cooper, and if I don't get it from you, I'll get it from your supervisor. Do you understand me?

There's some difference of opinion—Cooper sighed—as to whether the man even noticed your wife at all.

Tim Rule's face turned redder than red.

Do I care whether he noticed her? I care more if the moon is made of Stilton cheese, because that would make it a poor development bet. When you arrest the bastard, I'll take care of making a murder charge stick. That's all you need to know. Now find him, you hear me? If you don't, you're going to be handing out parking tickets at the Dadeland Mall.

Federal agents don't issue parking citations, Cooper said mildly.

Exactly my point, asshole.

Do you have to talk this way in front of your son? Cooper was genuinely pained for the child.

Worry about my wife and leave my child to me. She died gasping on the floor because of this dickhead, and I aim to see him brought in. My son needs to know how the real world works. He needs to know how a man gets things done.

At that moment, something blossomed inside Cooper, something which, if truth be told, had been planted that first night in Suzanne Emerson's bed. Perhaps it was some comfort dealing with the rich and powerful—there were increasingly frequent moments when Cooper imagined that he might someday himself be rich, if only by marriage—but perhaps it was something else, a self-confidence born of accepting the turns of fate life seemed to be bringing him lately; a conviction that no matter what he did, things were going to turn out the way they were going to turn out.

Sit down, he commanded sharply, and when Rule did not immediately obey, he took him by the shoulders and forced him into a chair.

Rule was so stunned that at first he didn't react. He couldn't remember the last time anyone had physically pushed him.

Now, I'm sorry about your wife, I really am, said Cooper. For you, for her constituency, and especially for Stefan here, but the fact is that I've spoken to the U.S. Attorney's office several times about this case, and it is their position that the thief is wanted for felony robbery but not for murder.

Rule struggled to stand, but Cooper held him down.

That's not to say there might not be a manslaughter charge—a manslaughter conviction, even—but I want you to understand that what we are looking for is a bank robber, not a killer.

Just tell me what you're doing to find him, Rule said stonily.

Stefan turned the Corvette over in his hands and sniffed the tires.

Real rubber, he announced in that high-pitched voice of his.

A huge amount of police work has been done and is being done. Interviews, forensics, dragnets, and a lot of nitty-gritty footwork. It isn't sexy stuff, but it's the kind of effort which typically produces results.

Sexy, repeated Stefan.

What produces results is money, snapped Rule, money and dumb luck.

Mommy's dead, said Stefan, no longer able to resist the temptation of putting the model car down on the rug for a run. I saw her turn blue.

Luck wouldn't hurt, Mr. Rule, but you can keep your money.

You're very lucky, Daddy, Stefan interjected.

A tiny professor of philosophy.

———————

Gant's first thought, the thought that stays with him through the whole morning and well into the afternoon, the thought that stays with him through cop interview after cop interview, the thought that stays with him through the recounting of the tragedy to persistent reporters and even through his second visit to the house, late at night, just him in his white limo come to call on the new widow, is that the kitchen smells of nothing so much as raw meat.

Raw brainmeat, because that's what's spattered on the Corian countertop, melding so intimately with the pattern of the stone that in less than half an hour a cop will place his hand unwittingly into a pool. Raw bonemeat, because that's what the white splinters and slivers are, including the one that goes crunch under Gant's penny loafers as he steps into the war zone. Raw blood, like what might drip off an undercooked steak, because that's what paints the white cupboard doors, one splotch low, for the little boy, and one blotch high, for the husband.

There are even a few drops on the note, which Caroline picks up and which Gant reads, over her shoulder, the smell of her sweat coming to him, the sound of her breath too, ragged over a cotton tongue, whistling over the scaly skin of suddenly parched lips.

There's no other way, Caroline. This is the only escape from the nightmare my life has become. I can't face anything anymore, not Xavier, not you, not the world out there, not myself.

Gant's glance flickers unwillingly over to the little boy's face, which lies on one cheek on the kitchen floor, surprisingly intact and calm, considering that the back of his head is missing. Amazingly, Gant thinks like an analyst, judging that Michael Hamilton shot his son in the back of the head, unable to look him in the eye.

Coward.

The note falls from Caroline's fingers. It flutters down onto the floor, landing facedown. Gant takes Caroline's hand.

Hard as an ax handle.

Cold as ice.

The trembling starts, then the shaking. Gant tastes bile and thinks that perhaps he is going to vomit, but that doesn't happen, largely because of the sound coming out of Caroline's mouth. It's a keening like Gant has never heard. Like nobody has ever heard, except perhaps if they have been to war, to a battlefield, which Gant has. The sound brings back the image of villages ringed by bamboo forests, of brown-skinned people in black clothing dashing from huts, gelfire on their skin, their hair, their lives, their souls. The sound rattles china cups in the cupboard. Strangely, it also makes the cord hanging from the wall telephone dance a rhumba, transfixing Gant's gaze, partly because he's rooted to the ground and can't do or say a goddamn thing, and partly because it gives him something funny to look at, for relief, something other than the revolver on the tile near Hamilton's elbow, not all that far from what used to be Hamilton's face.

Listening to Caroline scream, Gant has the ridiculously inappropriate thought, which he will never, ever share with anyone, that at least Hamilton's sinuses are clear.

The cord.

The phone.

Gant picks up the handset.

911.

It's hard to hear anything over the noise still coming out of Caroline, so he just talks.

Address.

Two dead.

When he's finished, he puts the phone down, wondering if anyone else has called, then figuring that the shots were probably quite muffled, having been fired at a range so cruel and close.

He puts his arm around Caroline and finds that she's a statue. She won't move. She can't move. She isn't screaming anymore, but her pulse is racing, he can feel that everywhere in her body, and she is sweating and rigid. Her legs don't work, her feet don't work, everything is locked. He picks her up—she's not a small woman, but lanky and busty and long and toned—and he carries her out of the kitchen, out through the dining room and the living room and into the sunshine.

As he waits, he wonders how he can possibly be so cool. A Jet Ski goes by on the Intracoastal out back. *Drrrrroooaan.* Then everything goes quiet. A cicada buzzes.

Then, finally, sirens.

As if all that urgency and drama are going to make a damn bit of difference now.

———

Pedro and Consuela Santana circled the new sofa like hyenas around a kill.

Leather, said Consuela. Where did you get the money for that?

I bet on the Marlins, Pedro defended.

You never won a bet in your life. You bet, they lose. I could bet on *that*. I could get rich on *that*.

You don't follow baseball. They won, countered Pedro, looking at his wife's cleavage as she bent over the yielding cushions and the welcoming hide. She put her fingers into the bullet holes—which she had made earlier—and she looked good doing it, even if she was a hooker. Maybe she looked good *because* she was a hooker. It had been a long time for Pedro. Years since he'd touched her, months since he'd touched anyone at all.

She looked up suddenly and caught him staring. A smile spread over her face. After all these years, the power still gave her a thrill.

What are you looking at?

You look good, Consuela, he said.

I didn't come here for your bullshit, Pedro I came here to find my son. We both know I look like a forty-year-old whore. When I was eighteen, before the boy, *that* was when I looked good. But you were too busy drinking to notice. You were too busy gambling and shooting. The big gang man. Gonna have your own club, you told me. Gonna buy me that Jaguar convertible I wanted. You remember that? *That* was when I looked good.

Pedro waved her away. He was tired of hearing it. He knew he had screwed up his chances with the Cuban mob by running on at the mouth, by not doing what he was told, by simply being the man he was. He ran the danger of falling face-first into a terminal stupor of self-pity if he listened to her too long, if he thought too hard about how right she was, about what his life had become, sitting there in front of the TV with his Hatuey and the game on, wishing the bet he'd just made with some of Umberto's cash *had* been a winning bet, instead of a losing one, like Consuela knew it would be.

You still look good, he said, because she did. Incredibly good. All that fucking and sucking didn't seem to faze her all. No disease, no drugs, just clean makeup and a trim figure. A businesswoman, that's what she'd become. And because you still look so good, I bought you something.

He pulled a cardboard box out from behind his chair, flat and big and wrapped in red. She recognized the wrapping as Victoria's Secret's—she'd received this kind of thing more than once or twice—but she didn't say so, she just took it.

Go on and open it, he urged.

She was surprised. He hadn't given her a gift since she left him and got her own apartment and started turning tricks, coming to see Umberto when she could, taking the boy to her mother's, leaving him there, bringing him back, an arrangement which had only broken down when Pedro confronted the old woman with the fact that her precious daughter did not, as she claimed, work as a secretary for an insurance company.

You want money, huh? she challenged. Or maybe a quickie?

He shook his head.

I don't want anything. It's for you.

He wasn't about to tell her it was a guilt gift, something he felt he had to do with a tiny fraction of the thousands Umberto had left him because, in fact, the boy had asked him to.

She tore the paper off, carefully, at the taped edges, so she could use it again. Her red fingernails matched the red paper. Off came the top. *Crinkle, crackle, tear* went the tissue paper, revealing a bustier—low-cut, sequined and blue.

To match your eyes, said Pedro.

What he meant, of course, was to match her eye *shadow*, but Consuela didn't call him on it because it was a beautiful piece of lingerie, and because she knew what he had been trying to say.

Are you drunk?

He shook his head.

Are you sick? You're not going to die, are you? Umberto disappears and then you die? Don't tell me.

Pedro puts his hand on her shoulder.

I'm not going to die. I just got you a present, that's all.

A little bell went off in Consuela's head.

You think Umberto's okay?

I think he needed to leave Miami.

Why? she demanded. She was thinking that her son was following his father's bum lead. She was thinking gang war. She was thinking crime.

Pedro shrugged, avoiding her eyes.

You know why! she screamed suddenly. She could do that. She was like a human volcano of sound.

I don't!

Yes you do! I can see it in your eyes. You can't lie to me, you bastard! Where is my son?

Consuela barely talked to Umberto. The boy knew who and what she was, and she knew that he knew. She knew that he held himself apart from her, as he did from his father, as he did from his lover, as he did from his boss and everyone else.

As he did from the FBI.

All of a sudden, you care? he said mildly.

They stood panting at each other, the blue bustier on the threadbare carpet between them. Something heated up in the room, something that hadn't been there for a generation. He'd gotten soft and fat, and there were clear traces of alcoholism in his lids and in his nose, but Consuela remembered suddenly what it was she had seen in him, all those years ago. The high cheekbones, the flat stomach—she wished *she* could drink like that and still be slim—the aquiline nose, that goddamn heartbreaking smile. She'd been on the street at night. She'd been yanked into vans and forced into corners and stripped down in motel rooms. She'd been leered at and winked at, chased after, and wooed. She'd been rubbed raw and beaten, and she'd been promised the world. Yet in all that, she'd never seen anything like Pedro Santana's impossible smile.

Goddamn you, she said softly.

He kissed her. It was a tentative thing, mouse whiskers against dandelion, and that's what made it work for her. If he'd been rough, if his beard hadn't been totally shaven, if he'd used his hands or pressed himself forward, that would have been it. She'd have been out the front door in a heartbeat. But instead, she allowed his affection, even put her hand down to measure his interest. He pushed her fingers away.

Just sit with me, he said. Sit with me on the couch. We don't have to watch a ball game. We don't have to watch anything at all. We can just sit and talk.

You're lonely, she said incredulously. You're lonely and you miss him.

Pedro shrugged.

Say it. Say you miss him.

I miss him, said Umberto's father, astonished that it was really true.

Consuela reached behind her and let her hair come down. She unbuttoned her blouse, showing him her bare back as she took off her lacy bra and slipped into the bustier, listening to him breathe.

I'm not what I was, she said, and he understood exactly what she was trying to say, understood that she was self-conscious, revealing herself in front of the man who was still, legally at least, her husband, after so many years.

A woman at twenty is like an unexplored country. He smiled, pretending not to notice the scratch mark scars on her fine skin. At thirty she is dark and mysterious. But at forty! Ah, at forty, she is technical perfection.

She raised her arms and pirouetted once and then sat down beside him on the new leather couch, bought from a store in Perrine with stolen money. He put his arm gently around her and pulled her so that she fit into the crook under his arm.

Are you all right? he inquired.

She tucked herself in tighter, smelled his smell.

I will be when my son comes home. She sighed.

Pedro Santana, the man who spent his life in front of the television, thought of the dead senator and the little boy and the angry, bereaved tycoon, and knew that it was Umberto who had done this thing and that he was proud of his son for pulling off something he himself could never have managed.

Don't hold your breath, he said, but too quietly for Consuela to hear.

EIGHT

❧

They are in Dove Creek, Colorado, just a few minutes from the Utah state line. There are heavy clouds in the distance, and Umberto is hoping it doesn't rain because his Michelins are bald. They were okay when he left Florida, but the heavy stresses of steering the big bike have eaten into the front tire, and his power smokeouts—performed before he met Gant, whose mere presence has inexplicably put a lid on such antics—have erased the tread on the rear. He knows he's best off taking things slow and easy, and he's finding it hard to keep up with Gant.

Normally, Gant rides smoothly, easily, and seemingly without effort, responding to nothing unless there's a real threat in it, leaning his bike effortlessly around potholes and gravelspits and moving deceptively fast. Today, however, he's as wild as a wounded cheetah. Umberto wonders if the older man knows what a fragile thing of flesh and bone he really is. He realizes that there's an irony in the young man showing more wisdom than the old. Still, he doesn't dare say anything. Not with the mood Gant has been in since the fortune-teller and some crazy ghosts named Xavier, Michael and Caroline.

Caroline! The way Gant ran! Umberto himself is almost believing the sheer madness of talking to spirits, partly because he thinks that he might be possessed by Graciela. He can't stop thinking about her. It's as if she's reaching out for him, like Gant's mystery woman, through the ether. He wonders why the warp and weft of his existence has not significantly changed, why he doesn't *feel* that different, why he hasn't immediately been struck in the head by the high life he was expecting. After all that has happened, he is still just Umberto. How, he wonders, can he feel so sorry for himself with well over $300,000 in his tailpack? How can he be so *stuck* when he's only seventeen?

Gant notices that the boy is having trouble keeping up, and at the Welcome to Utah sign he pulls over. The Manti-La Sal National Forest is less than ten minutes ahead, and Indian land is not far to the south. The edges of the road melt into desert, but there are mountains closer than the horizon, so that even now, in summer, both cactus and snow are in evidence.

You okay? the older man asks.

I'm the king of speed, *meng.* But ju never going to outrun that bitch that's grabbed onto ju, jes' in case that's what you're thinking. I been trying to do some outrunning of my own, and my bike's faster than jours.

Gant gives a start. He's been riding differently in order to follow his commitment to change one habit a day. He hasn't considered that he might be on the run. He takes a deep breath and smells the desert sage. How can this boy be so smart?

You love your girl? he asks.

Love? Umberto shakes his head in confusion.

Either you do or you don't. Love's like food. You gotta have it, but it can make you sick. You have to be careful. Eat the right thing and you're energized. You have a great taste in your mouth. Eat the wrong thing and, believe me, you have no idea what can happen. You want to call her up?

Nah.

But she's waiting for you, right?

Who knows what she's doing, *meng*. She's a woman.

Gant hits the kill switch on his bike, and Umberto follows suit, leaving them to the quiet tinkling of their cooling engines and the hiss of the Utah wind.

Ju figure I got entities too? Umberto asks at length.

Maybe everyone does. Gant shrugs. But a guy who robs a bank, there's not much doubt, is there?

Robs a bank? I don't know what ju are talking about.

Okay, says Gant, but we've flown without wings together, remember? Tell me, how do you feel about the senator?

Umberto gives him a blank look. Tim Rule's attorney Ron Bernstein is wrong about him. He isn't the type of crook who gloats over his crime. He isn't the type of crook who enjoys reading about himself in the papers or, God forbid, seeing his face on TV.

The senator? he asks slowly. His fingers drum his helmet.

Drum.

Stop.

Drum.

Stop.

It was all over the papers, says Gant.

I don't follow the news much.

Ah. Well, a woman had an asthma attack during your holdup. A woman with a little boy. She was a senator, and she died.

Umberto turns pale. Those thick clouds grow closer. Gant tries not to think of anything at all, and he tries not to move. It's as if he's got a fish on the line and he doesn't want to jerk the hook out of its mouth. Something's coming up, he can tell that much. Something is going to break the surface.

Umberto dismounts onto the Utah sand. Utah, a woman of proud character, a woman of frigid glances and heavy, hot embraces, has been watching the two men on their machines. She has already shown her charms in the form of this breathtaking landscape. Now she decides to show she can sting.

Xxxzzzz.

The ground speaks of rattler.

Don't move, says Gant.

Whoa. The boy smiles. That's some snake.

The rattler's tongue flicks out.

Back up slowly, Gant says tersely.

Check it out. She's tasting my foot.

Will you move now? Gant urges. He's thinking about just grabbing the boy and yanking him backward, but he's still astride his bike, and he's got farther to move than the snake does.

Ju think she's from the Devil? Ju think she's come to measure me out?

For Christ's sake, says Gant. We don't have to talk about it again if you don't want to. The robbery, I mean. The senator. The dough.

This could be a test, Umberto muses. I'm not giving an inch.

Back the hell up, will you?

Mi abuela, my grandmother, she pulls these funky black things out of people's ears and eyes and noses. Their asses too, by the way. Can ju believe that shit? Strange, huh? People come to her because they're bummed out or they got bad luck or they're afraid of dying, and she just sticks her twisted-up old hand right in and pulls those things out, drops 'em into buckets of bleach. I'm not kidding. I've seen 'em plenty of times. They look like black frogs without eyes. Black eels too, like my mother's Cuban heel stockings soaking in bubbles in the sink. Where do those fucking things come from, meng? It's no trick, I tell ju. This world, it's different than we think.

Gant's mind is a racing kaleidoscope of images, from his first memory, a cold metal trash can, to the last time he saw Caroline smile.

We can talk philosophy after you move back, he says.

Robbing a bank's not so bad. That shit's insured. Nobody's gonna suffer. Government just makes new money. Me, I've got dreams.

Let's hear 'em, says Gant, dismounting carefully, as if he were moving underwater, and beginning a careful shuffle in the boy's direction.

I gotta see everything in the world. I want to be a wise dude like ju. I want to travel, ju know, have experiences.

You don't have to give up on your dreams, says Gant. You made a mistake, that's all. I won't ask you about the money again. Now, will you please move away from that snake?

Umberto crouches down for a better look at the rattler.

Shit happens. I didn't know a lady died.

They're not blaming you for it.

Maybe they should. Maybe I was her angel of death. Could be, huh? Me, an angel. That's some funny shit, right?

No court will blame you, says Gant.

No court will get the chance.

Your lawyer will say you didn't have asthma in mind. It might not even have been the gun. There might have been perfume nearby. She might have had allergies.

It's sure true that I didn't have asthma in mind. Umberto laughs, dropping so low he's on a level with the snake.

The rattler puts out her forked tongue and touches the boy on the cheek.

Xxxxxzzzzzz.

Stop fucking around and stand up!

Snake breath is sweet, Umberto whispers. Listen, if I go, keep half the money. Just shoot the rest over to my girlfriend, okay? Her name's Graciela Perez and she works at the McDonald's on Federal Highway in Perrine.

Will you stand up, you crazy son of a bitch?

Umberto exhales in response. To the snake, it's a thunderstorm up close, something to flee from, but not something to bite.

There is, however, Gant's boot.

It comes sailing in at exactly the same time, darkening the sky and bringing a different wind, one that smells of oil and gas. The snake reacts in fear. Muscles from her neck power the attack. Tiny ligaments in her mouth swing her fangs forward, and they meet Umberto's chin at just the place where his few dark hairs grow. At the precise moment of impact, the snake's eyes dip down behind protective scales.

Umberto screams.

Gant's steel toe hits the rattler, sending it flying into the scrub.

Xxxxzzzzz.

Umberto flops over onto his side. Blood streams from two holes in his chin.

Remember Graciela, he manages to say, and then he faints.

Gant swears a streak that would shame a comet. He hops up and down, kicks the ground, punches the air. Then he drops down next to Umberto, puts his lips to the boy's chin, and sucks in warm blood just as hard as he can.

Suck.

Spit.

Suck.

Spit.

In the Utah background, on the edge of desert and hill, the mortally wounded snake flops onto its back, white ventral scales to the clouds.

Xxxzzzz.

Slap goes Gant's hand, when he can suck no more.

Red grows Umberto's cheek, while Utah stays quiet, watching.

Wake up! Gant shrieks, desperately scanning the horizon for a car, a truck, a train, a chopper full of medics.

He slaps Umberto's other cheek, and the boy catches his hand.

Chill out, Merc, he says. The bitch didn't juice me.

Gant thinks of the adders in Vietnam, the way they hid in the grass, the way they bit bare feet but sometimes didn't waste venom—a digestive enzyme—saving it instead for a mouse or a rat. He hawks and spits one last time.

Umberto climbs to his feet.

I'm Superman, he says, dancing around and beating his chest. Even snakes can't hurt me.

Gant grabs him by the collar, using a grip the boy cannot break.

Listen, amigo. You think your witch grandma is protecting you? Let me tell you something about life. The only thing protecting you is dumb luck. You feeling guilty about the senator? That's your business. You want to go kill yourself? That's your business too. Just don't do it on my time, in my space, on my personal stretch of road!

Finished, he pushes Umberto away. Angry, the boy walks shakily to his bike, dons his gear, and aims the big Triumph down the road all alone.

There goes Utah's silvery laugh.

————

What bothers me most, says the police lieutenant, standing in the slaughterhouse that once was a home, is that the bastard did it in the kitchen.

Caroline and Gant sit together on the couch, a proper distance between them. Gant's legs are crossed, a thin line of his white flesh visible above the dark sock on his right foot. He gets the crazy thought that he matches the giraffe rug in front of him. Caroline's knees are together and her elbows are in tight and all in all she's pretty much a human version of a night-blooming flower at dawn, totally closed in on herself, her beauty hidden by petals with their dull sides to the sun.

She's called her personal physician, or more precisely, Gant has called him for her. A highbrow Boca internist, the doctor has declined to make a house call, even to the Hamilton residence, even in the face of violent death. Accordingly, the paramedic has administered a tranquilizer, and Caroline has finally stopped screaming, although it has taken most of an hour to pry her away from the remains of her kid.

How long have you known the deceased? the lieutenant asks Gant.

Known him? I don't know him. Drove him to the airport a couple of times. Once to the symphony, once to a play. He uses the limo service, that's all.

Michael didn't even like Gant, Caroline interrupted. He thought he drove too slowly. He thought he had the hots for me.

This gets a couple of raised eyebrows from the cops in evidence, and a deep blush from Gant.

Is that true, Mr. Gant? Do you have the hots for Mrs. Hamilton?

Look, says Gant, spreading his hands. I drive these folks, that's all.

And you were returning from where?

I picked the lady up at the beauty parlor.

How long were you gone from the house, ma'am?

Caroline sniffles and blows a goose call into a Kleenex.

A few hours, that's all. Mr. Gant took me to the mall, then to my hair appointment downtown.

Do you always use a limousine service to go shopping?

Don't be an idiot, Caroline snaps. My Mercedes is in the shop and my husband said he needed his car. It takes weeks to get a hair appointment these days, and we were going out to an affair tonight.

An affair?

A benefit for children with AIDS. Caroline tries to wither him with a look.

The lieutenant doesn't wither easily. He's tough, and he's a natty dresser too. His shoes speak of slush funds and his tie is a kickback banner.

A guy shoots his kid instead of going to a benefit for children with AIDS. Meaning no disrespect, Mrs. Gant, but don't that just beat all?

Why don't you ease off? Gant suggests.

Why don't you answer my question? Do you find Mrs. Hamilton here a hot number?

If you're done with me, I'd like to go, Gant says, rising.

The lieutenant pushes him back down.

Answer the question.

Mrs. Hamilton is a beautiful woman. A blind man could see that. What's your point? How are you helping things here?

The cop turns to the new widow and rakes her with his steely gaze. In her turn, she looks at Gant as if she's seeing him for the first time. Something is going on in that head of hers.

Was your husband an alcoholic, Mrs. Hamilton?

He drank, if that's what you mean.

The lieutenant rolled his eyes.

I just can't get a straight answer out of anybody, can I?

What are you talking about? Gant snaps. You scum-buckets should be bringing her flowers, not lip. She's just lost her husband and her son and you're grilling her up like a sea bass. Why don't you clean up the kitchen and then get out of the lady's face?

The lieutenant regards him with interest.

I'm just trying to figure out what Mr. Hamilton was thinking, that's all. What would drive a man to get drunk and shoot his little boy in the head and then swallow a bullet himself?

I think you're garbage, the way you talk, says Gant. I think you're a piece of shit with a badge.

Yeah? Well this piece of shit wants to know why you

care how I talk to her, why you're still here. That's what doesn't add up, see. You drove her, you dropped her off, why did you have to come into the house?

He came into the house because I'd run out of cash and I needed to pay him, Caroline interrupted.

I'm sure he would have taken your check.

Caroline looks like she's going to faint.

The tranquilizer.

The shock.

I was going to give him a tip.

I'll bet you were.

Gant hauls off and punches the lieutenant in the mouth. It's a good right hand, and the cop swallows it poorly. His gun comes out. Gant's hands fly up. The lieutenant's beefy boys slap cuffs on him.

Great, mutters Gant. This is just great.

The lieutenant pulls a clean, starched, monogrammed hankie from his vest pocket and dabs at the blood at the corner of his nose. He reads Gant his rights.

You're a goddamn embarrassment, says Gant. Use that in a court of law.

As he is hustled out into the moist air, more cops stream into the house. They carry black bags like doctors used to, full of tweezers and vials and brushes and tape. Gant can't help but think they look like ants. Or soldiers. Or soldier ants.

Someone pushes Gant's head down.

He's alone in a police cruiser, but all he worries about is Caroline.

NINE

❧

On the morning that Ruth Bishop lost Audrey, Port Townsend was reeling from the effects of having its senses torn asunder. A low pressure trough of a magnitude never before recorded had descended over the town, spreading flat the sour cloud of paper mill gases which rose every day but Christmas. Typically, the gases were pushed along by breezes the natives had learned to read. If the breeze was offshore, the weather was likely to be fine. If the wind came in from the rain forests of the Cascades, fog and drizzle could be expected. If the wind came in from the ocean, the town braced for either a gusty day or, in winter, one of the fearsome Pacific storms which had been known to crash up over Water Street right to the foot of the basalt bluffs.

But that morning, the smell spread in every direction, and people walked around in a disoriented daze. Even feral dogs were confused, and business at the shoe store was so slow that Ruth loaded Audrey into the microbus and puttered up the road to the supermarket.

I can't find the ocean, Audrey complained, for indeed the bitter smell of wood pulp and bleaching agents had masked the briny tang of the harbor.

It's on the left, where it always is, Ruth replied absently. She was thinking about the birthday barbecue she

was planning for Audrey, down at the picnic tables by
Fort Worden. Ruth feared the party because Audrey
hadn't many friends and people seemed to be avoiding
the two of them lately, as if merely being in their presence might communicate ill luck.

Blind.

Orphaned.

Widowed.

Tragically alone.

You are practice-cooking in your mind, aren't you?
asked the little girl. Why?

Because I have to, Ruth replied truthfully. Because
otherwise things get salty or burned.

In the supermarket parking lot, Audrey tried to climb
into a shopping cart, but Ruth stopped her.

You're too old to do that, she decreed.

This slew the little girl utterly. Too old! Would there
be nothing left worth doing when she turned six? Hiding
behind oversized sunglasses, she followed Ruth reluctantly into the store, her fingers tucked lightly into the
back pocket of her grandmother's jeans.

You want corn on the cob, right?

I don't know, said Audrey.

But you love corn on the cob!

Maybe I do and maybe I don't. Audrey pouted.

The market was the biggest store in Port Townsend,
and served as even more of a meeting place than the
smoke-filled café at the end of Water Street, where the
tourist shops ended and the famous array of wooden
boats began. Yuppie housewives and working women
alike met at the supermarket, and men did too, on coffee
breaks, between jobs, between girlfriends, between fishing trips, even between jalopies.

Bragging.

Lying.

Desperate.

Laughing.

The energy of the place took hold of Ruth Bishop and

grabbed her by the throat, dragging her first to the produce aisle, where she picked up potatoes and corn, and then to the dairy case, where she selected maple-flavored yogurt for herself and two big cartons of Vanilla Fudge Häagen Dazs for whomever among Audrey's preschool friends might attend the birthday luau. The little girl followed her through the choosing of Tupperware food-storage items—in case the party was a total bust—and through the selection of paper cups and plates, plastic knives and forks.

Finally, when Ruth became involved with cosmetics, Audrey snuck off in search of an empty cart to ride. When she found one, she followed the sound of the cash registers to the front of the store and exited unmolested, partly because she moved with grace and confidence, bumping into precisely nothing, and partly because her RayBans lent her an authoritative air. Once outside, she placed one foot on the low bar of the cart and pushed herself across the parking lot as if she were skateboarding.

The shopping cart princess.

Meanwhile, inside, Ruth examined her eyebrows, which had diminished on a seemingly daily basis since Hiram Bishop was declared missing and presumed dead. She experimented with different shades of mascara, a dab of blue-black here, a smudge of dark brown there. She tried making arcs and she tried making lines, frankly confused by the contour of her own forehead. When finally she found the perfect eyebrow pencil, she discovered she was alone.

Audrey?

Ruth moved quickly to the end of the aisle, paused adjacent to specially priced blue corn tortilla chips, stacked like stones at Machu Pichu, and looked in every direction she could. When she didn't see Audrey, she went back down the aisle to the other end, and then down each of the other aisles, hawk talons around her heart. She went to the cash registers, where, driven by the strange weather, hordes of people were stocking up on such survival items as canned foods, batteries and water. Finally, in desperation, she ran outside.

By this time, Audrey had already careened across the road that led into town, riding on gritty black wheels, powered by the incline of the parking lot. She encountered no traffic, as it was stopped at the light, and followed the run and crown of the road right into the sandy entrance of the commercial marina. She passed varnished wooden centerboards and black metal engine cases. She rolled by rusted winches and peeling dry docks and fishing tackle and gas. Grinning, shrieking with pleasure, she steered with a combination of body English, foot pressure, finger nudges and the guidance of some magical internal map, completely unaware of the number of near misses she accrued. Her active right foot kept the cart going whenever its velocity flagged—all to the memorized tune of Rimsky-Korsakov's mad bumblebee—the normal mental warning bells all silent in the face of the mill stench and her childish enthusiasm.

Within minutes she was deep within the labyrinth of the marina—a place full of red and yellow and blue and safety orange she couldn't see, a place where entire oceangoing craft could be lost for months, and repairs might last for years. It wasn't until her cart ran straight into a suspended motor sailer that her ride ended, and with it her joy, for the impact sent her over the front of the cart and drove her forehead into the smooth, fiberglass keel.

Stars.

Blackness.

Quiet.

In the distance, just offshore, came the song of whales.

Nearer, but impossibly difficult to pinpoint through the forest of masts and hulls, came the onshore wail of one frantic Ruth Bishop.

Suzanne Emerson surveyed her garageful of motorcars, a cup of coffee in one hand, a sticky cinnamon bun in the other. She tongue-wrestled a raisin, listened to the hum of the dehumidifier, and considered her red Jaguar convertible. The car hadn't been right from the beginning, partly because it was red, partly because it was the wrong vintage, but mostly because it had never, unlike all the other machines in the garage, belonged to her late, beloved father. Late last week, a call had come from one of her father's former business associates, the man who owned Charles Emerson's *original* '66 yellow XKE convertible. The caller had said he was unwilling to take the time to restore it. Frankly, he said, he was too old and infirm to drive a ragtop anyway, and he wondered if Suzanne might have an interest in her old man's ride. She had jumped at the chance, and to make space in the garage she put the red car in the paper at once, generating an almost immediate call from a buyer who sounded Hispanic and excited. For security, Suzanne had asked Eagle Cooper to show up for the sale. She bought cars far more frequently than she sold them, and she wasn't sure exactly what might happen.

The buyer was overdue, a good thing, as a furious South Florida summer rain had set in and Cooper had yet to show up. The ozone crackle of a nearby thunderstorm crept in under the garage door, as did a thin line of moisture, and God drummed his fingers on the garage's peaked roof. Suzanne put a leg over the low door of the red Jag and climbed in, her eye instantly picking up the car's imperfections, the incompletely reconditioned Smiths gauges, the split in the dashwood, right above the central row of black toggle switches, the loose door handle, the rotting rubber window liner. It was still a fine car, but her father would never have let things get this bad.

Knock knock.

It was Cooper, at the side door, a soaking newspaper over his head.

I've been ringing the doorbell for ten minutes.

Sorry, Eagle. I didn't hear you over the rain.

Your buyers are in the driveway. From the look of them, I'd say we need to sneak out the chimney and get some lunch.

That bad?

A diesel Volkswagen with more dents than an overripe passion fruit.

Suzanne came into his arms, pressed against his wet sport coat, felt his muscles against her breasts, felt his gun.

I have a better idea. Let's just send them away and find something else to do, right here in the garage, with the rain coming down outside.

Smiling as conspiratorially as possums, they went out together into the downpour. The little green VW Umberto had bought and tuned for his father sat looking squalid in the rain, one right front quarter panel rusted, one wiper blade missing, its windows fogged up. Suzanne rapped on the window, and it went down immediately.

Can I help you?

We're here for the Jaguar. The convertible. For my wife, said Pedro Santana.

Beyond him, in the passenger seat, Suzanne saw a striking-looking Latina in a tan raincoat, street-worn and weary, but with a knowing, defiant gaze. When their eyes met, Consuela touched her hair.

I'm afraid it's sold, Cooper announced.

Consuela's face twisted into the look she reserved for lawyers and cops. Lies sounded the same to her whether they came from FBI men or parole officers or johns. Suzanne saw the change in her, and looked away to the green river of antifreeze emanating from the car. As if to reveal her dishonesty with strong light, the rain stopped and the sun came out, all in an instant. Steam rose off the driveway, and the Santanas emerged with great deliberation from their car. Pedro wore a sport coat and Consuela a classy pantsuit with a little too much costume jewelry.

My husband promised me a Jaguar, she announced.

Could we at least *see* it? Pedro pleaded, reassuringly squeezing his wife's hand.

It was that gesture that did it, filling Suzanne with shame. Without a word, she went and opened the garage to reveal the gleaming chrome and flowing fenders, and to release the faint smell of gasoline and the fine perfume of old leather. Pedro stepped back at the sight of the Rolls-Royce, but Consuela flew at the Jag like a honeybee queen.

Mira, she said. *Perfecto.*

In an instant, she was in the driver's seat, checking her look in the rearview mirror, caressing the shift knob with her hand. She turned the key with authority, giving the car just the right amount of gas, eliciting a roar from the engine.

Usually doesn't start so easily, Suzanne murmured.

My wife's father had one of these cars in Cuba, Pedro explained. He used to drive her down the canefield roads, very fast, when she was just a little girl.

Her father? Suzanne repeated, as Consuela cut the ignition and got out of the car to run her fingers lovingly over the long hood, a distant smile on her face.

She loved him, said Pedro. That's why I want to buy this car. I give you twelve thousand right now.

The price is fifteen, Suzanne steadily replied.

Twelve and a half.

Fourteen seven-fifty.

Twelve seven-fifty.

Fourteen and a half.

Thirteen.

Fourteen.

Thirteen and a half.

Thirteen, Pedro Santana said with a move of his hand that said it was his last offer.

Sold.

Pedro pulled a thick wad of cash from his jacket and began counting bills with shaky hands.

Something's not right here. Something stinks bad, Cooper's homunculus whispered in his ear.

Lotta cash, Cooper said casually.

People like cash. They don't know me, they don't want a check.

They *do* know you they don't want a check, Cooper thought.

But he didn't say it.

What bank do you use? he asked instead.

Ten thousand, eleven thousand, twelve thousand, thirteen, said Pedro, handing over the stack.

Que linda, cried Consuela. *Que bellisima*. Pedro, thank you. Thank you.

They filled out the paperwork on the hood while Cooper tested a random handful of bills with a verifying pen.

Never did get the name of your bank, he said. Later, he'd wonder why he pressed it. Cash, after all, was cash.

Homunculus.

Pedro ignored him, and Consuela slid behind the wheel once more, transported to Havana again, before everything fell apart. Behind the wheel of that car, she could pretend that Pedro's promises had been real ones and that the pillow talk of undying love, of fidelity, of wanting to father a tiny town full of her children and grow old with her there, him as king, she as queen, had been genuine.

Santana, Eagle Cooper mused, as the Jag disappeared, followed by the old Volkswagen and a cloud of smoke.

Seems like I've seen that name somewhere lately.

———

Caroline doesn't even see Gant at first. She just stands on the finger of the dock in a tight sundress, a tote bag at her feet, a Panama hat on her head, surveying the boats, thinking that if Michael had liked yachts things might not have turned out as they did.

These aren't yachts, of course, they're working boats. Commercial fisherfolk man them, and charter captains like Gant, who is newly out of the limousine business and has not yet learned that it's not the shine on the rail that brings in new business but the comments made on golf courses, and the billfish trophies gracing pool room walls and dens.

He steps forward with a can of brass polish in his hand, wishing he'd showered, wishing he wasn't wearing boat shoes, wishing his bluejeans weren't tattered, wishing his boat was bigger.

I AM A ROCK. She reads the name off the stern.

It's from the Simon and Garfunkel song, Gant explains, wiping his hands on his pants.

I figured. May I come aboard?

He offers her a hand, notices how she gives him more weight than would be strictly necessary, pressing their flesh together as she steps onto the boat, barely rocking it, as if she were just a tern alighting.

How did you find me?

The court had your forwarding address. It wasn't that hard.

I never thanked you for bailing me out. He smiles.

It was the least I could do. You were gallant. A gentleman. The only one there.

I was an idiot, says Gant. Hitting that cop.

A chivalrous idiot, she corrects gently.

If that lieutenant had shown up for my hearing instead of going to his kid's soccer game, I'd probably still be in the clink.

Probably.

They look at each other for a time.

So. Here for a charter? Gant asks finally.

I don't fish. She sits down on the sparkling fiberglass gunwale. But I'd love it if you'd take me for a ride.

This is something Gant hasn't been expecting. He's been trying to forget about Caroline, trying not to read every little newspaper item about the case, recognizing himself to be in danger of improperly using his fantasies of her to fill a vacuum in himself, a vacuum he was born with, a vacuum he's been nurturing for years. He has known he should start dating again, stop thinking about her crying on the couch, stop thinking about her all alone. He has known that at least he should go to a bar from time to time and put himself in a position to maybe meet somebody real.

Nothing would give me greater pleasure, he says solemnly.

That is possibly true. She smiles.

Weak in the knees and trying to stay calm and focused—boating is still new to him—Gant rechecks everything for the twentieth time and finally casts off. They head out of the Fort Lauderdale marina at no-wake speed.

How's the charter business? she asks, standing with him by the wheel, under the cover of the cabin, eighteen feet of boat before them, seven feet behind.

You're my second job. The first was a businessman who caught a minnow, then vomited. It wasn't pretty, but it was the fastest three hundred I ever made.

You poor guy, she says, which rankles Gant, because despite his self-deprecating manner he really wants her admiration, not her pity. He's not a pathetic man, he's just smitten. He turns his attention to the charts as they head into open water. The weather radio crackles. The day is going to be fine, but the seas are swollen.

Thunka, thunka.

Speedboat wake.

Are you still living in the house? Gant asks as delicately as he can.

It's on the market. I couldn't bear to be there. I bought a condo.

Are you all right, uh, financially?

She looks at him like a well-meaning princess addressing a serf. As if he knows anything about finance. Mr. Limo Service. Mr. Captain of the Good Ship *Vomitus*.

Michael had insurance, but it didn't cover suicide, she answers evenly. If there's one thing she's good at, it's controlling herself.

What about his business?

It's big and I think I've sold it. Men's clothing isn't exactly my trade.

What did you do before you were married?

For a while I went to school. Then I did nails.

A flying fish jumps up. The sea reaches up to catch it on the way down.

You were in hardware?

Caroline hits him on the arm.

Fingernails, Gant. Fingernails. As in beauty? As in salon?

Gant cannot imagine Caroline waiting on anybody. He cannot imagine her helping to make another woman more beautiful.

How did you meet your husband? he asks, trying to cover his surprise.

I won him at an auction.

What?

There was an auction for dinner with the most eligible bachelor in Boca Raton.

Come on. Gant laughs.

Believe it. Cost me three months' wages. There were five guys there. He was the youngest, the wealthiest, the most charming. Best catch. Isn't that a laugh? Look, let's not talk about him anymore. Will you take me to the Bahamas?

Gant is still chuckling.

The sea's a little rough for that, but I'll take you into Florida Bay if you like, maybe up to Naples.

We, ah, *I* have a condo in Naples, she says. Michael bought it before we were married. He used to take all his girlfriends there. It's right on the beach.

Naples it is, then.

Gant turns the boat south and the wind changes. Caroline stands face into it, and it blows her hair straight back. He watches her eyelids flutter. He watches the wispy hair at her temples dance like Medusa's halo.

Do you know what the police are saying? Caroline asks. They're saying I was having an affair with you.

Crazy. Gant shakes his head, tapping the gas gauge with his finger.

You think?

Gant makes a big business of studying the gas gauge, the temperature gauge, the oil pressure too.

I should get out of town. She sighs. I should get out of South Florida.

A gull cries, surprisingly close, hovering off the starboard railing, yellow beak slightly open.

You must think about your little boy every waking minute, he says.

Michael wanted more kids, she says distantly. A dynasty. Can you imagine what would have happened if there had been three or four?

Gant doesn't know what to say. He's struck by how strange it is that Caroline is there with him on his boat. He wonders if the cops are watching her, if he has somehow become implicated in this horrible tragedy by the fact that she wanted a boat ride.

Losing a child, he begins. Hard to know about that. My mother left left me in a trash can behind a coffee shop. An alley cat came across me and set to eating my umbilical cord. Started caterwauling when it was all finished. Wanted more, I guess. Some old guy came out into the alley with a frying pan planning to wax the damn cat. He found me and called the cops.

Caroline looks suitably shocked. Gant leans one way and then the other as a giant piece of swell comes in. It's as if an oil tanker has just passed by, or a blue whale has come up short, but there's nothing in sight. Caroline grabs a stanchion, but the rogue wave throws her against him. Heat comes off every square inch of her. She moves away, apparently embarrassed by the contact.

What did you do after that? she asks.

After what? Being found in an alley? I went into foster care, and I survived, that's what I did. Survival is my personal policy. A sweet kind of revenge. Tell me, why did you come to my boat today?

There is dew about her eyes when she answers, but he can't tell if it's from the wind or if it's something else.

I was sitting alone in my little apartment and I was trying to think of someone I could have breakfast with, someone I really wanted to be around, someone I could *stand* to be around right now

And you thought of me?

She moves her head. There might be a tiny sob coming up.

One minute I had everything, she said. The next minute I had nothing at all.

Gant's mind races. For some reason the fact that she used to do nails makes her presence on his boat easier. It's as if maybe he's in familiar waters, in his own territory, not reaching higher than he should. Maybe he's misread her all along.

Weird about your husband wanting a dynasty, he says carefully. Ironic, too.

I would have had another kid. I thought everything was going fine. I keep expecting them to tell me that they've found something wrong in his head, a tumor maybe, or that they've been going through the books at his office and have found out that he was a swindler or a crook. That would be easier to believe than that he would do something so crazy. . . .

Softly, she begins to cry.

Long breath in, staccato breath out.

Gant puts his arm around her, hugs her soothingly. Some seaweed gets into the propeller for a moment and the engine note drops, then picks up again.

You're not angry that I came to see you?

Actually, I'm flattered. But there must be someone you can talk to, no? Girlfriends?

I don't have any, she says, turning her face into his workshirt.

He steers the boat with her standing tight and close. They make their way down along the smooth coral shoulder of the Keys and turn into the protection of the lee at Lower Matecumbe. They pass Islamorada and enter Florida Bay. The water is calmer here, and the sun is hot enough to boil sawgrass. Caroline goes out to the front of the boat, strips down to a tiny red bikini, revealing a body beyond Gant's dreams, round breasts half out of the material, endless legs, a belly so flat and smooth Gant can't believe it once held a child.

She lies down, feet to the bow, head against the windshield.

You're going to burn, Gant shouts above the churning engine.

She doesn't hear. He goes forward to tell her. He really wants her to take care. He doesn't want the day spoiled by exposure.

I'm fine, she reassures him. Ultraviolet rays bounce off me.

Right then he sees a pod of dolphins off the port bow. He goes back to steering, maneuvers the boat in their direction until they are in close, riding the bow wave, their glistening gray flanks reflecting the sun like torpedoes.

If you hang over the edge, you can touch their fins, he shouts.

She pulls a face, recoiling at the idea.

That's disgusting. Get away from those things, Gant. Steer away!

Surprised—who doesn't love dolphins?—he goes back to guiding the boat past the outside passage west of Cape Sable and Ponce de Leon Bay, staying in close to the mouth of the Rogers River and the Lopez River and Chocoloskee, wanting to go into the 10,000 Islands of Everglades National Park, but not trusting the charts or his knowledge of the sandbars and the tides.

This wouldn't be the time to run aground.

Not today.

He throttles back to save fuel, scans the shallows hoping for a glimpse of shark or tarpon or snook. Half an hour later, she stands up right in front of the windscreen, right in front of him. A line of sweat streams down the hollow of her back. There's a dark stain on her suit bottom, turning it translucent, showing him the cleft and lines of her. She comes around.

Got any beer?

He gets that feeling again. Who is she, really? She doesn't seem the grande dame here at all. Not the woman dressed in fur waiting to be chauffeured to the plane to Telluride, not the grieving mother or the stunned wife or the tortured widow.

He pulls a Hurricane Reef out of the cooler.

Not that, she chides. A real beer.

He takes it back, digs out a Budweiser. She pops the top and slurps some of it down, then pours the rest straight into the nook between her breasts.

Thirsty? She grins, looking him in the eye.

It's like she's a whirlpool and he's a leaf. He's just sucked right in.

You're a good man, Gant, she says. How long till we make Naples?

A few hours, he mumbles.

Gently, she pushes him away.

Make it faster. I want you inside me at sundown.

Obedient and dry in the mouth, he rams the throttle forward.

TEN

❧

Pedro Santana.

There was something about that name and that face
that brought Eagle Cooper bolt upright from sleep in his
North Miami Beach apartment, his heart pounding, his
pillow moist with sweat. He'd seen both before, he knew
he had, but he couldn't place them. The coldly logical
side of him said, Forget it, there's no connection between a middle-aged Hispanic man in a rusty VW and
the biggest bank heist South Florida had seen in years,
but every time he lay back down to sleep, his little homunculus started whispering inside his head.

Check him out.

Follow up.

Run him down.

Finally, at 3:20 A.M., Cooper flung the bedclothes
aside and hopped onto cold white feet. Torn by conflict-
ing impulses, he went first to the bathroom, then to the
closet, getting dressed in fits and spurts, still not exactly
sure where he was going. He set out in his Bureau Ca-
price, and it wasn't until he was settled into the north-
bound fast lane of I-95 that he realized he was headed
for Boca Raton.

He got off at Hillsboro Boulevard, followed it east to
Federal Highway, turned north again to Camino Real,

and found himself at the big pink gates of the resort. A security officer stopped him, a big-bosomed woman with a doughnut in her mouth and a prize show playing on a tiny television in her booth. He flashed his shield, but she insisted on summoning the manager, a gay Brit with bags the under his eyes and a rumpled, seersucker tweed suit.

I need employment file access, Cooper told him.

At four-thirty in the morning?

It's the Senator Rule case.

I thought you guys had been through all those files.

How could Cooper explain to the guy that although his love life was better than it had been in years, at the office he was a bat without a belfry, flitting here and there, trying to avoid his boss, Nancy Fortier—who was feeling pressure from Tim Rule and his cronies—rather than admit to her that he had no substantial leads?

It's an emergency, he said. I've got to see them again.

The manager took in Cooper's unshaven face, the white crust of insomnia around his lips, his misbuttoned white oxford shirt.

Perhaps there's someone I could call to verify this?

If you called someone, it would be me. If this worries you, then why don't you come with me and stand guard at the door?

Reluctantly, the manager led the way back to the same room where just a few days earlier Cooper had pored fruitlessly through musty boxes of files. Following the guidance of the little voice in his head, Cooper found Pedro's photo after just a few minutes. It was an image from a time when Umberto Santana still rode a tricycle and hugged his father—who smelled of fresh-cut grass and the palm filaments and high-priced dirt—when he came home at the end of the day. In the picture, Pedro was grinning saucily, a man still optimistic about his future.

This gardening thing is just a temporary setback, *meng.*

I'm just doing this to learn how the other half lives.

I'm just taking a break from my *real* work.

Drinking.

It was probably just a coincidence, Cooper mused to himself as the night manager cracked his knuckles nervously. The bank robber had by all accounts been a younger, taller man. Still, the man had worked as a resort gardener and had shown up at Suzanne's with a huge wad of unexplained cash. And, of course, there was his arrogant grin, his crooked smile.

Cooper tucked the file under his arm.

You're taking that? the manager protested.

Evidence, Cooper declared brusquely.

He was in no mood for backtalk. He was ready for a big omelette and some comforting home fries. He was ready for coffee.

He was ready for a bust.

————

They call U.S. 50 the loneliest road in America, but they don't much talk about the heat. Or the monotony of the straights, for that matter, or the way the line west from Baker is punctuated by breathtaking views at Antelope Summit, views that take in 10,000-foot snow-capped peaks and high desert the color of Egyptian parchment, views that put a motorcycle rider on a par with circling vultures.

It is from that summit, a day after he and Umberto parted company, that Mercury Gant catches sight of the black Triumph once more. The boy is riding slowly down the grade into the Newark Valley, perhaps a dozen miles ahead, trolling along because he still hasn't made the required stop for a set of much-needed tires, and riding has gotten positively scary on this ordinarily high-speed road.

Gant trails him idly, then sets in motion, with a gradual turn of the throttle, a downhill rush that pushes the BMW to the limits. It's a squiggly mount, the German machine is, with a chassis that flexes and shocks that sag. In Gant's forceful hands, and with the heavy saddlebags in the rear and the thick summer air buffeting it up front, the bike begins to chase imaginary rabbits at 100 miles per hour, and by the time it shows 125 on its highly optimistic clock, Gant has to press himself against the tank and sway alongside the machine like a pendulum. He opens his mouth inside his helmet. The wind rushes in.

Aaaaaaasssssssh.

He pretends he's literally eating the road, pretends it's the refrigerator pie made from thin, black, chocolate cookies and whipped cream that his second foster mother used to make for him before she decided there were just one too many kids in that house.

You were the last here, she'd said, so you've got to be the first to go. It's not that we don't love you, Mercury. We hope you know that.

Sure.

Umberto doesn't notice Gant in his mirror because he isn't looking back much. He might be a bank robber, but he's not paranoid by nature, and the only vehicle he's seen all day is an Airstream trailer pulled by a badly chinked red Chevy waddling in the other direction like a silver tortoise.

Go! Gant screams, slapping the gas tank of his twin-cylinder machine. He can hear the valves begin to chatter, feel the thrumming of the driveshaft behind his right leg. He risks a quick look over his shoulder at the latches on the saddlebags. He's got what he tells himself is the prudent good sense to be concerned with those latches at speed, but he knows in his heart of hearts it is really an obsessive-compulsive problem with checking them again and again, whenever he is not at peace. And he's hardly at peace now, riding just as fast as the mountain will carry him.

He comes up fast on the boy's fender, computes the velocity spread, and slows down sharply with a handful of front brake. The comfort-oriented front forks dive hard, and Gant has to push himself up off the tank to keep from sliding forward. The rear tire chirps as the weight comes off it, and Umberto gives a visible start as Gant pulls up alongside. They stare at each other, riding not three feet apart, at perhaps fifty miles an hour. Umberto's heart pounds because he isn't sure what Gant is up to, and Gant, to his utmost astonishment, finds himself looking at the boy's eyes and wanting desperately for the kid to like him.

At Eureka, nothing more than a gas station, a few burned-out muscle car hulls and a post office that hasn't changed by so much as a spiderweb since the fifties, they pull in for fuel, acting as if nothing has happened.

How's the burned leg?

S'aright.

And the chin?

No problem, *meng.*

Yeah, well you have a problem with that rear tire of yours. Cord's showing through.

I'm gonna change it. I'm jes' riding a little longer.

The boy pays from a wad of fresh bills. Gant tries not to stare at them.

I just mention it because I'd hate to see you fall down.

Sure, I know, says Umberto.

Look, if you'd really rather ride alone, all you have to do is say so.

The boy can't figure Gant out. He owes the older man his life, at least once over, maybe twice. He knows Gant could have stolen from him already, too, and is puzzled that he hasn't.

Whaddya after? Umberto asks directly. I'm askin' whaddya want, exactly?

Just some company, Gant answers truthfully. It helps these days. I've spent too much time alone.

Driving limos and running boats, huh?

That's right.

Ju got your spirit to talk to, the boy says sarcastically.

I mean, you got Caroline left inside, right?

Gant winces.

Look, if you want to go it alone, then go. No problem.

Umberto thinks it through for a second, tries to get in touch with his real feelings, which is something he never does because it always brings him around to thinking of how his mother left him and what must be wrong with him for a mother to do that, and of what a drunk his father is, and of how Graciela is too damn good for him anyway.

It's true we both like riding motorcycles, he says.

Yeah, says Gant, smiling slowly. There's that.

What is it about bikes?

Freedom, says Gant.

Plus it's risky.

And graceful.

Power and speed too, says Umberto.

Inside, he's trying to justify his feeling for Gant, an attachment, an affection that he's been more aware of since riding off alone.

You fix your life by robbing that bank?

Sure. I'm making my dreams come true right now.

What if someone stole *your* money?

They gotta need it pretty bad.

And what if they needed it to buy crack cocaine?

I do dreams, not drugs, ju got that, *meng*? And like I said before, the money was insured.

Sure, I get you, says Gant.

So look, says Umberto, maybe we could ride together again. I mean just for as long as we both want to.

Gant nods, unaccountably grateful. To hide what might be the beginning of tears, and the anger he feels at himself for being so labile, he fiddles with his accursed luggage clasps, changes dirty fuel filters and checks his fluids. Umberto performs a useless measurement of his decaying tire tread with his thumbnail.

Finally, they take off together, over Scott Summit, past Austin and Cold Springs and Fallon. They come upon Reno after sundown, by way of Virginia City and the Geiger Grade, and pull off to stare at the neon magnet of a town from the shoulder.

A truck rushes by.

So big out here, Godzilla could fart and you wouldn't smell it. The boy shakes his head.

The way folks are building, it'll be covered with concrete in fifty years.

You think the world will last that long?

Of course, Gant replies.

I'm not so sure. How about we do a little gambling? Check out a casino? Roll the dice? Spin the wheel?

Be dumb to flash all that money around, Gant frowns.

I ain't gonna flash nothing. I jes' want to party!

So saying, Umberto takes off with a whoop, leaving tire smoke in his wake. Gant follows him, smiling in spite of himself, and they play tag down the grade. In town, they find the streets are full of motorcycles. Gant's been to the hullabaloo at Sturgis and the wild times at Daytona Beach, so he's seen rallies before, but Umberto can't believe it. They get off, stretch, and take a walk. They learn that the bike meet is a yearly gathering, put on by the town. The machines are Harley-Davidson cruisers to a one, simple, crude machines which Umberto regards with disdain. He is interested only in speed and handling, and the Harleys have neither. Gant, on the other hand, has a more elemental relationship with motorcycles, with their design and execution, their history, engineering and style, and he is fascinated by the assemblage.

Check out this bodywork, he says, pointing at a machine covered in swoopy, orange fiberglass.

That's some crazy shit, Umberto scoffs. Why would a guy spend forty, fifty large to build a machine that's still slower than a ten-grand crotch rocket?

An expert on high finance, all of a sudden.

Because it's unique, Gant explains. Because it makes a statement. Because it's his idea of what a bike should be. It's part of being an individual, and it's part of being free.

Being weird doesn't make ju free, *meng*, it jes' makes ju weird.

The boy is looking at the bikers, most of whom sport bellies and beards and tattoos, but more than that he's looking at the girls.

Think we could find a couple of hookers? he asks.

You're on your own, kid. I don't pay for it.

Umberto's surprised. He is thinking of his father, who doesn't get it any other way, and his mother, who doesn't give it without cash in advance.

Well anyway, I'm ready for a roll of the dice.

As if in celebration of that idea, a street band strikes up a country tune—Umberto makes a beeline for the nearest casino, a glitzy place on the main drag with a multitude of revolving doors, all opening in. It's a catacomb in there. The door has somehow disappeared around a corner, hosiery cracks like low lightning storms, coinage comes down like rain, ice tinkles and flashbulbs flare and cigarette smoke gets pulled up to the ceiling by giant hidden fans. Umberto's never seen anything like this before—the only gambling in Florida takes place on offshore cruises and Indian reservations, and he's never been to either. He wanders around with his mouth half open, finally buys a roll of dollar tokens and starts feeding the slots, pulling the lever like he sees blue-haired old ladies do, holding his plastic cup to the tray down below, staring at the blinking numbers atop a central podium.

$197,456.

Grand prize.

Easier money even than mine, he thinks.

He's more comfortable amid this din than he's been on the open road. In here—with those cute cocktail waitresses rushing back and forth with free drinks—he feels closer to what he thought his life would be like after the heist. Plus he doesn't have to think of that woman, whom he hasn't admitted to Gant he actually *does* remember.

The fat woman who had trouble breathing.

The little boy at her side.

A waitress brings him a screwdriver. He gulps the orange juice, blinks at the vodka, puts in another coin, pulls his money bag in tighter. He wonders how he can go about getting a hooker. He wonders if one of these cocktail girls will go to a hotel with him if he offers her enough.

Gant has followed, at a distance, and across the aisle from Umberto halfheartedly feeds a slot. He's not much of a gambler. He's more of a planner. Learned that in foster homes, perfected it in the army. He pulls the lever, watches the bananas roll down, and out of the corner of his eye sees Caroline again.

She's wearing the leather jacket he bought her, silver-tipped tassels and all, open over her snow-white throat, an expensive diamond necklace hanging down, catching the fluorescent light as if it's on fire. She moves like she doesn't belong here, sleepwalking with her eyes open. Gant leaves his machine still spinning and goes off toward her, but she melts away into the crowd. He pushes his way past a cluster of people, rounds the change booth, intent on Caroline's swaying, leather-clad hips.

Caroline! he calls out.

An old man turns nervously as he goes past, clutching a plastic pail with eight quarters inside.

Caroline!

She's moving faster now, floating over the floor. She won't turn and look at him. The faster he runs, the faster she floats.

GANT!

Umberto's bellow brings him up short. The boy is playing tug-of-war with a blue-suited security man, each with a hand on the money bag. Umberto's losing. Gant knows at once that this man was a soldier. His moves are as sure as forceps, deadly as a blade.

Gant shakes his head hard, and Caroline disappears. He sidles up to Umberto.

Hey there, he tells the rent-a-cop. Take it easy.

Is this kid with you?

He is.

I'll need to see his proof of age.

Gant grabs Umberto's ear.

Did you spend the hundred I gave you?

To his credit, Umberto catches on fast.

Not all of it. He trembles.

Proof of age, the security man repeats.

Gant pulls the coins out of Umberto's bucket.

Is this all you've got left?

I need to see that identification, the security man insists.

What were you? Gant asks the guard suddenly. Marine?

That's right.

Nam?

Three tours.

Me too. Charlie Rangers LRP duty.

Out of Phan Thiet? The marine looks mildly interested.

Yeah. Radio operator. Got my jump wings from the Eighty-second Airborne at Fort Benning. Look, I'll take the kid out of here now, okay? We won't be back. We're just traveling through, wanted a bit of fun.

Reluctantly, the security man lets go of the bag.

We bust people for this, he says. No kidding.

Gant nods, takes Umberto by the elbow, gives a quick salute. The marine returns it, out of reflex, and Gant can see that he's mad at himself for doing it.

That was close and you were stupid, he tells Umberto when they get outside.

Well I still wanna get me a hooker.

I'll take a thank-you, first.

Yeah, okay. Thank you.

A girl showing miles of bare leg comes walking

across the street with a smile on her face and a waggle
to her hips that knocks parked cars out of the way. She's
got sequins on. She's got white boots.

She's trouble in platinum blond.

Hey baby! Umberto croons like a Latino bandmaster
from 1952. Let me show you some Latin love.

Oh, give it a rest, mutters Gant.

The girl comes over. Umberto links his arm with hers.
At the feel of her flesh, he thinks of Graciela and wonders if he really wants to do this, wonders if he hasn't
proven enough already.

See how lucky I am, Mercury? He smiles.

The way the hooker grins, Gant figures the kid might
just be.

Some towns spread like day-blooming flowers, their
roots running far and wide but never deep, their inter-
connections spread shallow, just under the surface. Other
towns ramble like vines, with life taking hold wherever
it can, relying on the strangling force of grasping peti-
oles. Still others, and Port Townsend is one of these, are
built vertically, like a saguaro cactus, with a nourishing
underground network far deeper and larger and more
ramified than what one can see from above.

When Audrey Bishop disappeared, the town showed
its roots. Employees from the supermarket poured out of
the place like ants from a poisoned nest, covering the
parking lot, the adjoining strip mall, the base of the
nearby cliff, the thick local ground cover and sidewalks
as well. Sympathetic shoppers, some of whom knew the
little girl and some of whom did not, joined in the
search, cruising the streets in station wagons and vans
and rusted-out pickups, all with the windows down and,
inexplicably, the headlights on as if for a funeral.

Cry out till you're hoarse.

Beat the streets with her name.

Ring the town like a bell.

When the police were finally called in, it was as an afterthought by the store manager. Port Townsend was not a place where people relied much on cops. Folks were there because they wanted responsibility for their own lives, and control of the same. When a patrol car showed up, it fit right into the array of vehicles cruising for Audrey, taking only the briefest and most cursory statement from Ruth, who provided shoes to the small police department at a discount and whose devotion to the little blind girl was known to one and all.

Few people strayed across the street to the commercial marina. This obvious oversight would later be blamed on the cloud of mill stench which persisted over the city in a disorienting blanket. Nobody could think clearly with that odor dripping over everything. It was too much to expect. There was also the fact that a little girl wouldn't wander into such an obviously inhospitable place, a world dominated by men wearing beards and paint-flecked suspenders, a labyrinth devoted entirely to the conquest of fishes. What could she do there? What *would* she do there? Before anyone would consider the marina, they would consider abduction.

And carefully.

Within a few hours of Audrey's disappearance, Ruth found herself sitting in the Water Street police station, across from her store, giving the whole story once again to Officer Sam Patch, a man with a twenty-eight-inch waist and a little brown mustache, a man who wore the shoes she sold him, three pair a year, and who tried to protect her, with a closed door, from the references to ritual murder band sexual abuse being made in the squad room outside.

Eyebrows, she thought guiltily. Mascara. What had she been *thinking*?

It happens, soothed Sam, who had been known to buy peppermint saltwater taffy for Audrey. You're not perfect, Ruth. You're not a machine. People look away for

a minute. Is there anyone you know who might have
taken her?

Taken her, Ruth repeated.

Kidnapped her.

Who would want a blind kid?

She's a beautiful little girl, Sam replied, immediately
regretting it. Then he said there might soon be a ransom,
or maybe a note. Wishful thinking. Sam knew that rarely
happened. He knew such disappearances tended to be
final.

I don't have any money. Ruth fought back tears. Without Audrey, I don't have anything at all.

We'll get her picture in the paper, Ruth. We'll do that
right away. Do you carry one with you?

Still crying, Ruth dumped the contents of her purse
out onto Sam's desk. Included in the pile were makeup
and pens and keys and loose change. Included too were
her driver's license, Dr. Pearson's business card, a re-
ceipt from a wholesaler for a major order of gum-soled
fisherman's boots, and a copy of a letter addressed to a
man in Deerfield Beach, Florida.

Here, she said, sliding an outdated picture of the little
girl out of her billfold and handing it to Sam. This is all
I have.

Sam takes the picture, soon to give it to the newspaper, soon to have it spread all over town.

Audrey lies in a sandy spot on an otherwise gravelly
beach. She is wearing a little flowered swimming suit.
Her body is inert and her gaze is vacant, but her mind
is full of jasmine and Mozart and Brahms.

When the call came in, it was early in the morning, and
Tim Rule's soft round body was immersed in a warm
Jacuzzi tub.

Touch up those sideburns.

Stay busy with the small things.

Time to dye the hair again. Time to think of women.

Stefan needs a mother, after all. Listen to him secretly crying behind the thin wall of his closet, where he thinks he is safe. Where he thinks nobody can hear.

And Vicky barely cold in the ground.

Brrring.

Hello?

The FBI has a lead on the killer, Ron Bernstein announced. Rule pressed the receiver to his face, covering it in shaving cream from his chin.

How do you know?

My source at the Bureau tells me Agent Cooper is moving on it now.

Rule was into a towel before his soap bubbles hit the ground.

Give me the address.

Rule scratched the digits out in the fog on the gold-rimmed mirror above his washbasin, but that was hardly necessary. The information was already a permanent addition to his brain, and within minutes he was in his big Bentley, going to the scene, the home of Pedro Santana, down deep in the bowels of Cutler Ridge.

Pedro lived nowhere near the shopping malls on Federal Highway, nor near the discount tire stores or the electronics warehouses, but close instead to the corner stands of grapefruit and melon and guanabana and mango, closer still to the BMX dirt track where Umberto learned to add body English to a turn, to power his bicycle down the straights, to rev up when all seemed lost, even if the engine was only his own two legs working in concert with his hurting lungs and bursting heart.

Rule arrived in Pedro's driveway right along with Agent Eagle Cooper, who wasn't the least bit pleased to see him.

What are you doing here, Mr. Rule?

I understand you've got the man who killed my wife. Let's get inside and grab the bastard.

Cooper took a deep breath, surveyed the size of Tim Rule's belly, the size of his car, tried to make himself understand how grieving might mix with intoxicating power to spur on such an outrageous piece of behavior as showing up at a suspect's house, fed by inside information, shameless as a shitting crow.

This is a law enforcement matter, sir. You can't be here.

But I *am* here.

Nevertheless, you must leave.

Fat chance.

We're wasting valuable time, Mr. Rule.

Then let's get started, said the real estate tycoon, swaggering toward Pedro's door.

Tim Rule carried a handgun in his car, for those necessary trips to South Miami–Dade, but it was a revolver, big and shiny, and he shot it only once a year and his hand was always sore afterward, and his ears rang. He fought with attorneys and contracts and lawsuits, not with bullets. The sight of the ugly black Glock in Cooper's hand made his mouth go dry.

You're holding a gun on me, he said, trying to keep his voice steady.

You are interfering with a federal officer in the performance of his duty, Mr. Rule. That is a felony. Please go home. If there's a real break in the case, I promise, you'll be the first to know.

You'll call me? Rule asked, the braggadocio gone now.

I will.

Would it be all right if I just watched from my car? It's got bulletproof glass, you know.

A special executive option.

No sir, it would not, Cooper asserted.

Rule considered arranging for Ron Bernstein to make trouble for Cooper, but apprehending the bastard who killed his wife was more important to him than anything, and he realized that his meddling might slow things down.

I'll be waiting, he said with a nasty smile.

I know you will.

As soon as he was gone, Cooper rang the doorbell, and Pedro—who had been watching the scene play out through a crack in his living room curtain, trying to figure out what a quarter-of-a-million-dollar car was doing in his driveway—answered right away. Through the screen door, he recognized the FBI man, and at the sight of his shield remembered the way he had tested Umberto's money with his pen. He found himself praying the bills hadn't been marked. It was an important moment for Pedro, the first time that denial receded and he was forced to face the possible consequences of what his son had done.

Is there something wrong with the Jaguar? he asked, trying to buy time.

The car is fine, Cooper said patiently.

It's not hot?

Transfer of the vehicle was perfectly legal. But you never did tell me the name of your bank, Mr. Santana. The bank from which you withdrew your cash?

Ju are here for what reason, exactly?

Ms. Emerson is a personal friend of mine.

So this is a social call?

The name of the bank?

Am I under arrest?

Now why would you ask that?

Because ju jes' showed me your badge.

Do you have something to hide? Something you should tell me about?

I'm not hiding nothing.

Well then, how about something cold to drink? It's roasting out here.

Pedro narrowed his eyes. Drinking with a cop. On the list of things to avoid, this was right up there with getting caught picking a lawyer's pocket.

Refrigerator's empty.

Could we at least talk inside?

With great reluctance, he stood aside and let Cooper

into his house. The cop looked around at the worn carpet, the holes in the brand-new leather sofa, the framed photograph of Umberto on a fat-tired bike.

You sure you don't have even one cold beer?

Damn, the man was persistent. And irritating too. Pedro hadn't dealt with cops in years. He'd forgotten how they could be. Give them an inch and they'd take a mile. He brought Cooper a cold Hatuey.

Thanks, Pedro. By the way, who shot the couch?

Ju got some imagination, that's for sure. Pedro laughed uneasily. I smoke, *comprende*? Those are cigarette burns. I fall asleep on that couch sometimes.

Really. Say, you used to work at the resort in Boca, am I right?

The question caught Pedro off guard. That was so long ago! Besides, he hadn't done anything over there, no fingers in the till, no persuading of any kind. Why the hell would this guy want to know about that?

Yeah. What about it?

What did you do for them?

Trimmed hedges, Pedro answered. Cut grass.

Cooper took a sip of the beer.

Your wife enjoying the Jaguar?

Sure.

And where were you on the morning of June seventeenth?

Pedro gasped a silent prayer to his Santeria gods.

What day of the week was that?

A Friday.

Friday mornings I go to the barber. Same haircut every week for twenty years. I don't lose it like some guys, he said proudly. Cuban blood is strong.

Cuban blood, whispered Cooper's homunculus, right into his ear.

I could check that out? he asked.

You mean is that an alibi?

You said it. Cooper smiled. I didn't.

Sure. Go ahead and check. Lotsa guys were there. What I need an alibi for, anyway?

Right now you just need to give me the name of your barber, Cooper said, pulling out a fancy red pen and a notebook. After that we'll talk again. By the way, he said, pointing at the photo of Umberto, who's that?

Pedro the con man grinned broadly.

That's me.

I didn't know they had those high-tech bicycles back when you were a kid.

Pedro didn't know why, but since Consuela was back in his life he seemed to have his old nerve back. He hated to admit it to himself, but it was as if she were the keeper of his balls.

Sure they had 'em, Pedro bluffed. And I was one hotshot on two wheels!

Cuban blood, the homunculus repeated one more time in Cooper's ear.

ELEVEN

❧

Graciela Perez ignores the winks and the tongues and the lewd comments and the body odor of the stripe-shirted service station men and stabs at the little icons on her cash register. While she totals their order for seven Chicken McNuggets, five Diet Cokes, ten orders of Supersize Fries, and four Big Macs, they fumble for change and shove at each other in an effort to get close enough to her to look down her blouse.

I'd like to order you, honey.

Will you eat my Biiiiiig Mac?

What time you get off, darlin'?

Yeah? And what time you go home?

You gonna get in trouble with your wife, talking like that, she admonishes playfully.

What my wife don't know ain't gonna hurt her. Now, when you going on that Caribbean cruise with me?

Yeah, Graciela. You got us dying over here. You're breaking hearts all over Miami.

She can't help but give them a little smile. They are, after all, her public.

Go sit down, all of you, she commands with mock testiness. I'll call you when your order is ready.

They go, reluctantly, each one harboring his own private thoughts about the top of her white lacy bra and other, muskier places.

The chicken comes up while she pours the drinks herself, trying to avoid the leer of her manager, who, out of a perverse proprietary sense, gets aroused when others ogle her.

It's not even noon yet and already she's getting it from all sides. The fact is, she's too busy piling burgers onto trays to notice the television crew—a well-known blond reporter; her fat, bearded cameraman; a svelte, elegant producer—until they're at the counter.

Hola, Graciela, the producer says easily, reading her name tag.

Try English, she replies.

Okay. The man smiles. I'd like to speak to the manager.

Graciela's boss appears as if by magic.

Can I help you?

CNN Cable News. We're doing a piece on the Biker Babe giveaway.

No kidding. How come?

It's a big story. The hottest Happy Meals giveaway in history. Kids are scrambling for them. A teenage girl came into a McDonald's in Aventura this morning and shot the place up because they told her she couldn't have one.

The manager covers his mouth in horror.

We're all out, says Graciela.

Everybody's out. That's the story. Our news team has been searching for hours and we haven't come up with one yet.

Let's get this over with, the blond reporter says, irritated. It's disgusting in here. The grease is clogging my pores.

Graciela notices that, up close, the reporter doesn't look as good as she does on TV. Her skin is bad and her nose is too big and she's wearing colored contact lenses.

I have a Biker Babe right here, Graciela declares.

All eyes swing to her as she reaches under the counter and pulls out one of the little plastic dolls, clad in a black, zip-down neoprene riding jacket and skimpy shorts, a tiny, well-fashioned helmet on its head, red bangs, green hip boots, a pierced navel, and tattoos that a Barbie would never have, covering the arms and thighs.

This is what all the fuss is about? The reporter snorts, snatching the doll.

It's our own fault, Graciela says.

Really, the producer asks, signaling the cameraman to roll tape. Why is that?

Kids get seized by impulse, Graciela explains, trying not to let the reporter's glare disturb her, trying to do her best for the camera. After all, adults are the ones who raise them. We live in an instant gratification society. If we don't get what we want, we take it. That's what self-help books tell us to do, right? That's how we're supposed to live our lives. These kids want Biker Babes, and when they can't have them, they freak. Like I said, it's not their fault, really. It's ours.

The reporter's mouth is open, and the producer's mind is racing. By now he has noticed Graciela's hazel eyes and her beautiful skin and her pouty lower lip and he is smitten by the sultry vibe of her.

How exactly did you get *yours*? the reporter challenges.

Graciela gives the camera her best sexy smile.

I took it, she says.

The reporter knows what's good for her, and what's good for her is not Graciela. She bats her baby blues and moves off to another corner of the restaurant. The cameraman dutifully follows.

That's the situation in South Miami–Dade County, she says as she walks. Children reaching out to take the latest promotional toy item, then blowing up, literally, when they can't get what they want.

You were terrific, the producer tells Graciela. I mean that.

Really? Graciela asks breathlessly. The man's cologne is so fine, and his seersucker suit is so handsome, she hopes he can't hear how hard her heart is pounding.

Really.

Thanks. She blushes.

Look, why don't you call me in the morning? He hands over his business card. I think I can find you something better to do than turn burgers.

Are you serious?

Definitely.

Definitely, Graciela repeats, her body shuddering as if the word is a prayer.

Are you sure you want to go in here?

Don't tell me Mr. Special Forces is afraid of a couples' joint, Caroline teases.

You put it that way, let's go, huffs Gant as they step into the dark interior of the club.

It looks innocent enough at first blush: couples standing around with drinks in their hands, a little floor show going with mirrors and lights, the smell of whiskey and toilet deodorizer, the occasional sound of laughter. Gant tries to relax, but it's hard, dressed in chinos and a blazer and Docksiders as he is, with Caroline in a skintight black leather bustier and skirt, her muscular arms showing, and her strong legs too. He wonders for the hundredth time how she can have such tone. She'd have to work out every day, and he knows that she doesn't. He's been with her around the clock. Can it be steroids? Can it be genes?

A big-breasted black woman catches Gant's eye, and Caroline notices.

Someone you know?

Caroline's possessive. Gant's got to keep his gaze on the floor. It's tough sometimes.

Nah. Just reminded me of someone.

An old flame? Do tell.

Not my style.

That's right. You're a man of character. A war hero.

No hero, says Gant. Just a soldier. I got drafted, I went, I did what I had to do.

You've got medals, she counters.

He wonders how she knows that. She must have snooped in his drawers while he was sleeping.

All kinds of people get medals, he says—although the medals mean much more to him than she could possibly know—you can get a medal for getting your legs shot off.

So tell me about your old girlfriends. I want to know about them all.

The music picks up.

Forget that, he says. I don't kiss and tell. Let's dance.

She follows him onto the dance floor, right into the middle of the crowd, under the lights. She rubs herself provocatively against him, then moves away, raises her hands over her head, gyrates slinkily, thrusting his way with her hips. She closes the distance, licks the side of his face, strokes him between his legs.

Old girlfriends, she whispers in his ear.

Oh for God's sake.

At least tell me what they did for a living.

One was a cocktail waitress.

Yeah?

She's not interested. Station in life is everything to her.

Another was an airline pilot.

You went out with an airline pilot?

Jets, he affirms. Big, big jets.

Mile-high club?

Cockpit club, he replies.

Now that's something. What did she look like?

No kiss and tell, remember?

Was she blond?

What did I just say?

Redhead?

You're ridiculous. He laughs, yelling into her ear over the din. Most women don't want to know this stuff.

I'm not most women.

They move off to stools which afford a good view of the gigantic aquarium behind the bar. She has a gold margarita, Gant orders a bourbon, a boutique brand this time, distilled, the label claims, in small batches. He watches disk-shaped reef dwellers with black bars and yellow stripes, he watches the predator needlenose, the floating angels, the wrasses and the eels.

I love the lionfish, Caroline says, twining her arm up in his, breathing close to his ear so that he can smell the tequila on her breath. He gets a spear in his heart. He's still not sure about her. What's she doing slumming with him? She's a social climber, that much is obvious. Why isn't she jetting about in somebody's Lear? He's afraid of how hard he's fallen for her, feels like he's waiting for the boom to drop, for her to tire of him. He doesn't like feeling this way about her, and he doesn't like feeling this way about himself. But she's addictive. So gorgeous, so complex, so goddamn sexy.

Which is the lionfish? he asks, putting his arm around her silky bare shoulders.

The beautiful one with the spines floating near the front. It just eats and swims around like a great glorious queen, but if anyone fucks with it, boom, those spines are deadly poison. One touch, one tiny prick, and you're dead.

I like the eel, says Gant. He just finds a hole and he sticks to it, watching the world go by.

I've pulled you out of your hole, haven't I, Gant?

I do believe you have.

Are you happy about that?

He allows that he is. They drink more. Sometime after midnight, the bartender feeds the fish. Flakes fall down into the water like rain. Tiny piscine mouths snap hungrily. Inspired, Caroline nibbles on Gant. His skin exudes a smell like hickory-smoked ham, from the fermented fragrances of his chosen American whiskey. Industrious as she is, her tongue could get her drunk.

It's time to visit the back room, she whispers.

He's too far under her spell to resist. Too tired too. He's been working all day on the boat, in the sun, getting things ready for a big charter coming up. She guides him through a door he had assumed led to the kitchen, but which, in fact, leads to the pulsing central organ of the club. It could be a gymnasium, the way belts and pulleys come out of the walls, but a gymnasium wouldn't have the chains.

Uh oh, says Gant.

Forget fear, Caroline urges. Get bossy or get passive. It's the only way to survive in here.

In the corner, a young blond girl has a man chained up. There's a leather hood over her face and she's doing something to his groin with a pair of pliers. He writhes. Farther along the wall, which Gant notices is covered with acoustic tile, two redheaded women enact a love opera with a whip and a spiked collar and a leash.

Crack.

Bark like a dog!

Do it now!

Jesus, says Gant. He's seen shit like this before, in Saigon. He didn't like it there, and he doesn't like it here.

Playtime, Caroline coos.

I don't think so.

Oh come on, have a little fun with me. There's another room, for groups, if you don't like this stuff.

I like you, says Gant. You're enough for me. I've had enough pain. It's the pleasure I'm after.

Everyone's after pleasure. Caroline smiles. It's where they find it that's interesting.

Someone whimpers. It's a bald bodybuilder, maybe 250 pounds, facing the wall, his hands in chains while his male lover, a gimp as agile as a monkey, runs a pizza knife up and down on his back, bringing a tiny thin line of blood.

Just come to the wall with me for a minute, she implores.

Gant can't imagine Caroline's dead husband in a place like this.

The luggage is waiting for you by the front door.

I'm not into this, Caroline, he says.

You are now, she says, shoving him over to the wall.

He's surprised. He hasn't expected her to force him, and he doesn't want to force back, which is what he would need to do, because she is made of real muscle. He can't believe how strong she is.

I'm not kidding, he protests, forcing a laugh.

But she's already got the cuffs on. One, anyway. He reaches over to take it off, and she slaps him in the face. Hard. He can feel the red fingermarks rising. Stunned, he waits too long to resist the cuffing of the second hand. *Click.*

Lionfish? Shark would be more like it. He knows some guys who'd get off on this, on her taking control, on being hurt. He's just not one of them, and she won't listen. There's this look on her face. She's into it like a robot at its task—welding in an assembly line, laying pipe. She's not going to stop, no matter what he says. It's her breathing. That's what reveals her commitment.

He brings his feet up in a scissor around her waist, twisting her forcefully. He's not fooling around. He's a strong man and he's got a boater's legs now.

Stern and aft.

Starboard and port.

Their wrestling gets a few glances from the rest of the room, but no more than a few glances. Each couple is a private party here. Caroline gets something up to Gant's nipple, inside his shirt like a surgeon. A clamp. He yells, but nobody hears him.

The acoustic tile.

He pulls at the chain, hard as he can. It must be.concrete back there. It is concrete. And an eyelet the size of an apple. He can feel the blood coming up under his skin, contained, a bruise. He roars and kicks out at her hard enough to crack ribs.

This brings her out of it. Holding her side with one hand, she unlocks the cuff with the other. She's furious.

Fuck you, she spits bitterly.

Not tonight.

TWELVE

❧

Coming down out of the Tahoe National Forest, the need for ocean seized Umberto and Gant by the handlebars, yanking them violently forward like Neptune possessed. They didn't speak of it, talked not at all of destinations, but were both aware that they were in the clutches of something manic and salty and wet.

Dune fever.

A kelp addiction.

A yearning for cliffs, rocks, and foam.

Sporting new tires all around, they crossed California's great central valley, battling the heat through Smartville and Tierra Buena and Colusa. When they reached inaptly named Clear Lake—it was opaque as pea soup from algal overgrowth—they surrendered to the sun and pulled up to a hot dog trailer. A hot wind blew in from the growing fields, and since rain had been scarce, dust came along with it.

California. Umberto shook his head. Amazing.

You think you can ever go back to Miami?

Sure, Umberto bluffed. He heard himself say it and felt bitterly and hard how, in such a short time, he had become just like his father; a bullshitter so talented he almost convinced himself.

Three hundred and forty grand. Gant pointed his chin

at the bag. That's what the papers said. It's not as much as you think it is. Not anymore. You'll still have to work, you know. You'll still need a job.

Ju such an expert on work, what ju doing out here on a bike, huh?

I've got more in the bank than you've got in your bag, kid. And I didn't steal it, I worked for it.

So how come ju ride that old piece of shit? Where are ju kids, *meng*? Where's ju wife, ju house, ju Cadillac, ju gold Rolex watch?

Gant couldn't help but feel sad that he was running from the very life the boy thought he should have.

I had a Cadillac once, he said.

Driving a limo doesn't count.

It does if you own it. I had a ragtop DeVille, too. And an apartment. Had all kinds of stuff. It didn't do that much for me. It wasn't the answer.

Sounds like ju asking the wrong question. Umberto snorted, and went off to the trailer, where he ordered lunch from a wizened old vendor with a red bandanna around his neck to hide his skin cancer scar.

This is a special hot dog, the old man told him, his accent still dripping Greece. You never had a dog like this. You see how it's white? That's veal. Chews up like bratwurst, but less fat. Spices I bring from the Mediterranean myself. And the sauerkraut! The sauerkraut's from New York. Bun's baked fresh just down the road in Ukiah. Ten grains in that bun. A bun like this every day, you live a long time, believe me, and never get sick.

Jes' tell me it tastes good, Umberto replied, forking over a couple of bills.

The heat had Gant's appetite, so he just sat by the polluted lake and watched Umberto's soda can sweat, watched the tiny rivers get down to the dry planks of the table, watched a squirrel circle in, edging the muddy lake bed, fixated on Umberto's food.

A Caddy, but no wife and no kids, right? Umberto pursued.

Right.

But ju had somebody special?

Thought I did one time. Turned out she was something else.

Umberto bit into his hot dog. Mustard foamed out over his lip.

Awesome hot dog, *meng*. Ju should try one. So this chick did a number on ju, huh?

A number, repeats Gant. Yeah. She did a number on me all right.

I got Graciela. She's beautiful. Really. Ju ever try musk cologne? Ju know, like they sell at expensive drugstores?

I've tried it.

Her whole body smells like that. But natural. I tell ju, it's like almonds or something. She doesn't put anything on.

I bet you she does.

Umberto shook his head.

No way, *meng*. I know her.

Women have a way of doing things when you're not watching, said Gant. Of keeping secrets you wouldn't believe.

Ju don't know Graciela like I know Graciela. Umberto chewed.

A gull fluttered around the table. A wasp bombed by. Gant tried to remember what it was like to be in love when he was seventeen. He thought briefly of a redhead he met while waiting tables in a restaurant. After sleeping with her for a week, he would have laid down on railroad tracks for her.

But you keep secrets from her, right?

Na. Umberto shook his head.

No? So you told her you were going to rob a bank?

The boy snorted.

Ju don't talk about shit like that with women, he said. Tell the truth, I never talked about that shit with anyone, till I met ju. I don't want to go to jail, *meng*. I want to live free.

So what now?

The wasp alit on the end of Umberto's hot dog. He looked at it coolly.

I got a plan.

Gant nodded, got up and bought himself a ginger ale. They sat staring at the lake for a while. Bluebottle flies swarmed over the riparian mud.

The money marked?

Umberto reddened. Ju think I'm stupid?

You can't control everything. You couldn't control Vicky Rule's lungs.

I asked for old bills.

Gant laughed. Umberto balls his fists. His accent thickened.

Ju laughin' at me?

Hundreds of thousands in old bills? You gotta be kidding. Banks don't keep money like that around.

Umberto dashed to his tailpack, ripped it off the bike, came rushing over to Gant and thrusted it, half unzipped, into his face.

This bank did.

Gant stared up the money for a second, takes a long last swig from his can, shrugs himself into his sweat-soaked coat.

Let's go, he said.

Umberto throws the squirrel the last little piece of hot dog, and trots after him.

When ju gonna toss that crazy coat, huh? S'bad for my image be seen ridin' with ju.

Gant, who didn't care for leather, and who knew that the oil-soaked cotton kept him from dehydrating in the heat, didn't answer.

One of these days ju gonna call the cops on me, huh?

Gant put on his helmet.

Not likely, he said, stunned by the sudden realization that he found being around a criminal exciting.

Feeling desperately defective, he started his machine.
Back at the table, the wasp claimed his ginger ale.
Up ahead, far ahead, the ocean called on, lovingly.

———

Eagle Cooper nestles comfortably against Suzanne Emerson's naked breasts.

I pick up the yellow Jag tomorrow, she murmurs, her eyes closed in bliss.

I love that you know those cars like you do.

You don't think it's too masculine?

I think it's adorable.

I bet I find something of my father's under the seat.

Like what?

I don't know.

A watch? A slip of paper with someone's name on it in his writing? A pen?

You're such a detective. I don't care what it is, as long as it belonged to him.

You loved your dad, huh?

I didn't know my mother. My dad was everything to me. Hey, what happened with that Cuban man who bought the car? His money's legit, right?

I don't know. I've got a feeling about the guy, Cooper says vaguely. I'm closing in on something, I know I am. I can hear the little voice.

An armed man with a badge listening to voices is a scary thing. Anyone ever tell you that?

Not voices plural, just this particular one.

She flops over on her back, palms turned up like a floater.

Just one, huh? Is that supposed to make me feel better?

I'm going to talk to the wife, Cooper says suddenly.

I don't like the idea of you alone with a hooker.

He rises up on an elbow.

What?

I'm the jealous type, I admit it.

You think she's a hooker?

You're a cop, Eagle. Don't tell me you don't know a working girl when you see one.

You sure?

Suzanne trumpets like an elephant.

I love the way you're innocent at the same time as wise, Eagle. I really do.

But they're married.

How the hell do you know what they are?

They have a kid together. I saw his picture in the house.

Suzanne sits up at this one.

Really? They have a kid?

Guessing by the picture I saw. And I think I need to talk to him.

Cuban blood, the homunculus whispers, one more time, in Cooper's ear.

There! Cooper fairly shouts. Did you hear that?

———

Audrey moved like a ghost in a Dickens novel, her hands out in front of her, her head throbbing where she'd hit the keel of the sailboat.

Grandma? she said quietly. She was still seeing stars, but they weren't the stars on her bedroom ceiling, they were the spasms of peripheral blood vessels, the pulsing of petechial insults to her cranium.

She recognized certain smells, although their attribution was scrambled in the initial moments after she came to. She thought that varnish was oysters, for example, and that oysters were rubber cement. She tried touching things as a braille reader might, but she got only rusty nails for her trouble, and the smooth, seemingly endless expanse of keel into which she had catapulted. She confused a sawhorse for the aisle of the grocery store, because she had forgotten the last few moments before losing consciousness, and remembered only that she had gone shopping with Ruth.

Where was the cold smell of meat? Frozen pizza? Pears? Ajax? The warm, heartening odor of wrapped paper towels?

Grandma! she cried, louder this time, but her voice was trapped within the valley of the hull, and bounced back at her as a cruel mockery on slight delay.

Grandma, Grandma, Grandma! Oh Grandma, where are you?

Never, not even when her mother died, had Audrey been so alone, and never had she felt that loneliness so keenly. She dropped to the concrete, felt with her fingers where the weather and years of storms had worn the smooth surface down to sand and grit, felt the sand on her bare little knees and sobbed. She was thirsty, she was hungry, and all she could do was think of Ruth.

Miles away, Ruth received the broadcast and returned it, from her bed, but Audrey was in transmit-only mode. She wasn't relaxed and happy and open enough to mentally receive anything from her grandmother. She could barely manage a clear impression of her surroundings. One thing she did know was that it was nighttime. Port Townsend gets much cooler at night, washed by ocean winds and deprived of the warming sun. She shivered. A rat scurried by, and Audrey heard its claws on the ground, heard its tail drag, heard it make tiny sniffing noises as it investigated the soles of her child-size Birkenstock clogs. She couldn't smell it though, as her senses wouldn't sort out for another hour or two from the bump.

Here, little dog, cooed Audrey.

Away in the forest on the south side of town, Ruth rose and went to the little girl's room. Sobbing at the sight of the tiny, empty bed, she reached out her hand to touch Audrey's lace-trimmed, peach-colored pillow and found it sopping wet. Her first instinct was to look to the roof for a leak, but when she saw none, she raised the fabric to her tongue and tasted it.

Salty as tears.

The riders were four hours above the Golden Gate Bridge, right on the Pacific Coast Highway, north of the eco-dream called Sea Ranch and north too of Gualala, Point Arena, Little River and Elk. This was a part of the coast that never warmed past pleasant, and Gant found that his crazy flapping coat was just right, while Umberto, who had stowed his leathers, had gooseflesh rough as barnacles and a keen yearning for a roaring fire.

But the views made enduring the fog and the drizzle and the endless overcast worthwhile, for here was a coastal mosaic that drew in the whales, the albatross, the frigate birds and those martens of the sea, the shellfish-cracking otters. These were the crags and the vistas and the deep brown forests of kelp which shaded the seascape in such a way that Umberto found himself wondering if the waters off Miami, populated mostly by Jet Skis and displaced reef fishes and drug runners and yachts, really qualified as ocean at all.

At times, when the road turned inland, the attention of the riders was commanded by the tarmac itself, by the way it banked and trammeled and pounded and swept. At one point, they slowed together for a hairpin, and came to ride side by side.

First time I did this road, I followed a friend up from Santa Barbara in the pouring rain, Gant called over. When the rain let up, at the end of the day, a fog rolled in, and since he was a better and faster rider, all I could manage was to follow his taillight. It was like a red beacon in the night.

I feel like the goddamn Silver Surfer, Umberto responded, like I'm zooming past planets and shit. Whoever laid out this road was a genius.

God laid it out, Gant yelled back. The engineers just followed his plan.

The ride was so glorious that for a period of hours Umberto forgot that he was a fugitive on the lam, and

Gant forgot the challenge that lay ahead. Finally, with dry gas tanks and empty stomachs, they stopped at Mendocino. Gant selected an inn overlooking the mouth of the Big River, the glinting tips of sailboat masts far below them, along with bright red fishing net floats and yellow crab trap buoys and whitecaps. Saddlesore and happy, they walked the streets, looking at the art galleries and the furniture shops, and items made from local timber by men and women who smoked the weed that made Humboldt County famous. There was a certain aesthetic to the artistic creations they saw in windows, a combination of Oriental spareness, lighthouse loneliness, and the pioneer spirit of the West. Gant noticed it, accustomed as he was to the Caribbean feel of Florida, but Umberto didn't, because he was too busy checking out the girls.

It was there, on the streets of Mendocino, that Gant finally began to face the face that his criminal fetish was gone and he had come to regard Umberto as a son. Not precisely the son he'd want, but not precisely the sort he wouldn't want either. The boy might have made a mistake, admittedly a big one, and he might have been caught up by the Fates and put straight into their boiling cauldron, but he was a good kid underneath it all—in many ways differing only from an average teenager in the degree of his nerve and the steel of his resolve. As they dined together, in a seafood restaurant on a back street, Gant asked him about his family.

Ju don't want to hear that tired stuff, *meng*.

You're running from them, then?

Umberto laughed the bitter laugh Gant hadn't heard since the face-off with the rattler.

I don't *run*, I ride. Anyway, I told ju, I got dreams.

Gant leaned closer.

Things you haven't seen yet, right? Things you haven't done?

Now ju got it.

Their young waitress—a California surfing babe with

three earrings in each ear and hair pulled back to show freckles, put Gant's lobster bisque in front of him and served up Umberto's calamari appetizer.

How about your father? asked Gant. What does he do for a living?

My father? He drinks beer. He watches ball games. He fucks whores. But not my mother, even though she is one.

The calamari slipped from the waitress's hand.

Cocktail sauce on Umberto's mandarin-collared shirt. Long grease stain on the tablecloth.

Umberto pushed his chair back, angered more by what Gant had brought out of him than what the girl had brought down. She rushed away muttering something about napkins, but when those finally arrived, along with soda water for his stain, they were brought by a different server, a cynical guy from New York who, it was agreed in a quick kitchen powwow, could handle any table on earth.

Do they know what you did? Gant inquired quietly after the mess was cleaned and a fresh portion of squid laid out.

They don't know dick about me, okay? They've got their own problems, their own quicksand, their own lives.

And your girl, Graciela?

Look, Umberto said, putting down his fork. How about we don't talk anymore? How about we just drink this wine?

Main courses arrived, orange roughy for Gant and swordfish for Umberto, because he'd never had it. They ate in silence for a while, each trying to pretend he was alone at the table, until Gant finally spoke.

You're a pretty good bullshitter, aren't you?

I ain't bullshitting nobody.

Except yourself. You're just waiting for someone to notice you. Waiting to be caught, waiting for someone to show they care.

Fuck ju, Umberto said loudly, and then he got up, and then he left.

Gant, who had endured land mines and napalm and the screams of Vietnamese children in the last days of the war, ate his dessert alone.

Crêpes Suzette. His favorite.

———

When he got back to the hotel room, he found Umberto watching television.

The Jap stock market's way down, reported the boy.

Is that a fact?

Lotta dudes falling on their swords today. Umberto sniffed.

A weather report came up after the financials. Forest fires were burning in California's southland, fanned by Santa Ana wind, and the Malibu horse ranches of two famous Hollywood actresses had gone up in flames. The horses, including an Arabian stud worth a reported $5 million, were presumed dead. In world news, a Palestinian car bomb had killed four clerks and a geophysicist in the produce section of a Tel Aviv supermarket, the vice president of the United States was on a fact-finding mission in Brazil—something about rain forest destruction. More, a teenager had opened fire with a handgun in a Miami-area McDonald's that morning.

She couldn't get some giveaway doll. Umberto shook his head. Look, I'm sorry, okay? I jes' don' like talking about my family. Ju were in the army, right? Why don' you tell me about Vietnam?

That was a war, Gant snorted.

Ju got ju war, I got mine, Umberto said, kicking off his shoes and climbing under the covers.

But sometimes it pays to surrender, said Gant.

Kids get seized by impulse. After all, adults are the ones who raise them.

Graciela's voice was like a cruise missile exploding inside Umberto's heart, disrupting the flow of blood, destroying his equilibrium, driving the pump into overload due to the dropping pressure and the massive leakage, making him leap from the bed, his trembling finger pointed at the TV set.

Check it out, *meng*! the boy whooped. Graciela's on TV!

Gant leaned forward for a look. The camera lingered on her as if the lensman himself liked what he saw. And for good reason. The girl was stunning. Many of the Latina girls Gant had come to recognize as familiar in South Florida had something small in their faces, a limitation of view, perhaps, a cramping of their souls by the machismo of their culture. Others had a defiant look, as if broadcasting through the ferocity of their expressions their resistance to domination, losing sight of the fact, in their eagerness not to be trodden underfoot, that rebellion is not freedom. But Graciela was different. She was neither constrained nor defiant, she was genuinely independent, and from that independence sprang a deliciousness of purpose, a joy in her own convictions.

She's fantastic, Gant declared. Tell me about her.

She looks at me sometimes like she knows shit I don't, Umberto answered, staring at the TV. That kinda pisses me off, but hey, it's probably true. She says shit ju wouldn't expect, too.

Like what? Gant asked, fascinated. There was nothing of the Latina stereotype in this girl. She wasn't bottom heavy. She wasn't dark. She didn't overdo her makeup. He'd never seen anyone like her.

Like one time we were fooling around and she said to me, there ju go, ruining a great evening by biting me on the butt.

These kids want Biker Babes, and when they can't have them, they freak. It's not their fault, really. It's ours.

Like I said, Umberto murmured, sitting on the bed in his underwear, his long legs bopping a song on the inn's carpeted floor, she knows some shit.

As the camera moved to the reporter, the blond woman with the expressionless face and the purple eye shadow and the flashing white teeth, Graciela's ghost remained on the screen, in the barest outline, as if the picture tube itself was in love with her. Watching the photons fade, Gant felt the rumblings of an idea.

If that's really your girl, you're an idiot for leaving her, he said.

Umberto didn't even hear him.

He was lost in private, intimate thoughts.

THIRTEEN

❧

Crisp, thinks Consuela Santana. How did he get the sheets so crisp? She is beginning to feel a grudging respect for her estranged husband. She isn't certain that he picked up laundry skills from her, the bleaching, the starching, even ironing—to save bills—but she suspects it. What she is sure he did not get from her is the rose petals in the bed. That, she knows as surely as she knows the outline of her own triangular bush, is another woman's work.

Mmmm, Pedro sighs, nuzzling against her. He still loves her smell, that much hasn't changed, as indeed it cannot, since Consuela has learned, through years of experience with a multitude of men, that each one is directed by an inborn and inviolable preference. There are sniffers, there are listeners, there are men who rely only on an exquisite sense of touch, and there are those who live solely in fantasy or memory, who use a flesh-and-blood woman only to concretize their dreams.

What made you think to put flowers in the bed? she asks. That's the way she is. She can't leave well enough alone.

I saw it on TV, he answers too quickly, his eyes still closed. Do you like them?

Sure. She sighs.

He's naked, but she's still wearing her Cuban heels. It's something she does for him. Those, and the garter belt, so his access is free. No panty hose for Pedro. Not now, not ever. She fluffs up the pillow, a new case to match the sheets, she notices, and slides back so she's sitting up in the bed.

Tell me about the money, she begins.

I told you. I won it gambling.

And I'm Castro's mother.

Sshhh. Pedro touches her lips. He wants to preserve the delicious feeling; he wants to avoid the shitstorm ahead.

But sex doesn't mean what it used to mean to Consuela, what it meant to her when she was a virgin, what it meant the first time with Pedro, clutching him so tightly to her that she scarred his back forever with her nails. Sex is irrevocably tied to money now, and it is money she thinks about as she fingers the new linen and thinks of the Jaguar convertible parked outside.

The money comes from Umberto, doesn't it? You've gotten him into something. Drugs, right?

Pedro waves her away with a sleepy hand.

Girls then? Is it girls? She sits up savagely erect and smacks him on the head. Tell me my son's not running girls.

There's no girls, okay? Pedro says, grumpily protecting his head. And no drugs either.

There's the girl who was here.

I don't know anything about her.

I'm supposed to believe that?

Consuela, please.

She decided to let it go. It couldn't lead anywhere good anyway.

But he gave you the money, right?

Pedro reluctantly acknowledges this with a nod.

To get money like this, he had to do something bad.

I don't know. Pedro shrugs. He's a hard worker, our boy.

You think I'm an idiot? Consuela rages, swinging her legs out of bed. If you know it's not girls and you know it's not drugs, that means you know something you're not telling me!

Pedro protects his balls in case she loses her temper completely, but before she can hit him, someone announces himself at the door.

Knock knock.

You got no pimp now, right? Pedro asks nervously.

Nothing he could have said would have hurt her more. It was a delicate thing, this reparation of a marriage, this business of pulling something sweet back from an abyss of bitterness, and in asking that thoughtless, stupid question, Pedro lets the rope slip so far that Consuela ends up ankle-deep in the mire again.

Like father like son.

She slips into her dress, picks up her shoes, dangles the straps over her thumbs, and retreats to the bathroom, where she can cry unseen.

Knock knock.

Coming! Pedro yells.

He answers the door in boxer shorts, and finds Eagle Cooper there, wearing sunglasses, not smiling.

May I come in?

Is this about the car?

It's about your son.

My son? I don't have a son.

Eagle presents a piece of paper. Pedro squints, thinking it's a warrant, but gets a horrible feeling in his belly when he sees that it is Umberto's birth certificate. He moves out of the way, and Cooper blows by him like an angry wind. He snatches up the picture of the boy on the bicycle and is still holding it when Consuela emerges from the bathroom. She's all made up again, externally perfect, not a hair out of place, as if nothing at all has happened.

She's practiced at this.

She can do it anywhere, anytime.

She can hide bruises, she can hide tears, she can even hide blood, if she has to, but she can't hide the hurt of what Pedro has said to her, not from him, anyway, because he knows her too long, and, in his own clumsy way, he loves her.

You're a cop, she says to Cooper. It's not really a question.

Special Agent Eagle Cooper. FBI.

I fucking knew it. You're going to take back the Jaguar, right?

In fact, I'm here to speak to your son.

Get in line.

I don't do that, Cooper says, waving his shield. This means I jump right to the front.

She shrugs, fumbling for a cigarette in her purse in order to give herself something to do with her hands, and her little gun falls onto the floor. Before she can reach it, Cooper snatches it away.

Baby Browning, he says approvingly. An original too. Wouldn't stop a squirrel, but it's a nice little gun. He looks up at her. You got a permit for this?

She produces a plastic card from her purse.

She's licensed to conceal.

The proper, legal hooker. Pedro is downright amazed. Cooper, for his part, spins the gun around his finger, then lets it slip into his pocket.

Even so, I'll keep this for a while, he says. So it looks like Umberto is seventeen years old. You sure he's not around?

Consuela lights her cigarette and blows a little smoke.

I'm sure, says Pedro.

Then I'll need to see pictures.

We don't have pictures.

Cooper is impatient now. He's finished dancing around.

I'll come back with a warrant, he says, suddenly

fierce. Then I'll rip this goddamn place apart. After that, I'll start on the two of you. Your secrets, your friends, the places you eat and drink. I'm not kidding around. I'll make your lives a living hell.

Go ahead, Consuela spits. You think you're going to find gold in this shithole? You think you're going to find platinum?

Cooper softens his tone because he's ashamed of his outburst. Strong-arm isn't really his style.

Look, he says. The truth is, if you care about your boy, you really need to help me. There's a murder involved, see? I don't think he did it, but there are others who do, and they are powerful. I want to help him. I want to crack the case, but I want to see justice done. I can smell a lynch mob growing. I really can. If I don't get to him first, things could get ugly.

Pedro pulls Consuela to him because he can tell she is going to make a grab for her gun.

My boy is no killer, she says, trembling with rage.

A senator died, Consuela, Pedro interjects sadly.

What are you talking about?

Your son robbed a bank, Cooper explains. A senator, a woman, died from asthma while it was happening. She was scared to death. Any good lawyer will blame Berto, and there will be good lawyers involved.

Don't call him Berto, Pedro interrupts. He doesn't like Berto.

Consuela watches her last hope for a decent life head like a lemming for the sea. She's drowning in self-pity, and in fear for her boy. She can't think, she can't see straight, she can hardly breathe air.

A senator, she murmurs faintly. She gets it now. She puts it all together. Prostitute yes, dummy no. She reads the newspaper. My God, I should have watched over him, I should have kept him closer to me. I should have loved him more, I should have worried about him more, I should never have let him fool me with those eyes of his and the way he can talk.

I'm sorry, says Cooper, because he really is. He really wishes the robber were some prick with a record, some seasoned bastard with a known modus operandi who could take care of himself in the joint.

You want pictures? Consuela hisses, suddenly savage. I'll give you pictures. She reaches into her purse and hurls a tattered plastic photo case at Cooper. It unfolds upon impact, accordion style.

Here is Umberto in a crib, showing only his red face and a crooked little pinkie.

Here is Umberto at the beach, holding a plastic yellow toy shovel nearly as big as he is. There's that pinkie again.

Here is Umberto beckoning with the pinkie for someone, perhaps his mother, to come closer. He's almost in puberty now, a thin line of black hair down the center of a tanned chest, muscles not yet grown to man size, tight bathing trunks.

Umberto on a push bike.

Umberto in the backseat of a car.

Umberto on a motorcycle.

Beckoning with the pinkie.

Come ride with me.

Seeing Cooper's cop mind at work, Pedro snatches the pictures away. He is privately astounded that she carries these pictures in her purse. If he were a john, pictures of a kid—so *many* pictures!—might be off-putting.

Cooper is thinking about Umberto's little finger. His pinkie. The way it beckons. Nobody beckons with the pinkie. He is trying to imagine that handsome boyish face declaring its intentions to a trembling bank teller, when the doorbell rings.

The Santanas look at each other. Cooper feels for his gun. Nobody moves.

Is one of you going to get it, or am I?

Disheveled and smelling faintly of sex, Pedro goes to the window and peeks out. The way he groans, Cooper figures the boy has come home. Gun at the ready, the FBI man yanks open the door, but it is Graciela, not Umberto, who stands in the doorway. The summer sun strikes her, morning rays on her forehead, partially reflected by her tan skin, partially absorbed by her dark eyes. Cooper hastens to holster his piece. Graciela tries to wither him with a look, brazen for a girl who's just confronted a gun.

Is everything okay? she asks.

Fine, says Pedro. Everything is fine.

I was just wondering whether you had heard from Umberto.

Graciela won't set even one toe over the threshold, seeing that Consuela, the gunslinger, is there. What is it with this house and guns? she wonders.

Cooper takes her gently by the elbow.

Special Agent Eagle Cooper, FBI, he says. Please come in.

She shakes loose.

FBI?

She gets a terrible feeling deep in her bones. What is going on here? Where is her boyfriend, the father of her unborn child? First there is television and now there are cops.

I'm looking for Umberto too, says Cooper. You his girlfriend?

She nods.

Have you heard from him at all?

If I had, do you think I'd tell you?

I'm here to help him. He robbed a bank.

He might have put it differently, might have pumped her for confirmation or information or facts, but there is something special about this girl that's making it difficult to think straight. Her legs are one problem, bare as they are, and smooth, with incredibly muscular thighs.

You've got the wrong person. She juts her jaw out stubbornly.

A momentary colloquy takes place, silently, between

the Santanas and the girl. There is to be a conspiracy of silence here, Cooper can feel it. He writes down everything he can about Graciela, where she works, where she lives, her telephone number, her driver's license number. Then he gives everybody his card.

I could have come here with cops and warrants, but I wanted to work this out quietly. I still do. If any of you hear from Umberto, I expect you to let me know at once. I want Umberto in custody, but I also want him safe.

Copper's Sherlockian homunculus clears his throat.

Fat fucking chance.

Except for maybe the girl. She's got something in her eyes.

Could be love.

Could be more.

What's more than love?

What indeed?

———

Another Bloody Mary, Caroline told the waiter.

Gant stayed with coffee. It was too early in the day for him to drink. Booze robbed him of energy.

I've got things to do on the boat, he explained.

The boat, she scoffed, her voice slurring slightly. Why don't you sell that fucking thing?

She'd been drinking more and more in the four months they'd been together. It was as if she was challenging her fine young liver to a duel to the death. Gant hated her drinking. It turned her into somebody he hardly knew.

The boat's my living, he replied simply. He wasn't ashamed of that. In fact, he was proud of it. Being a captain, any kind of captain, said something for one's sense of dignity.

And sense of destiny.

I'm your living, she said, snatching the drink from the waiter before it even hit the table. How many was that, anyway, Gant wondered. Five? Six?

That's a hell of a thing to say.

Well, I don't like how much time you spend with that boat. I want to travel. I want to go to Europe. I want to go lie on a beach in the South Pacific. I want to dance all night in Paris and eat all the pasta in Rome.

Gant found himself staring at the smooth white crease of her arm, where it bent inward at the elbow. How could anything be as perfect as that pale curve of flesh?

Then travel, he said. I've got to work.

The drink disappeared in a couple of long gulps. There was only the celery stalk left. That, and a wash of red on the glass which made Gant think of the Hamilton kitchen.

Maybe I will.

Fine with me.

Are you saying it's over? she inquired tightly.

He found himself unable to meet her eyes. Those hazel, blazing, crazy eyes. She always won their face-offs, and it always made him feel less than a man.

I'm saying if you want to go, then go. I'm trying to build a charter business. I can't just take off.

She leaned forward, pushing her braless breasts against the table so that they came up out of her white shirt, squeezing together to exaggerate the cleavage she knew he loved so much.

Do you know that Michael had you followed? she said.

He could smell the Worcestershire on her.

What? Why would he do that?

Because of the way you looked at me that time we went off to Colorado. He thought we were having an affair, just like that cop did. Everyone could see we were drawn together like magnets. You were the only one slow on the draw.

Gant pushed back from the table and crossed his arms. He remembered that look, remembered the feeling of his heart in his throat when Caroline took off her sunglasses for the first time. He remembered it, and he wanted the feeling back, and he knew, sitting there at the Polo Beach Country Club, with the shiny new gold Rolex she had bought him on his wrist and her empty cocktail glass on the table, that he would never have it again.

I didn't realize Michael was so possessive, he said quietly.

He was a control freak, she snorted. A jealous, manipulative bastard. I wanted a life, see? I had dreams and ambitions. I had things I wanted to do. He closed me down like one of his lines of suits. Nobody could live like that.

The waiter passed close by carrying cocktails for other diners, and Caroline deftly reached up and snagged another drink for herself off the tray.

Come on, Caroline, Gant growled. You've had enough.

Glug glug. Good-bye Chardonnay.

Her eyes grew red rims.

He was a jealous prick, she said, and he got what he deserved.

Caroline! Gant was horrified.

She leaned across the table.

And the kid was a spoiled brat. You should have heard him wail as an infant. Christ, he was all lungs. And just because I took myself away.

Away? Gant repeated, confused and full of dread. Something terrible was coming.

I gave him the bottle, that's all. I didn't want to ruin my tits. I didn't want to sag.

Lots of women feel that way, he said, relieved. Lots of women use a bottle.

Poor dumb Gant, she slurred, stroking upward with her fingernail on his forearm, following the flow of venous blood to his heart. You still believe I'm like lots of women.

She was drunker than he'd ever seen her, and he'd had enough. He wasn't going to see her again. Not for a while, anyway.

The waiter went by again, with the replacement Chardonnay, giving Caroline a wide berth this time, and a glare. She stood up suddenly, those endless legs of hers showing in her too-short tennis dress, and blocked his path to steal a drink again.

Do you mind? snapped the woman who was waiting for the wine. If you're that thirsty, perhaps you should go for a swim.

They all knew her there. Caroline Hamilton. For months there had been nothing but talk of her, and her money.

Caroline the victim.

Caroline the lamb.

Caroline the slut.

Wasn't that the limo driver she was with?

Go fuck yourself, Caroline snapped, throwing back her head and downing the wine.

That's it. We're out of here, said Gant, rising.

We. Always the gentleman, it wasn't his style to simply walk out. He was still being considerate of her, chalking the boozing up to bereavement, to what she'd been through and what she'd lost.

Obstinate, she sat down hard and fell silent. Figuring food would help, Gant ordered a chicken salad for her, pasta for himself, wondering all the while how things with her had gone so quickly and tragically wrong. Was it her? Was it him? She had seemed so right at first. Caring for him the way nobody had, the way his mother never had, doting on him, buying him things, telling him how handsome he was, how good he made her feel. Not only had she not left him in an alley, she had devoted herself to him totally. She had given him four of the best months he'd ever had with a woman.

And then the death spiral. The whole room was looking at her, and it was up to Gant to put out the fire. He was doing it, succeeding with his disarming smile, when she started in again.

I hate this fucking place.

I'm sure this place feels the same way about you. Now will you keep your voice down? Your food will be here in a minute. You'll feel better after you eat something.

The patronizing way he said it was what finally did it. That he would dare talk to her that way. Mercury Gant, her walking alibi. Full of nine cocktails, she lurched to her feet and put her mouth to his ear.

I killed them, she whispered.

I shot the jealous fucker dead.

And the little witness, too.

FOURTEEN

❧

The good ship Merryweather was a yachtsman's dream. For years and years, she brought smiles not only to her owner but to the people of Port Townsend and boaters on Puget Sound. John McCarthy had commissioned the 120-foot ship to be built right there in the heart of wooden boat country, having seen its lines and its portholes and guardrails and cabins in a dream, much the same way he claimed to have conceived the comic strip character Nodel, a mute, sleepwalking boy whose antics found a great audience in the comic strip section of newspapers nationwide.

Like Nodel, *Merryweather* was chock-full of whimsy. She had two funnels, though she needed only one, and these were done up with sky-blue caps and a general configuration not dissimilar to that of the giant cruise-ships of the Cunard Line. At a time when tropical hardwoods were rarely seen but still politically correct, her decks were teak and her rails rosewood. Her portholes were oval, a trick of master carpentry. Her graceful, up-swept bow was designed by Hiram Bishop—the man who later captained her and then turned in agony to salmon fishing when she was destroyed—to conquer the nastiest seas the Strait of Juan de Fuca could dish out. Her stern, at least the rearmost portion of it, was an exercise in optimism, as it was open to the elements in a climate where even sea lions took on extra blubber. It was said that McCarthy sat there often, bundled in a scarf as long as Isadora Duncan's, with a Greek fisherman's cap pulled low over his brow, a bright yellow oilskin sou'wester, and a Meerschaum pipe covered with a metal damper to keep it lit in the rain.

Parties were often held aboard *Merryweather*. Mostly these were for the publishing crowd—including a bevy of little-known novelists who made their home locally or in neighboring Port Ludlow or Sequim—but also for the common folk of Port Townsend. On Independence Day, local children were treated to a rain-or-shine sail tour of the sound and an endless supply of chocolate doughnuts with a liberal dusting of rainbow sprinkles. McCarthy claimed he gained inspiration from the kids. He showed them his famous art collection. He showed them Rembrandt's famous painting of lions, and he shared with them a room full of stuffed animals with which he was rumored to sleep when his critics were nasty or one of his many licensed Nodel products sold shy of expectations. The parties, the cruises, the well-paid contented crew, and the glad energy of the megalomaniacal comic strip artist all imbued the very wooden frame with a glowing energy. The perfectly smooth hull defied friction and slid through the sea as soundlessly as time. It also defied barnacles, a mystery which just made Hiram Bishop smile knowingly when he was asked about it.

Merryweather couldn't defy the greatest storm of the century, though. The rape of the Olympic Peninsula by the monsoon which washed away the Hood Canal Bridge and stranded island folk for weeks took a nasty toll on the ship. Even though she was battened down and shored up and tied tight and sealed, she needed drydocking when the storm had passed, and it was in drydock that she stayed, for years, because John McCarthy's aorta exploded just one week later, while strolling to his mailbox, the latest instalment of Nodel in his hand. He was mourned, of course, but somehow his memory was eclipsed by the need to rebuild homes, roads and bridges.

With McCarthy gone, the battered *Merryweather* sat and decayed, ignored by all except Hiram, whose love for the vessel could not be quenched. It was into the musty, termite-infested skeleton of this once-wondrous yacht that Audrey Bishop inadvertently wandered, in her own darkness, hungry and thirsty and completely alone. She gained access to the cabin by climbing a ladder that had been set against the hull years before by her grandfather, at a time when the supermarket across the road—the place where she and Ruth had last touched hands—didn't even exist. The ladder was gritty and weathered but sound enough to hold thirty-five pounds of child, and Audrey, who had been quietly formulating the idea that she had fallen into some kind of a hole, assumed that it might lead upward to salvation.

It had been three days since she disappeared, and while the town was abuzz with her imagined fate, while Ruth remained frantic, and a clue simmered in Officer Sam Patch's mind, Audrey had already begun to adjust to her new reality. Like a child in a concentration camp or a foster home—or indeed, a child sold into slavery—she adapted far more quickly than an adult might to her circumstances. It was not that Audrey didn't love Ruth, it was just that her brain chemistry had not yet hardened. Neural pathways were still soluble, and the habits, ego-centrism and grim outlook on life that characterize the adult mind would elude her for some time to come. More, she was emphatically different, being a special kind of blind. Without visual clues to orient her, a large portion of her brain, centered about the frontal and optic lobes, remained at loose ends, facile, ready, indeed eager, to work at creating new touchstones.

Mold spores gave the old yacht a familiar smell, one which Audrey connected to Boccherini's Cello Concerto in G, the music of the moldy storage room at Ruth's store. As she crossed the open stern deck where once other children had reveled, Audrey was feeling better for the music she fancied she heard. By the time she reached the doorway to the long passage that led to the galley and the sitting room—sans Rembrandt; some distant cousin of John McCarthy had seen to that—she actually began to smile. She ran her hands lightly over everything, letting her fingers make whirlpools of knots in the wood and chopped forests of the legs of tables and chairs. She inhaled metallic odors.

Copper.

Brass.

Silver.

To her nose there was a difference.

She smelled the fungus on the pages of the books in John McCarthy's great floating library—books on swords mostly, as he had a fetish—and the moisture the mahogany shelving had absorbed during the storm decades before. Then, at last, she detected the odor of algae flourishing in the galley drain.

The galley!

There were myriad fragrances there, and Audrey's spectacular nose sought them out. Driven by the only keen hunger she'd ever felt other than to feel her mother's touch just once, she found first the dried goo of plums a generation old, stuck to the bottom of the vegetable tin in a large refrigerator whose door was ajar. The Olympic environment was so moist, and the confines of the yacht so much like a cigar box—some of the walls were cedar—that pits, stems, and even skin remained. Audrey wasn't hungry enough yet to eat them, as bacteria had lent them a sulfur smell, but she was close.

Next, she discovered a plastic bag that had once held asparagus. A dinner party had been planned for the vegetarian society of which McCarthy had been head, but the storm had ruined the evening. All that was left of the asparagus was thin black strips where the stalks had been, and thorny outcroppings that had once been delicious heads. After that, she discovered the rice, sealed in shiny plastic paper, and still edible, with the addition of boiling water, of course. It was a streaked, wild rice, with a chewy outer husk, all the better to compliment the squashes and mushrooms and carrots enjoyed by McCarthy and his herbivorous kin. All those vegetables were gone now, leaving absolutely nothing for a starving little blind girl to eat.

Except in the tins.

There were better than a dozen of them—sweet corn and broccoli and sauces and soups—samples for the tasting of a vegan king who, at the monthly meeting of his like-minded clique, had announced his impending departure for the Orient, there to pursue the acquisition of the world's ultimate katana.

But Audrey would never have found any of them—her nose was good, but no nose can smell clear through aluminum—if not for the aid of her grandfather's ghost. What remained of Hiram Bishop, a confluence of energies and intentions and sorrows, pillowed by seaweed and shrunken by brine, all hanging off the gaunt, efficient frame of the longtime fisherman, came sailing down the hallway at the sound of the little girl's puttering—unlike Caroline's ghost, he was a floater, not a walker; there is a difference, but only ghosts understand its full significance—until he stood right behind his granddaughter. He stroked her ash-blond hair with hands she didn't feel, and marveled at how much of her mother there was in the shape of her head and the way she held her shoulders.

I'll be damned, he said to himself. She's growing so fast.

Audrey sniffed the air like a coonhound. There was something new in the breeze, something like what she smelled after a big boomer out over the water.

Storm, she muttered at Hiram's ozone.

Baby, he replied. Your grampa's here.

Audrey turned, so startled her heart went off like a marching band.

You're not Grampa. Grampa's dead.

I'm still him. Hiram chuckled. Just thinner.

It was dark inside the yacht, and they were almost nose to nose.

You sound the same, but you smell funny.

That's because I'm dead, he said.

You can't be dead, silly.

He left it at that. Some things are not for a six-year-old's ears.

Your grandmother's worried about you, he said.

She's worried about you too. You should go tell her we're both okay.

Hiram couldn't explain to her that Ruth wouldn't be able to hear him, that only certain people could, and that such talent couldn't be learned but only inherited from just the right bloodline.

Grampa? I'm hungry.

Follow my voice, he said, because he couldn't touch her in a way she could feel.

She did, and ended up in front of the pantry, really nothing more than a tall, thin, vertical closet.

Here, he said. Canned vegetables.

Just not Brussels sprouts. I hate Brussels sprouts.

No Brussels sprouts, then. Reach up. There you go. Your hands are on spinach now.

Yum, said Audrey, rolling the can in her hand as if it were gold.

What's this one?

Beets.

And this one?

Corn.

And this one?

Those are the Brussels sprouts.

Yuck!

They continued through the inventory, finding broccoli florets and sweet potatoes, lentils and black-eyed peas. They found water too, from an alpine source, bottled in plastic with twist-off tops. It tasted like plastic, but it was wet.

Grampa, Audrey said at last. What about a can opener?

Hiram led her to the right drawer and talked her through fitting the tool. When the can was open, he watched her eat.

Dribble.

Slurp.

What a wondrous thing is a child's face.

Outside, the town grew more and more frantic.

Audrey?

Nancy Fortier comes spilling into Eagle's nest like boiling water from an overfilled kettle. She's dressed like a schoolgirl in a Black Watch plaid skirt, a white blouse, black stockings and flats. The Sig Sauer nine-millimeter in her shoulder holster looks completely ridiculous, but Cooper knows better than to laugh. She has won the division marksmanship trophy four years in a row and holds two black belts in Korean karate.

Plus, she's the boss.

You have a suspect, she declares.

I'm working on something, Cooper carefully replies.

She draws a deep breath. It's as if her mouth is on fire and the air is going to cool her.

Here's what you're going to do. You're going to turn over a copy of everything you have to me, and we're going to put an all-points out on the guy.

Actually, I'm thinking I can do it faster my way.

Nancy closes her eyes for a moment. She doesn't want to lose her temper. Cooper's a valuable man.

The homunculus!

Do you have any idea how many people Timothy Rule knows? In Washington, never mind Miami? Do you have any idea how much clout that guy has?

I can imagine, says Cooper.

I doubt that, I really do. I'm telling you we need a bulletin on the guy. We need to set up a net.

He didn't kill the senator, says Cooper. He came in, got lucky with the cash, and went out again. There's no evidence he even saw her choking.

So what if he didn't? If he hadn't pulled the heist, she'd be alive today.

If she didn't have asthma she'd be alive too. Her lung condition was not the kid's fault.

Now you're being ridiculous, Fortier snaps. A person has a right to go into a bank without expecting a robbery.

And a robber has the right to pull a heist without expecting asthma, Cooper says desperately.

Fortier frowns.

You're joking with me, right?

I'm not.

You'd better be.

I know, Cooper says miserably.

Fortier draws up to her full five feet and two inches.

Perhaps I should just take you off the case.

You don't want to do that. I tell you, I'm closing in.

What the hell is going on here, Eagle? How old is this kid, anyway?

Seventeen.

And is your interest personal? You know him or something?

Cooper doesn't know him. Not really. So why *does* he give a shit? Is it because if he were going to do what the lad has done—not that he ever would—he would like to think he would do it just the same way?

Walk in.

Get the money.

Don't even talk to anyone but the teller. Don't go yelling for everyone to get down. Don't go advertising the gun. Just let fears and instincts unfold on their own, then take the loot and leave.

Cool and faux blond and invisible.

Eagle Cooper might be a cop, but that doesn't mean he can't admire the bastard.

Of course I don't know him, he tells Fortier. He intrigues me, that's all.

Intrigues you. Christ, I think you like him.

I've met his girlfriend, his family. His mother's a hooker.

Boo hoo. Fortier sighs. I've heard it all before. Product of his environment and all that. The jury's business, not ours, but Rule can buy any lawyer there is, so I bet they try him as an adult. Don't get too attached to him, 'cause he's going down hard and he's going down big.

Kid made a mistake. He deserves another chance.

He'll have one, says Fortier. In his next life.

Damn it, Cooper curses. Look, at least let me bring him in. I don't want some trigger-happy sheriff whooping it up over a bank robber collar.

No can do. He goes out on the wire today. Now hand over the file.

Give me forty-eight hours, Cooper implores.

Not a chance. The kid could be in Rio by then, which would mean your shield and probably mine.

Then let me stay on it. Put him on the wire if you have to, but let me chase him down.

Fortier considers the whole thing carefully. Her first and probably her best instinct is to take Cooper off the case right now. There's plenty of other work at the office. But there is also the agent's uncanny sense of things, the way he always ends up right and always ends up with his man. In the end, it's the tiny creature on Cooper's shoulder, the creature nobody can see, who gets Umberto his reprieve.

All right, she says. You're on. But find him fast, and don't do anything Rule can bitch about.

She turns on her heel, leaving a faint hint of the lemony designer fragrance. Cooper, who has never had a sexual thought about her beyond idle underwear speculation, finds himself thinking that lemon is not something Suzanne would wear. Cinnamon is more her style.

Really, he's trying not to think of Umberto Santana out there somewhere on the run. He's trying not to think of the gears and chains and pulleys of the vast law enforcement machine that has been set in motion by Tim Rule's hurt and Tim Rule's ire.

If only Vicky Rule hadn't died.

Death just somehow changes things.

————

Officer Sam Patch has a sleep disorder of the highest magnitude. If anyone knew how bad it really was, knew the disorientation that develops in him after night after night without sleep, they'd never let him have a gun. And yet it is guns that fuel the problem, or, more precisely, his *passion* for guns. He's a collector, and he specializes in .22 caliber pistols, the machines of yore, made by Belgian and German craftsmen who fled Europe between the great wars and ended up in American's finest arms shops.

Sam's devotion to his collection is legend. He's a bachelor, which is fortunate, because he lives like a marten, in a den which hardly qualifies as a house, not far from the wooden boat docks and the saddest motels, at the far end of town, on a filled-in sandbar at which the mad ocean patiently licks. It's not good for his guns to be so close to the salt, a fact which creates inner turmoil for Sam, because he loves his weapons and the sea equally. In order to juggle his passions, Sam has to oil and clean his treasures every night.

Banish the rust.

Dismiss all signs of lead.

Thank God for insomnia.

He stores his goods in airtight cases stacked ten high inside his closet, four or five to a case, depending upon the models. These are target models, designed to put ten bullets through the same hole at twenty-five yards, and they feature such things as barrel weights and recoil compensators and featherlike triggers and polished sears. There are slant-gripped military High-Standards and early Woodsman Colts, and there are firing indicators and original boxes—the best of this and the rarest of that. His collection, which numbers perhaps a hundred guns, represents the entire income of his working life, and although he is only thirty-two, it is a truly substantial portfolio of steel and wood, a record of what can be accomplished by focus.

With all this, he is a terrible shot, and he seeks to live down that shame by becoming the ultimate gunsmith, working, as he always does, with a high-wattage bulb and fine cotton swabs and a dental pick, beneath that true testimonial to random good chance, his one and only bull's-eye-struck paper target. He is removing a large flake of lead with relish when something utterly unrelated to guns comes into his head and stops him cold.

Deerfield Beach, Florida.

What would Ruth Bishop, who he happens to know is connected to Florida only by tragedy, be doing writing to someone down there? He pries out the last remaining chunk of lead from the recoil-reduction ports and glances over at the clock. It is 2:20 A.M., and the little girl is still missing. It is time to act.

He takes the police cruiser, which he uses as his personal car, and drives out the long road to Ruth's place. He loves the aromas summer makes up here, how the heat loosens the sap on the evergreens and lets it run, wild as liquid gold, all the way to meet the dark soil. He loves imagining that there are fairies in the woods, and goblins and ghosts, not just the occasional potsmoking backpacker or white separatist afield with garrote and knife.

After a good stretch of road, he turns the car into Ruth Bishop's driveway. He sits finishing a cigarette, and is surprised to see lights on and Ruth's shadow moving

behind the window. Cooking, it looks like. For whom?
He doubts she'd be hungry. She has seemed in quite a
state, and there are no cars but his in the driveway.

He goes to the door and knocks.

The door flies open.

Sam! Yes! Any news?

Mind if I come in?

The color drains from her.

What is it? What do you have to tell me in the middle
of the night?

Nothing bad, he reassures her hastily.

Her face loses twenty years in sheer relief.

The longer we go without word from her, the smaller
the chances of finding her, you know, Ruth announces.
That's what the TV shows say. That's what it says in
this book I read. Here. Look.

She holds up a paperback about the tragedy of children lost in America. It's called *Vanished Angels*.

We're working on it, Ruth. We really are.

I can't do anything but think about her, Sam. I just
can't. I can't eat, I can't concentrate on the shop, I can't
sleep. Here, have a cookie. I just baked them with or-
ganic oatmeal and carob. You know, I just keep turning
that shopping trip over and over in my head, wondering
what I could have done differently. I was looking at
myself in the mirror, did I tell you that? At my eyebrows, if that doesn't beat all. I'm such an idiot woman.

She starts to cry, and Sam pats her hand. He glances
around at the immaculate house, at the crayon drawings
on the refrigerator, as strangely hued and inchoate as
they might be, created by a blind hand.

Ruth pulls herself together.

What are you doing awake at this hour, anyway, she
asks with a strong attempt at warmth. Polishing your
pistol?

The double entendre hits them both at the same time,
and, like a pair of chameleon eyes, one looks up, the
other down at the floor.

About this man in Florida, he begins.

Ruth gasps.

How do you know about that?

You had a letter to him in your purse when you came to my office. Do you want to tell me about it?

Not really.

There's energy attached to this issue, Sam Patch can see that much right away. She was wet and she was weepy and now she's like the guard on a fencing foil, all round and hard and shiny.

Tell me anyway. There might be some connection to Audrey.

Ha, says Ruth.

You're sure there isn't?

Ruth pauses a moment, as if looking at the world for the first time. Her eyes open wide and her hand flies to her mouth, and suddenly, without any warning, she starts to cry.

I've been such a fool, she moans.

Sam pats her shoulder and offers his handkerchief.

She dabs at her tears with it, smelling the gun oil.

FIFTEEN

❦

To Eagle Cooper, Graciela Perez's apartment was nothing so much as a three-dimensional *People* magazine. The white walls were like shiny paper stock, and all but obscured by clippings of fashion models and secret weddings and sneak photos of shocking trysts and movie stars.

Most of all movie stars.

What do *you* want? Graciela asked, barring the door. She was clad in a T-shirt cut off to show her smooth belly, and a pair of sprayed-on bluejeans with horizontal tears at the knees. She wasn't sure she should let him in. She knew about cops, saw them swagger into the restaurant, listened to the way they chatted among themselves their terms for her people, their us-and-them mentality.

I want you to help me save Umberto's life, Cooper replied.

She turned and moved away, swaying her hips. At first, Eagle figured she was trying to seduce him—and he felt smugly immune to her charms, taken as he was by the wholeness of Suzanne Emerson, her smile, her touch, her voice—but something told him that this was just the way Graciela walked in front of men.

Creature of habit that she was.

You got some kind of a warrant?

Not that can force you to talk to me.

She paused for a moment, considering the unborn child inside her, and then reluctantly cleared a place for him at the kitchen table, an unsteady job of thick white plastic with matching chairs. This required pushing Hollywood clippings aside, but also grocery store coupons and the tool she used to cut them.

Look, you obviously read the paper, so I'm guessing you've heard of Senator Vicky Rule, the one who died of asthma during a bank robbery? She saw Umberto's gun, see, and she died gasping for breath in front of her seven-year-old boy. Nobody helped her. They probably could have, but they didn't.

Graciela didn't move a muscle. Cooper had to admit to himself that she was one self-possessed young lady. Cool like her beau, but not cool enough to stop the blood draining inexorably from her face.

This senator, Cooper went on, she was married to a rich and powerful guy. He builds houses, and he has friends in the Justice Department. Those friends are interested in seeing Umberto caught, no matter where he is, and then tried and sentenced as an adult. He could get the death penalty.

The death penalty? For a lady's asthma attack? Graciela bristles. She's caught something she can hang on to with angry fingers—an injustice—and she's no longer dangling over the abyss.

Or life without parole. If he hadn't robbed the bank, the senator would be alive today. That's the way they'll argue it. The whole FBI is out looking for him, Graciela, and they will find him, believe me, no matter where he's hiding. When they do, they're going to use tear gas and bullets and helicopters and dogs. They're going to bring him in, dead or alive.

Dead or alive, Graciela murmured.

I'd like it to be alive. I don't like lynch mobs, and

that's what I think we're going to have here. So, to save his life, I need you to help me.

How can I help you? I don't know if he did this, and I don't know where he is.

Let's say I believe you. Cooper leaned back in his chair. Sooner or later, he's going to contact you. When he does, I need you to convince him to surrender.

Fat chance, she said, an expression she'd learned from Umberto.

Listen. If you trust me, and can convince him to trust me, then I can protect him, bring him in safely and quietly. Surrender will help him in court too. Juries like people who surrender. It shows they have a conscience, that they are willing to face up to what they've done, to atone. It will help his attorney assure that he is tried as a minor, which might keep him from the chair.

The chair?

The electric chair. Old Sparky. *Bzzz*, no more Umberto.

Graciela shut her eyes and squeezed her fingers together so Cooper wouldn't see her shake. She thought of Umberto's cheek on her thigh and the way he held his head.

Umberto hates gangs and he hates guns, she said. You don't know how *snotty* he is about people who use violence. How much he despises them. He's a dreamer. An idealist—a person who wants to lift himself out of this life and into another, better one.

So you two have a plan then? You're going to meet him someplace?

Graciela stands up and turns her back to Cooper and bites her hand so she doesn't cry. He *can't* have left her. This is all some kind of horrible lie. But where is he? Why doesn't he call? Why doesn't he write? How could he let this terrifying man come to her kitchen?

We have no plan to meet, but I'm sure he would send for us eventually.

Us?

She's thinking of the baby.

Me, I mean. He would send for me.

Cooper nods slowly.

So you have no idea at all where he might be hiding?

None. Her composure was back. Her makeup was barely smeared, and she hadn't shed a tear in front of this bastard. She would look this good in the middle of a slaughterhouse or even tennis ball–size hail. She'd never let anyone see her sweat. She was going to be an actress.

Right there, Cooper decided he had no choice but to bug her telephone.

Here's another card, in case you lost the last one I gave you, he said. If you hear from him, you let me know, okay? I would hate to see this end badly.

He got up and went to the door, and when he reached it, she finally spoke.

Umberto isn't the hiding type. Seems to me he might take off somewhere.

Like where?

I told you I don't know. But have you found his motorcycle?

———

At Leggett, some thirty-six miles north of Mendocino, the coast highway turns inward, leading the riders down a cool and magical path of flickering forest sunlight and damp, mossy, sensual aromas. This is the land of leprechauns and legend as well as the land of hidden hemp and helicopter raids and the occasional mountain lion mauling. The plates underlying the earth move differently here. Shifting tectonic energies meet whirlpools. Prevailing ocean currents eddy, and cool soil conspires with damp wind to produce the kind of humid conditions which over the course of time make for the deepest possible bedding of pine.

The mystical nature of those first inland miles suspends the squabbling between Umberto and Gant as surely as if it were a spell. In truth, each of them is too occupied with his own thoughts to worry much about the other. Gant feels an apprehensive constricting of his throat as the latitude rises, the temperature drops, and he draws closer to his destination. Umberto is taken by thoughts of how very big the world is and how absolutely impossible it would be to ever see it all, no matter how much time and money he had, and no matter how few cops were on his tail.

They pass through Piercy and stop briefly for a bite at Benbow—home to an incongruously grand inn with white walls and red shutters and the dim, darkwood interior ambience of a Swiss chalet—and then press on to Garberville and Rio Dell, riding together with the well-oiled precision of a police drill team, but automatically, as if more out of habit than choice. They pass Fortuna and Loleta, where the road rejoins the ocean once more, and in the shadow of the Trinity National Forest, on the downslope to Crescent City and the top of California, they watch the sky turn the color of singed ivory.

Industry.

Millwork.

Myriad tiny particles of sawdust refract the sun, forming a blanket over the long flat highway. Gone are the scenic cliffs. Gone too are the avenues of giant redwoods, whose fronds—had they been allowed to stand—would have cleansed even the thoughts of so rough a crowd as the timber haulers and the woodcutters. Gone, in short order, is California.

The state line. Brookings. Carpenterville.

Pistol River.

Boom.

Oregon. The state is so exotic to Umberto that Gant has to coach him to pronounce it correctly. The cypress hedges and the lily beds, particularly at the mouth of the Coquille River at Bandon, give the coastline a feel quite distinct from dramatic Big Sur. There are dune-sheltered lakes between the coastline and road, covered with furze

and punctuated by stands of Oregon white cedar and
cranberry and huckleberry, rhododendron and azalea.
Umberto slows the pace, in part because he is so taken
by the beauty of the coast, and in part because he is
thinking about Graciela.

So is Gant. As surely as if she were on his pillion,
thoughts of the girl are gradually displacing thoughts of
his own destiny. Without knowing anything about the
delicate toe dance she is doing with Special Agent Eagle
Cooper, Gant is trying to figure how the girl might help
him steer Umberto away from disaster. Gant knows the
world is after the boy, and every small-town cop car that
whizzes by, every sheriff's speed trap they motor sedately past, fills the older man with terror, not because
he fears his affiliation with the criminal but because he
knows Umberto has a young man's heart and therefore
views death as a lion to be wrestled with and conquered,
not an inevitable monster to be feared and forestalled.

Claws like handcuffs.

Breath like shotgun pellets.

A gaping maw like a jail cell.

The thread that holds them together stayed intact just
as far as Coos Bay, which is a picturesque enclave, sit-
uated on the southern edge of a bay shaped like a croc-
odile's jaw and bordered by a lighthouse and a point of
dunes onto which crash waves which occasionally bring
flotsam from Japan. Everywhere there are vendors sell-
ing key fobs and soup bowls and salad forks of polished,
satiny myrtlewood. The whole place is pervaded by the
smell of curing salmon and boiling Dungeness crab, raw
razor clams and pungent simmering chowder.

Check this place out! Umberto exults. It's a fucking
fairyland!

He points to the boardwalk and the marina and the
trawlers and sloops. He dances with circling seagulls and
cracks mussel shells under his boots.

Listen, says Gant. I'm going to make a call. Wait for
me, okay? We'll grab some lunch.

Umberto narrows his eyes suspiciously and Gant sighs theatrically.

What, you still worried I'm going to turn you in? Do you know how many cop cars we've driven past in the last two days? What are you thinking? I have a life outside your thievery, all right?

It is hard for Gant to get this out, but indignation helps fuel the fire of his deceit. He would have an easier time if he knew that at the very moment the lie was passing his lips, modem lines from Baltimore to Sault Sainte Marie and San Diego were alive with chatter of Umberto Santana. There were printouts in FBI offices in New York and Chicago, and there were E-mail blurbs with his description appearing in communications booths and small offices in local police departments and town halls.

Yeah, okay, says the boy. He is hungry, that's the thing, and the longer he dallies, the longer he has to wait for one of those fine-looking crab sandwiches that have caught his fancy.

Gant leaves his machine with Umberto in the corner of a gas station and wanders across the street to the seafood restaurant where he figures they'll eat. It is a single-story clapboard structure—nobody would have had the audacity to put up so much as a widow's walk so near the ocean for fear of obstructing the tourists' view—and there is a pay phone alongside.

Maimi, please, he tells the information operator, tapping his foot on a sidewalk made of hard sand.

What listing?

McDonald's restaurant in Perrine.

Be at work, he mutters to himself as he waits.

Be at work, and love the boy.

Here's your number, says the operator.

He looks at his watch. It is mid-afternoon there on the edge of the Pacific, which means the Florida sky is already turning that delicious pale blue that June nights bring. He prays Graciela works this shift. He clicks off, gets a dial tone, uses up a pocketful of change, and punches in the number.

Rrriiing.

Rriiiing.

Across the road, Umberto turns away from the service station vending machine with a soda in his hand and gulps a long, cold bubbly draught. He can't see Gant. Who could the old guy be calling? His stockbroker, probably.

McDonald's, can I help you?

Graciela Perez, please.

She's busy.

It's an emergency.

Christ. Hold on. We got a store full of people here.

Umberto strolls around the bikes, the can of soda in his hand. Damn if one of those BMW hard cases isn't half open.

The stupid latch. Mercury is always fiddling with it. Reaching back to check it while he's riding. Ridiculous. The boy prefers soft, zippered luggage, the kind you can jam oodles of money into. He doesn't like the way hard cases confine and limit things. He doesn't like to be limited at all. He doesn't like to be confined.

He pushes against it with his knee, reaches down to latch it shut with his free hand. Something is sticking out. An envelope. He tries to push it back in with his free hand, but it won't go. He takes another sip of soda—it's hot in the sun—and pulls the envelope clear, intending to lay it back in on top, where there's room. There's a photograph inside. He can see the rectangular outline through the white paper. He looks around. No sign of Gant.

He opens the envelope.

Back by the restaurant, Gant steels himself as he hears a clattering at the phone.

The waiting is over.

This is Graciela.

Such a clear, strong young voice.

Hello, Graciela. You don't know me. My name is Gant. I'm a friend of Umberto's.

Graciela slumps against the wall near the deep fryer. She's nauseated. She has been since morning. It must be the baby. It's all she can do not to drop the phone and run to the bathroom. She takes a deep breath.

Is he all right?

He's fine.

She runs her hand over her belly, massaging it in circles, as if maybe she can calm things down.

It's about your father, she whispers downward, hand over the phone.

Back at the service station, Umberto pulls out the photo. It shows a little girl, maybe four years old, with ash-blond hair. A pretty kid, but with a strange, vacant stare.

He unfolds the letter and begins to read.

Dear Mr. Gant,

Thank you for replying so quickly, and for submitting to the medical test. Life is sad and strange, sometimes. You cannot possibly imagine the pain Caroline has caused—perhaps torment would be a better word. In any case, words don't seem adequate to the task of conveying my feelings about what she has done, and how her mind could have gone the way it did. Time, however, has passed, and although the wound hasn't healed, it does seem somehow less in focus. With my husband gone, I am bent to the task of raising Audrey, and that in itself is a therapy, although there is always, I confess, a terrible fear that whatever went awry inside Caroline might happen again in the child.

If I hadn't attended the trial, I doubt I would ever have even heard your name—that's the amazing part. Caroline never said one word about you, and the idea that she kept your own daughter's exis-

*tence a secret from you is something, like so much
of what Caroline did, that is completely beyond my
comprehension. By the same token, I hope you can
understand that given who Caroline was, the number of possible fathers was shockingly high, which
explains, I hope, why I didn't contact you sooner.
The fact is, however, that the DNA results are con-
clusive. Audrey is your daughter. I don't exactly
know what the law says about our situation, but I
do know that I am 66 years old, and while my
health is generally good, I know I'm not going to
live forever. I have to think about her in a future
without me, and I hope you will too. I can't bear
the thought of her being alone in the world.*

*I hope you can see something of yourself in this
picture of her, and I look forward to meeting you
in the near future.*

Sincerely,

Ruth Bishop

The reason I'm calling, Graciela, is that I'm hoping
you can help me help Umberto.

Help him how? she asks cautiously. There's bile down
deep in her chest now. She doesn't know if it's from
hormones or nerves.

I have to make this brief—he doesn't know I'm calling—so forgive me for being blunt. Have the police in-
terviewed you yet?

The bile rises high, acrid on her tonsils. She swallows
hard, but it doesn't help.

The police?

Banks have video cameras these days, Graciela. And
a senator is dead. Now have you heard from anyone?
The FBI, perhaps?

Maybe.

I'll take that as a yes. Now listen to me carefully,

because I'm sure they've bugged your telephone at home. They may even have done so there at work.

Graciela is stunned.

They've tapped her phone.

The world about her roars dully. Fast-food orders fly, and there are smashed French fries on the floor. The milk shake machine whines. The dessert pies rotate in the warmer.

My phone, she says dully.

Is there an FBI man you feel you can trust?

I don't trust anybody. I don't trust you.

Fine. Okay. Good. Does this FBI man seem a good man or a bad man?

Graciela thinks about Eagle.

He's okay.

All right then. Get in touch with him and tell him that there might be a way to get Umberto to surrender.

He wants to give himself up?

He might. If he does, will you help me?

Graciela's mind is a hurricane. She doesn't say anything for a long, long time.

Graciela?

I gotta go, she says. She sees that orders are piling up. She sees that customers are getting impatient.

Will you help me?

All right.

Good. I'll call again.

Gant. Listen to me. Tell Umberto . . .

Yes?

Nothing.

Good-bye, Graciela.

When Gant hangs up, his hands are shaking. They haven't shaken this bad since he looked up out of the mud, leeches twisting inside his fatigues, to the sight of four NVA soldiers stepping through the jungle just ten feet away. He takes a couple of deep breaths, wrings his hands out like they are dirty towels, and heads back across the street, where he finds the boy just finishing up a soda.

Ready to eat? Gant asks.

SIXTEEN

✿

Gant's distaste for the lieutenant didn't make what he had to do any easier.

The limo-driving lover, the dapper cop said, blowing cigar smoke in Gant's direction. To what do I owe the honor? Conscience bothering you?

It was expensive tobacco, that much was obvious, and the ring said Havana. The forbidden, illegal leaf. It figured. Gant's head was suddenly filled with images of depositions, reporters, courtrooms. He looked around the office, feeling exhausted. The lieutenant had a taste for the good life. How he managed it on a cop's salary was anyone's guess.

I have information about the Hamilton murders.

Did you say murders?

She killed them both, he said simply. She told me.

Is that right?

Gant isn't getting the response he expected. The damn cop hasn't even asked him to sit down.

She confessed. She was drunk. She bragged. The marriage was too confining for her. She set the whole thing up.

The lieutenant took a long drag. He licked his lips lasciviously.

So she unconfined herself with you, is that what happened? Big strong guy like you took the lady to bed and helped set her free?

I didn't sleep with her when she was married. Gant sighed. I didn't even know her then. I don't even know her now. Why won't you believe me on that?

Because I'm a piece of shit with a badge, remember? I don't believe people very often. Being skeptical makes my job easier. You got some proof of any of this?

What do you mean by proof? She confessed.

You figure if I go arrest her now she's going to admit it? Think she'll testify in court that yeah, she told her lover she killed her son and her husband? Florida's a death penalty state, Gant.

What are you trying to say?

I'm not trying to say anything. I'm saying it. There is no proof. If there were, we would have found it. The insurance policies were intact, although there was a heavy one out on the kid, but hey, rich people do weird things sometimes. The weapon was on the scene, and ballistics confirmed it. So unless she kept a diary detailing her plans, we're shit out of luck.

Gant's palms prickled with sweat.

You mean she's going to get away with it?

She already did.

Gant slid down in his chair. If his feet hadn't hit the legs of the lieutenant's desk, he might have kept right on going to the floor. None of his muscles were working. He was as limp as overcooked fettuccine.

She shot her own baby in the head, he whispered. The husband I can understand, I mean crimes of passion happen, but the kid . . .

I got news for you, Gant. This was no crime of passion. She planned the whole thing, down to the last detail. The note, having you walk in there with her. She went out to the beauty parlor afterward, for Chrissake. You drove her!

These thoughts had woken Gant the night before, while he wrestled with himself, alone between the sheets, about what exactly he was going to do. There was no denying anything anymore, not the handcuffs, the sex club, the shiny revolver. Life had dragged the eel right out of his hole, and it was murder out there all alone.

She's a monster, Gant whispered.

The lieutenant put down his cigar and took out a gold nail clipper decorated in mother-of-pearl. He commenced trimming and snipping, pushing his cuticles down with the blunt end. He had noticed that they had run amok and were obscuring his digital white moons.

He liked his digital white moons.

My job is full of them, he said with great largesse. I'm president of the monster-of-the-week club.

Gant swallowed hard and stood up.

I've been to war, he said. I've seen a thing or two also.

I know you have, Gant. I know everything about you. Army Ranger, medal of valor, decorated for bravery in combat. And I know that even if you've seen things, it's different when it's a woman, especially if you're banging her.

Gant grit his teeth.

So now what?

Nothing, unless you help me get evidence.

What kind of evidence?

The lieutenant slipped on a nail, drew a little blood, sucked it hard.

She duped you so now you want to help, is that it?

Just tell me what it will take.

You want to know what it will take? Really?

Tell me.

Okay, Gant. It will take a wire. You're going to have to wear a wire and you're going to have to talk about the murders and get her to give you every delicious detail for the tape.

That's the only way?

You got it, soldier.

Gant stood up. It was all so clear to him now.
It was all so simple.

———

Hiram Bishop's ghost slides under Audrey's head and
runs his insubstantial hands through her dirty hair. He
remembers how that hair smelled on the last day he was
alive, when she brought him lunch down at the boat, and
he wishes he could smell it again, here and now. He
thinks about Audrey's mother, his own daughter, Caroline, and almost doubles over with the pain that his own
flesh and blood had brought him. Why can he feel pain
in his heart but not detect aromas? It's so unfair. And
the little girl can't feel his lap or his hands or his tears,
nor can she see him at all.

But she can hear him crying.

Grandpa?

Sleep, he says.

Outside, a summer storm is raging. It's not like the
typhoon that nearly sank the *Merryweather*, thank God.
If it were, even in dry dock things could become peril-
ous. No, this storm is just enough to give Port Townsend
pause, to prompt some folks to open windows because
the smell of warm rain is so rare up here.

Tell me about my mommy, Audrey prompts, curling
up on herself.

She was beautiful, he says, biting his own ghostly lip
with his own ghostly teeth.

There are still stalks of kelp dripping from his fingers,
Nereocystus, the bubble seaweed whose inflated sacs
support the marine forests of the northern Pacific, the
same kelp in which he was tangled to drown in the frigid
waters off Orcas Island, in the winter, in the Strait of
Juan de Fuca.

How beautiful?

Very beautiful.

Tell me about her voice. What did she sound like?

Convincing, Hiram says, with a twinge of sadness. She could make anyone believe anything.

He wishes he could make Audrey believe that she's going to be okay, but he senses she's got a gift for knowing. He can't bring himself to tell her that there are only two cans of food left, and that she's already opened the last bottle of water. He wishes he wasn't stuck here, within the confines of the yacht, by whatever rules there are to his stage of the game.

Limbo.

Lonely limbo.

Until she came along. And soon again.

Could my mommy change the weather?

Hiram is astonished by the question.

What?

Like, could she move clouds around and stuff? She sent me whales, you know. A mother and a baby. As a sign she was thinking of me.

People can't change weather, says Hiram.

I bet if all the people in the world got together and prayed for it, if they thought about it, they could make it rain. Or stop raining. Gramma says there is too much rain in some places. She says that people drown. She misses you, you know.

I miss her too, says Hiram. He's wondering, with a sudden feeling in his throat, if Audrey might possibly be an angel. But how could God let an angel get so dirty and so gaunt? How could he let her little knees get bruised and her palms skinned? How could he allow that great blue bruise on an angel's head? Is this all some kind of test for him? After all this time?

Tell me more about Mommy.

The little girl's voice is weaker now, as if the visionary outburst has cost her what energy she had left. Her head is heavier in Hiram's lap, although all she can feel is the hard mildewed cocobolo of the *Merryweather*'s sitting room bench.

Hiram tries to think of a bright side to Caroline, some

shining piece that hasn't been totally obscured by her dark soul and her horrific end.

She was smart, he says. She could figure things out faster than anyone. She treated life like a chess game.

That's the game with kings and queens, right? And princesses and princes?

Yes it is, and your mother was good at it.

I want to learn chess, Audrey declares faintly.

And you shall.

Mommy was a princess, wasn't she? I just know she was.

You're the princess, Hiram says, his voice thick with heartache.

So Mommy was the queen?

Sure, says Hiram. Now it's time for you to sleep.

Okay. She sighs.

And she does, beneath a torrent of ghost tears.

———

Gant has to work hard to get Caroline to see him. She doesn't want to. Not anymore. She's done with him and she's too hardhearted to respond to his pleas, to his claims that he's lost without her. She already knows that. She thinks he was lost before he found her. That's why she used him so easily. That's why he fit so readily into the plan.

In the end, he has to come to her apartment in Boca Raton, the new condo she's bought with Michael Hamilton's money, not five minutes from her former mansion on the Intracoastal. Gant wonders what self-congratulatory megalomania would drive her to live so close to the scene of the crime. He bets that she would have kept the murder house if it wouldn't have looked suspicious.

At the small of his back, taped right above his coccyx, he wears a tiny transmitter. The delicate wire from it runs around to the front of him, up along the seam of his polo shirt, so it can't be seen even if he sweats. The lieutenant's men wanted to put the thing in his crotch, but Gant made it clear that the crotch wouldn't be safe from her, not even after she said she never wanted to see him again. One could never tell with Caroline. Her moods could change like the wind.

The building was half empty because the condos started at one million, but there was still a security force, and they wouldn't let him in.

Not authorized.

Ms. Bishop doesn't want to see you.

Ms. Bishop. She'd gone back to her maiden name. It helps, she said, to avoid pity and attention.

Let him in anyway, the lieutenant instructs, appearing from out of nowhere like a dark wizard.

The security guard backs down, but Gant can tell that he wants to call and warn Caroline. She must have something on this guy. Maybe she's been teasing him. Maybe she's stroked his cheek one time.

Maybe she's stroked something else.

Gant shakes off the thought, steps into the elevator.

That's what things have come to, he says aloud to himself. There's no telling what she might do. No telling whatsoever.

Her apartment faces the ocean, of course, and there has been some discussion of the transmitter getting through the walls and down to the garage, where the original plan had the surveillance van waiting. At the last minute, partly because he is hell-bent on the collar and partly because he has such a taste for fine things, the lieutenant has borrowed an expensive Cigarette speedboat from the DEA. He's put the radio in the bowels of the thing, below the waterline, with a couple of his men huddled there too, waiting to give the high sign that self-incriminating words have been spoken.

Gant knocks on the door.

There's a long pause, then the *click-clack* of high heels on tile.

High heels. Does she have company? The cops have

sworn to him that she's alone. It's key to the operation.

Who is it?

Gant.

How did you get up here?

I was charming, he says.

Jesus, she says. Why can't you just drop dead?

Gant wonders how she can use the *J* word. He's not a conventionally religious man, but hearing it makes him wince.

I need to talk.

Then buy yourself a shrink.

He realizes in that moment that nothing he can say about himself is going to advance the cause. She no longer cares enough about him to open the lousy door.

It's about the police, he says through the heavy door. They've been asking questions. I think they know.

You think they know what?

That you killed Michael and the boy.

Click.

Snap.

The door opens.

They don't know shit, she says.

She's naked, wearing only high heels and shades, and she's illuminated from the back by the crisp winter sun off the water, coming in through floor-to-ceiling windows. She's shaved herself completely—something he often asked her to do—but she's also changed the color of her hair. She's a blonde now. Honey, not platinum. She watches his reaction with amusement. He swears she can see him get weak in the knees.

So it's true. She smiles coldly. From the look on your face I'd guess blondes really do have more fun.

He takes in the apartment. He's never been here. All their time together, and she's never once invited him up. It wasn't ready, she told him. It was better if they stayed together in a motel, or if they stayed on his boat, or at his place in Deerfield. Under construction, she'd said. Not the building, but the condo itself. She claimed walls were being knocked down. She claimed they were creating a new kitchen and the marble was taking forever to come in from Italy. She said the mess bothered her, and the dust.

There's no mess and there's no dust now. There is only glass. Not just the glass of the windows—beyond which is the Atlantic, and the floating hot islands—but the glass of sculptures. They're everywhere. It's a goddamn indoor sculpture garden. There are young men at engorged salute, with even their glass biceps bulging. There are imprecating maidens in frosted glass gowns, their hands outstretched, long locks of cold, glassy hair streaming down. There are mermaids with glass tails and jaunty imps with glass boots, and there are dragons, satanic, not oriental, with gleaming glass teeth and forked glass tongues and glass talons that could rip your heart right out.

Gant's been wondering what she did with Mike Hamilton's money, and part of the answer is right here, for these are full-size sculptures, not delicate little table pieces. One huge dragon takes up a whole corner, its spiked mane nearly touching the ceiling. The mermaid lounges in front of the white leather couch, and is fully as long. The men, ah, the men are full-size. With just a breath of blood and heat and guts and lymph, they could be functional enough to service their owner.

This place, he says. It's you.

You just couldn't stay away, could you? You always were a weak-willed bastard.

I came to warn you, that's all.

She comes up to him, stands so close her nipples graze his shirt, barely inches from the wire.

You haven't *really* heard from the police, have you, Mercury?

They told me about Xavier's insurance.

Breathing through his mouth so he won't smell her, he moves past her and into the forest of glass. This insurance detail is the thing he and the lieutenant have agreed to reveal, to tease her, because there is no way Gant could know it if he hadn't been told by the cops.

Obviously jolted, she follows him, her hands out by her sides, touching her glass townsfolk as if for reassurance, a finger on a glass hip here, a finger on a glass ear there.

The kid was insured. So what?

For four million.

That's not so much, she shrugs.

Gant wonders how her perspective can possibly have changed so quickly, this creature who less than ten years ago painted fingernails for a living and bid on rich men at auctions.

There's something I've been wondering, he says.

I'm sure there are a lot of things.

He has reached the patio now. He opens the slider and steps out. It's cool out here. She won't come out. He looks straight down. It's quite a fall. There are multi-colored umbrellas on the beach, and from here they look like they might be made of paper, like the tiny ones in Chinese rum drinks. He sees a little kid maybe Xavier's age run at the incoming tide, attack the froth with his tiny, baby toes, and then run back, his hands held high as a meringue dancer's. Out farther, on the water, is the lieutenant's red Cigarette boat, quietly cruising back and forth, its antennas fully alert.

Gant resists the temptation to wave.

You need to go, she says. I'm packing.

From where he is, he gets a glimpse into her boudoir. Sure enough, there are suitcases open on the bed.

Running from me? he asks.

She looks at him as if he must be crazy, and even with that incredulous, loveless gaze, she is so painfully beautiful, her body so breathtaking, her features so sublime, that he wonders for the hundredth time how it is possible for such incredible evil to exist inside such a magnificent shell.

She sees the look on his face, which she reads as frank

admiration, and she comes over and takes his hand, gently.

Before I go, there's something I want you to do, she says. Her voice is gentle. She's his lover again, not at all the same woman she was just a nanosecond ago.

He doesn't know what it is she wants, but he nods in agreement. She leads him over to a glass statue by the kitchen. It's six feet tall if it's an inch, naked, of course, and with wings on his heels.

Mercury, the messenger of the gods, she says. It even looks like you. Take off your clothes and stand next to it for me. I want to see the two of you together.

Incredibly, Gant begins to undress. Whatever willpower he had moments ago has fled. It's as if he's under her spell again, the one she cast, right at the beginning, in that terrible, bloody kitchen. He's ready to strip down to the wire, and then he thinks of poor little Xavier, missing half his head, and a moment of pure internal alchemy ensues. Atoms rearrange themselves, subatomic forces come into play, molecular bonds shift and realign as new chemical allegiances are formed, and suddenly, right there in Caroline's apartment, right there by the beach sand and the clear water and the sun and the sky, the old Mercury Gant is gone, transformed into a being of new substance entirely.

What I've been wondering, he says—the microphone burning at the base of his spine, his heart a cannon in his ears—is how you got Michael to swallow the gun. You did that, right? I mean you didn't put it in his mouth yourself?

Oh, he did it himself. I wouldn't get that close to him. She smiles. I hadn't let him touch me in months. I was already thinking of you.

Really?

Gant outdoes himself with that word, with the eagerness, the feigned, vapid adoration. No actor has ever done better.

Oh yes. And it drove him crazy. I tortured him. I'd

leave moist panties in his car, but I wouldn't let him near me.

A flash of teeth.

A pretty laugh, like a bell. She might as well be watching a sitcom on TV. She might as well be at a comedy club, front row and center.

Poor Michael, says Gant.

You have no idea. Now move a little to the left for me, she says, motioning with her finger.

It's as if she's framing a picture.

Gant moves.

There. Now strip for me. I want to remember this just so. You really are a hunk, Mercury.

This is the first time she's called him by his first name. Even in the heat of passion, even with him inside her, it's always been Gant.

So what would make a guy do that? he asks, unzipping his pants. Put a gun in his own mouth, I mean?

Can't you figure that out? I just told him if he didn't swallow the gun, I'd kill Xavier. Michael was obsessed with perpetuating himself. He had a dynasty complex, I've told you that. He used to call the kid his ticket to immortality. The little bastard could do no wrong.

But you killed him anyway.

Sure I did. What else was I going to do? He witnessed the whole thing, and he was old enough to talk. Think what *that* would have done to the freedom Michael tried to take from me, she says bitterly. Michael couldn't *stand* the idea of me being free, of me not worrying about the things he worried about, of me going and coming as I pleased. He couldn't stand the way I talked back to him. He hated my spirit.

Gant feels the microphone taped to the small of his back burn with the heat of the truth.

Didn't he figure that you would just shoot Xavier? he pursues.

People don't think of a mother shooting her own, she

says. As if there's something special about motherhood. Cockroaches have babies.

Cockroaches, repeated Gant.

Rabbits too. But Michael never was very smart about me. He never was much good at thinking under pressure. He just opened and said aaahhh and I drilled him with his own finger on the trigger.

Down below, on the boat, the cops get every last word on tape.

Up in the apartment, Gant undoes his belt.

Here comes the show, he says, and believe me, Caroline, you've never seen me like this.

Down go the trousers. Off comes the shirt.

Down go the skivvies.

Gant pirouettes, especially for his love, just so she can get an eyeful of what he's wearing underneath it all.

SEVENTEEN

❧

Emergencies in Port Townsend tended in the direction of the medical and the maritime. Little girls didn't disappear too often, and the nefarious activities of hate groups, mere splinters of more serious Idaho crowds, never really reached Waco-esque proportions. Any small town in the Northwest could host sociopaths with strange ideas about race, creed and religion, but Port Townsend, known mostly for its artist's community and as a getaway for Seattle yuppies, was hardly a hotbed of crime.

Accordingly, the police force was small. Officers tended to run their own cases, and there was little department politicking or meddling. The guys on the force, most of whom knew Ruth Bishop because they bought shoes from her, were concerned about Audrey but were happy to let Sam Patch work the case. Such disappearances rarely turned out well, and nobody was looking forward to finding the little girl's mutilated body somewhere, or to bringing bad news to Ruth's door. Thus, Sam was working alone and unfettered on the police computer, his elbows leaning on the desk he shared with a cup of black coffee and the trigger mechanism from one of his target pistols which he felt needed a crisper release. No matter how many databases he searched, however, Sam could find no trace of the man called Mercury Gant.

The fact that Gant had no record—his brief tiff with the lieutenant at the scene of the Hamilton murders was not entered into any official log—frustrated the hell out of Sam. He had been certain that the South Florida man would turn out to have a sheet as long as an ostrich's neck, but instead the guy didn't even seem to exist. Florida's Motor Vehicle Department showed the same Deerfield Beach address to which Ruth Bishop had written, but the telephone company showed the account as having been terminated and paid in full.

Sam contemplated the screen, and finally made an entry requesting the apprehension of one Mercury Gant for questioning in connection with the disappearance of Audrey Bishop, age five.

That done, he went home to polish his guns.

———

Tim Rule holds his Cuban Montecristo cigar out behind him, daintily, as a flapper from the twenties might, ashen tip pointed down, away from the crack in the door, so that the smell of smoke, which little Stefan hates, won't alert the boy to his presence. This is the only Montecristo he has left—having recently given his last box to a friend of his, a lieutenant on the police force—and he is loath to miss even one inch of the fine tobacco.

He peers into his son's room, which his Brazilian housekeeper has told the boy is bigger than the São Paolo apartment she shared with her entire family. The room is decorated with football pennants, astronomy posters, and dinosaur mobiles. There is also a rock tumbler, a telescope, a herd of Steiff animals, and four racks of expensive adult air rifles, including the Daisy Red Ryder Tim himself treasured as a child. Stefan sits in the middle of floor, surrounded by the entire collection of vintage, wind-up Shuco racing cars from Germany, with their real rubber tires and their steerable front wheels and their huge metal keys.

Zoom, he says, pushing a little red Mercedes race car along the tile which just two days ago was carpet but which Rule agreed to replace—despite the fact that Vicky always thought tile was dangerous—because he can no longer deny his son anything.

Stefan forces the expensive little model into a tail-over-nose tumble.

Kerkrash, he says.

The plastic driver falls out.

Ding dong the driver's dead, ha ha ha, the driver's dead. Ding dong, the little driver's dead.

Tim blanches. During the last week and a half, despite his already slim frame, Stefan has lost seven pounds. Worse, death has become his theme song.

Get him to eat, the pediatrician has ordered Rule. I'm telling you, do whatever it takes, pancakes, candy, ice cream. And take him fishing or to the video arcade or something. He needs to have fun. He needs to play and remember what being happy feels like, even if neither of you can sustain it.

The turn's not banked! The turn's not banked! Stefan shrieks, another toy car, a yellow Lola, in his hand this time. Oh, my God, the camber's wrong!

Camber? Tim wonders where he could have learned such words. He himself is not sure what camber means.

Paboomsh, cries the boy, twisting the Lola so that it barrel rolls along the floor. I can't breathe! I can't breathe! Oooooh, the flames, the tank's gonna blow, I'm gonna die. Arrrrggghhh.

Tim Rule feels his eyes filling. Goddamn Umberto Santana to hell, he thinks.

Putting his Montecristo back in his mouth, he takes a long puff, then turns and pads away. He goes down the great, winding marble staircase, taking it carefully, because he knows he's a little drunk and he knows his life is extraprecious now, because if something happens to him, Stefan will be totally and completely alone. He crosses the onyx floor of the entrance hall, passes through the dining room where only two weeks ago Vicky hosted a dinner for the Daughters of the American Revolution, and pushes his way through the swinging doors and into the kitchen.

The Brazilians are asleep, as he and Stefan should be, and the only light comes from the hood over the stove. Tim makes his way to the restaurant-size Sub Zero and opens it up. Inside is Stefan's favorite—Mercury Gant's, too, but Tim will never know this—refrigerator pie.

Tim cuts off a little piece.

He wants to bring Stefan the whole damn dessert, but he's learned from breeding miniature pinschers—the dogs are boarding now; they were the objects of Vicky's affection and for some reason he can't bear to look at them—that everyone eats better if they think the supply is limited.

Offer a full plate and they turn up their noses.

Offer a tidbit and they fight over it like jackals.

He looks for a fork, but he can't find one. He opens drawer after drawer, yanking them hard enough to rattle whatever's inside, turkey basters and cheese graters and carrot slicers and grapefruit spoons. He grabs handfuls of potholders, tips cigar ash onto coasters, plunges his hands deep into Tupperware, but fails to find a fork. By the time he gets around to the drawers beneath the oven, he is crying terrible tears.

Victoria!

Outside, crickets are singing and cicadas are buzzing and herons are hunting and gators are gnashing their teeth. Upstairs, Stefan is running another race to the death. Tim sits on the floor, beside the butcherblock island, and shakes with rage and frustration and most of all with missing his wife. Finally, a beaten tycoon, he takes the cake upstairs with a wooden soup spoon, walking carefully. He passes the guest bathroom and puts his cigar down on the edge of the counter.

Wait there.

Don't you dare go out.

He knocks softly on the door and goes in. Stefan is asleep on the floor, surrounded by an army of tiny cars, all of them upended or nose-to-nose and up on their rear wheels, little pyramids of disaster.

Tim passes the cake under the boy's nose, in hopes the aroma will wake him, but to no avail. In the wash of the ceiling fan light, Stefan's skin looks deathly pale, and the arteries and veins just under his skin are in ominous evidence of the lack of substance. He scoops the boy up, and holding him close, switches off the light and carries him to the truckle bed Vicky had insisted on because she wanted a second child.

He lies down carefully. Stefan mumbles, wipes his nose with the back of his hand, and snuggles against his dad. Tim stares at the ceiling for a long time, not thinking at all of his cigar, which has fallen off the counter and set the fluffy white rug in the bathroom to smoldering.

The boy's breathing finally lulls the builder to sleep, as the rug begins to burn in earnest, igniting the cabinet, the shower curtain, the paint. As the fire gathers force three doors away, Stefan dreams of chocolate and his father dreams of love. The smoke detectors don't go off because the batteries in them have not been replaced on time, and room by room the fire sets about devouring the house. Before it gets to Stefan's room, before it heats the chambers of a dozen air rifles and causes them to go off, *pop pop*, it takes the material leavings of Senator Vicky Rule, negligees which have, admittedly, grown tight these last years, jewelry which, even melted, will later be worth salvaging, papers and books and letters and shoes, most of all shoes, including the pair of high-heel red ankle boots which Tim has recently, secretly, taken into his bed.

When at last Tim Rule wakes up, it is by the force of his young son shaking him, and not because he smells smoke. The alcohol has numbed him to that.

Fire, Daddy! Fire! Stefan cries.

Tim opens his eyes and is instantly alert. He moves to the door, burns his hand on the knob, tests the ply-wood center. Something he does, one of the little custom touches on all his homes, is to put garage-rated foam core doors on all the bedroom jambs. He's happy for it now, as it buys them a little time.

But help will not come soon enough, he knows that. If the smoke detectors aren't shrieking, and they're not, the alarm system has not been triggered, and the police and firemen have not been notified. Given that, he is going to have to rely on a neighbor to see flames, and that's unlikely. The hour is late, and the homestead is remote.

Leave me alone, world.

You won't find me in these 'Glades.

Go to the window, he urges Stefan. See if you can open it.

But we're high, the boy protests.

Smoke is creeping in under the door. Tim is deadly calm. So calm it scares the kid, who does not yet un-derstand that his father shares with the late Michael Hamilton a preoccupation with dynasty characteristic of most extremely successful men. Tim Rule is not about to let the fruit of his loins perish in a fire. Not when there are so many things he can do to prevent it. The door is one, the smoke detectors another—only because of his grief has their battery schedule been neglected—and the emergency ladder is a third.

Stefan has forgotten that it's even there, at the back of his closet, but Tim remembers. He's a builder, after all, and is therefore a slave to this kind of detail, even with a quarter of a bottle of gin in his belly. He claws through Stefan's stuff, a veritable geologic record of youth, with Lego toys at the top, wooden blocks in the middle, stuffed bears and bats at the bottom.

He throws things out behind him like a woodchipper

until finally he reaches the lightweight aluminum rungs and drags them, unfolding right on top of the toy cars in the center of the room, until he reaches the window, which Stefan has managed to open.

He attaches the hooked end of the ladder to special eyelets in the floor, and then feeds it quickly out into the night. When the end touches bottom, he lifts the boy over the sill and fixes his hands to the top rung.

Are your feet touching?

Daddy, I'm afraid.

I'm afraid too. Now, are your feet touching?

Yes.

Okay. Now climb down.

What about you?

I'll be right above you, Tim lies.

If he thinks the ladder would hold them both, he would have gone down first, to protect Stefan from falling, but when he clicked the ladder to the floor, the eyelets moved. They haven't been fastened properly, and they're just plain unsafe.

Shoddy work.

In the boss's own house.

Someone's going to pay for this, and it's going to be Tim, because he's got to stay behind and hold the ladder down.

Daddy! Stefan calls up, a moment later. Daddy, I'm on the ground.

Right here, Tim Rule calls back, just as the fire dragon's teeth rip the door right off its hinges and throw it into the middle of the room.

Now the little cars really *are* on fire.

Now the little drivers are *really* burning up.

As he shields his face, Tim hears voices down below. The Brazilians.

Mr. Rule! You must come now!

Tim tests the ladder with his hands; it wiggles.

Daddy! Stefan screams. You can't die too!

This, Tim knows, is the God's honest truth, so he

vaults out into the night. His feet catch the rungs, and he half slides, half climbs toward safety.

He makes it almost halfway down before the eyelets come out of the floor, shooting like projectiles into the ceiling, going through the plaster and into the attic, where are stored manifestos of Tim's building empire, tax records and deeds and some letters from old mistresses which he has taken great care to hide.

As he falls, headfirst, he smells the swamp around him.

Instead of panicking, he inhales deeply.

Franklin Morehouse was the type of guy who could lift the rear end of a Triumph tourer with one hand, while his other hand worked a stubborn nut. He was big and black and short-tempered and queer, which gave him a curious sensitivity to engines, or anything else that required a light hand and a careful ear, but made him angry at the world and most of the people in it.

He didn't like cops much either. Eagle Cooper, however, he found kind of cute.

Sure, I know Umberto, he said, putting down a Snap-on wrench and wiping the sweat from his brow on a shop rag. He worked for me.

This surprised Cooper, who was there only because the DMV records on Umberto's Triumph connected it to the dealership. He looked around the shop, which was big and spotless, with five mechanic bays and glass doors leading to a showroom floor crowded with scooters and dirt bikes and tourers, repli-racers and personal watercraft.

Yeah? What did he do for you?

Mechanic, Franklin replied. I got four of 'em. We do a lot of volume. The kid did mostly prep work, you know, taking new bikes out of crates, setting them up. He had a flair, and he was careful. Methodical. Flaked on me, though, so you can tell him he's fired if you see him.

What do you mean by flaked?

He just stopped showing up for work.

A big drop of sweat escaped the red mesh of Franklin's tank top and fell to the floor from his glistening, smoothly shaven chest. Cooper stared, and Franklin felt a twitch in his pants.

You're pretty good-looking for a cop, he remarked.

Cooper cleared his throat. The situation was not entirely new for him. To his continual embarrassment, he seemed to have a look that stirred male blood.

Thank you. Can you tell me exactly when Umberto disappeared?

Been about ten days now. I'd have to look and see. Why do you want to know?

FBI business, said Cooper.

Aw, come on. You can do better than that.

He might have committed a robbery.

Yeah? Franklin replied, surprised. He didn't seem like the type to me. Quiet, you know, but honest. Shit, you think he had his fingers in the till over here?

I couldn't say.

You know, it's a funny thing to say, but I always wondered what he was thinking. He had another agenda, you know what I mean? Dreams. He was a dreamboat, too. Man, what a looker.

He didn't tell Cooper that he'd put the hustle on the boy repeatedly and been soundly rebuffed each time.

Do the girls like him?

Cooper was thinking that maybe Umberto was two-timing Graciela, that maybe he had a piece of honey somewhere else, a girl who was hiding him right now. He'd be a fool if he did, but then geniuses only rob banks in the movies.

Shit. *I* liked him. Franklin grins. But yes, the ladies took to him like flies to fruitcake. There was this one, worked the coffee wagon, Mexican, I think, she offered him a free ride one time, I heard it while I was putting cream in my coffee, but he turned her down. He's got a steady girlfriend, used to come by and get all the straight guys hot and bothered. Hey! Speak of the devil. That's her right there.

Cooper whirled around. What was it with Graciela and doorways? She always managed to bathe in a halo of light, even standing five feet from a crumpled fiberglass motorcycle fairing, a bunch of rusted mufflers, and a cardboard box full of tangled Yamaha wiring harnesses. It was obviously her day off, because she wouldn't wear those high heels to flip burgers, and she wouldn't wear that see-through sleeveless sundress either, or G-string panties and a lacy bra.

She literally jumped backward when she saw Cooper.

You! she exclaimed.

Ms. Perez. What are you doing here?

Nothing.

That right? Have you heard from our boy?

I told you I'd call you.

Cooper took a deep breath and thought of Nancy Fortier, of the pressure she'd put on him, and of the tight timetable she'd constructed.

The state troopers have been mobilized, he said. They're using hollowpoints and grenades. They're going to waste him, I'm telling you. And you're going to have it on your conscience.

Hey, said Franklin. Take it easy.

Graciela's heart started skipping. She thought of her baby.

Your daddy was blown away by policemen, little one. I could have stopped it, but I didn't.

A friend of his called yesterday.

What friend?

Someone named Gant.

You know the guy?

Never heard of him before.

How about you, Franklin? You know Gant?

The big man turned up his palms.

Gant, Cooper muttered. Gant, Gant, Gant.

He wants to help, said Graciela. He thinks he can get Umberto to turn himself in. He said he'd call again.

Cooper considered the news. A good samaritan? Not likely. Maybe the guy was going to move on the take.

Where were you when Gant called?

Well, you've bugged my home phone and this is news to you. You figure it out.

He gritted his teeth in response. He'd begged the tech guys to put a tap on McDonald's, but they said it was a challenge to do a restaurant with multiple lines and hundreds of calls per day.

Graciela watched him crack his knuckles and she watched him lick his lips. She watched him give her a rueful smile. Most men got angry when you did them one better. Especially most cops. She decided she liked Eagle Cooper, and she decided she could trust him.

She smiled back.

EIGHTEEN

❧

Caroline Bishop sits on her hard little bed with her shaven scalp in her hands. She caresses her earlobes with her fingertips, feeling the soft skin. She reaches up to her temples, where she knows the electrodes will go. Word is the Florida chair is outdated. Word is, it should have been replaced decades ago. Word is her death will be slow and it will be painful. Word is that her skin will burn and her brain will boil.

She lies back down on the bed, one arm over her eyes, one leg up, the other down, the foot tapping on the ground. Images of her life run before her. She thinks of the trial. Of that Judas, Gant. Of the grim faces of the jury, the judge, the prosecuter, that frame-up artist.

Everything this woman did, from the purchase of a large insurance policy in Xavier Hamilton's name to her liaison with Mercury Gant, was part of her murderous plan.

Caroline thinks of her boot-licking lawyer.

No sane woman could plot the death of her own child. No sane woman could kill a man for loving her too much, especially not a man who had changed her circumstances from those of a strip mall beautician to those of the most privileged life a wealthy South Floridian could enjoy.

Caroline remembers the videos they showed at the trail. There she is, waving happily from the driver's seat of her new Mercedes Benz convertible. There she is, draped in her favorite Van Cleef and Arpels baubles, hugging Hamilton on the golf course. There she is, building castles with Xavier on the beach, even letting the boy cover her up all the way to her face.

Trying to bury her, even then.

She thinks fleetingly of Gant's baby. Odd the little thing should come to her now. She hasn't given it a passing thought since it was born, which was a year ago today. It came out, it cried, she smacked it hard on the head to shut it up, they took it away. Her mother adopted it, they told her, and her father. Good fucking luck second time around to the two of you. I never liked your skinny legs, Ma. Good thing I didn't get them. I never liked your stupid boat, Pa, good thing I wasn't a dreamer like you. *I* really made things happen.

Outside, she can hear the low murmur of the gathering press.

Vultures.

The governor is coming to watch her die. A news reporter, some popular blonde from CNN, is going to be there too, even though she told them she didn't want to look at any blondes, told them she wanted all the women with hair to cover it with hats or kerchiefs. Some of the women agreed, out of respect. Others didn't.

Out of all the things they've done to her—locked her up, chained her down, poked, prodded, and injected drugs—cutting her hair off was the worst. At least the drugs are gone now. She's asked to check out awake. She wants to feel everything, that's what she's told them. She's told them she thinks it will help her repent, help her find mercy in the eyes of God. She knows what to say. She's a fast learner.

So she's free of chains and thinking like her old razor-sharp self. She picks up her head and she looks at the clock. Eighty-seven minutes until show time. She stares at her last supper. Here is the golden flatware she requested, inspired by Alfredo's of Rome and taken by special dispensation from the Hamilton estate. Nobody to object, save the lawyers, because Michael Hamilton was an orphan. Here is a chocolate soufflé from the best bakery in Orlando. Here too are the two petite filet mignon steaks—why not? she hardly has to worry about her figure now—donated by La Veille Maison, her favorite Boca Raton restaurant, out of mercy, for old time's sake, and brought up by a women's rights organization.

She takes a bite, savors the meat, sucks a strand between her teeth.

'Bout time you ate, observes Leah, the guard who has been assigned to watch her during her last hours.

Bet you thought you were going to get it.

Leah just chuckles. She's a bull dyke, and she's had her eye on Caroline since day one.

Sometimes more than her eye.

Caroline knows that the big bitch has been watching her. In the shower. On the toilet. Getting dressed. She knows Leah felt her up when she was too groggy to move, but to tell the truth she wouldn't have moved anyway, because it felt good to have somebody touch her. Anybody. She misses sex a lot. The only thing wrong was that Leah had been in control.

Slowly, Caroline slathers the baked potato with sour cream, then, looking straight at the guard, she licks the spoon, up and down, up and down. This whole plan would be easier to pull off if they had furnished a knife, but she thinks she can do it anyway, mostly because they're not watching now, not expecting it. She has lost a little muscle tone in the last nineteen months, waiting for the appeals to run out, enduring the change in tranquilizer doses, missing her gym workouts, but she has remembered every calisthenic, every Yoga posture she's ever been taught, and has stayed strong by performing them all, one after the other, right there on the cold, hard floor, big Leah getting all hot watching.

Yum, she says, now running her tongue over her lips. May I ask you something?

The guard grunts.

Do you think I'm pretty as a picture? she asks. Be honest now. It's your last chance.

What's wrong with you, asking me that? Leah swallows hard.

I'm going to die, that's what. Wouldn't hurt to have someone I've admired, someone I think of as a friend, tell me I'm pretty.

Leah gets up out of her chair and comes over to the bars.

You look good, Caroline. You even have a pretty head. No bumps or nothing. I've seen some, you know, didn't look so good.

Caroline gets up slowly from the bed, carefully, so she doesn't upset the food tray, and reaches through the bars, very slowly, very gently, and touches Leah on the cheek. Lord, Leah wishes she'd done that months ago instead of biting and kicking and struggling.

Thank you, Leah. Tell me, do you think I'll go to heaven?

I guess that'd be up to God.

You know I've repented. Asked him to forgive me.

Well then, I reckon you've done everything you could do.

Nodding, Caroline goes back to her dinner, pushes the potato aside, and brings her chocolate soufflé front and center.

Shit, I can't eat this.

Go ahead and enjoy it, Leah says.

I really can't. You couldn't either if you were about to die.

This is probably not true, and Caroline knows it. Leah is the chocoholic to end all chocoholics. She's never without a Mounds bar, or a Snickers, Hershey's with almonds, or Toblerone. Hundreds have passed down her gullet since Caroline's been in the clink. The soufflé has to be driving her nuts. It is. Caroline knows it is. That's why she ordered it.

Come on, eat up. You got nothing to lose.

No. I really don't feel like eating.

Come on. At least eat the soufflé before it collapses. Calculate the pause.

Wait.

Wait.

Okay.

Now.

Why don't *you* eat it? That way it won't go to waste.

I couldn't, says Leah.

You'll eat it after I'm gone, right? While they're unstrapping my dead body from the chair?

Don't be crazy, Caroline.

It won't taste good cold, Leah. And a microwave will ruin it.

Leah blinks.

Share it with me at least?

You know I can't come in there now.

Who's going to know? Caroline smiles seductively. I'll feed it to you.

Leah's heart is racing. She dreams of Caroline night and day. Caroline is the most perfect, the most beautiful, the most incredible creature she has ever met, and tonight she's going to die.

I can't, Leah whispers.

Caroline carries the soufflé, on fine china, with the golden fork laid out beside it, right up to the door.

This is our last chance, darling, she says. If you don't share this last thing with me, you'll never know what you missed. Forever's a long time to be sorry.

Big, fat, sweaty Leah looks up and down the hall. Nobody's around. It's grown quiet as a tomb. She can't even hear the reporters anymore. That means they've all moved off to the chamber. That means time is really growing near. It's always like this right at the end.

Quickly, she pulls out her keys and lets herself in.

Caroline sits down with the dessert and pats the bed beside her. Leah lumbers over. Caroline digs into the soufflé and takes a bite.

Wow, she says. Delicious.

Leah sits carefully beside her. She smells like a college locker room.

May I kiss you? she asks.

Caroline smiles. They kiss. Leah is incredibly gentle and sweet for such a big woman. Her mouth tastes of tobacco. She's an enthusiastic smoker.

Caroline digs the fork in one more time, bringing up a big piece of soufflé.

Say ah.

She does, and Caroline drives the fork up through her hard palate and into the base of her brain.

Hard.

As hard as she can.

As if it's her next-to-last act on Earth.

Leah rises.

That is, she actually manages to stand.

She stares. She gurgles. Her eyes seem like they're coming right out of her head. She reaches up to pull the fork out, but her hands start to shake and her eyeballs roll up and suddenly she's flopping and twitching all over the place. The brainstem gives up control of glands and smooth muscle, and the diaphragm spasms and Leah urinates. Then she dies, gasping for air, thinking of a little pony she had as a child, and how it felt between her legs.

During the next few minutes, Caroline Bishop pushes the body onto the floor, pulls the sheet off her bed and rips it into long strands which she winds together. She opens the cell door with Leah's key, ties one end of the rope she's made to the horizontal bar at the top, drags the bed over and stands on it. She ties the free end of the rope tightly around her neck and kicks the bed out from under her.

Jolt.

Pain.

Shock.

Blackness.

I told them I'd be damned before I let them take my life!

Such beautiful stars.

NINETEEN

❧

They rode the lie together, up one of the most beautiful coastlines in the world, at sunrise. They passed Hauser and Lakeside, Florence and Yachats, and at Seal Rock they pulled over into the park. A thick fog had come in, and despite the Oregon summer sun, they found themselves transported to a dark and windy place where headlights looked like moons, and the ocean, periodically visible through floating wisps of fog, might have been the roiling waters of hell.

They parked their bikes by a craggy cliff and watched young lovers climb out of sleeping bags, shiver in their underwear, and run for the rest rooms, hair like quail, sleep still in their eyes.

Those girls make you think of Graciela? Gant asked.

Everything makes me think of her, *meng,* Umberto answered nervously. He found himself wanting to ask about Audrey, but he didn't dare reveal his riffling.

Maybe you should give her a call.

Yeah. I'll do that soon.

What are you waiting for?

Umberto didn't want to admit that he didn't know, that he was less and less sure of his plans every hour, that somehow simply accumulating experiences wasn't giving him the sense of freedom he had hoped it might.

The right time, he replied.

They sat sideways on their bike seats and ate dough-nuts and drank coffee, which Gant sweetened exces-sively.

How come ju go crazy like that with the sugar, *meng*?

Because it's my first time.

What?

Every day of this ride, I made up my mind to do something differently than I've done it before, explained Gant.

Out over the ocean, south and west, Seal Rock itself jutted out of the water. There was an old lighthouse atop it, but when the fog broke, as it occasionally did in the face of the gathering morning, the pair could see that it had fallen into disrepair, the spectacular lens of the old beacon yellowed with salt and grime and age, replaced by a stronger, automatic beam higher up.

No more manual warnings.

No more lonely lightkeeper.

No more romantic glasses of wine at sunset, nor grim faces in a storm.

No more secret trysts with the girl who delivered fresh bread and rare mail.

What a life that must have been, said Gant, staring at the old tower.

A seal barked like a dog. Then another. Then another.

Coyotes of the sea.

Ju kidding me, right? Ju would have to be some lonely bastard to live out there, waiting for dead bodies to wash up on those rocks, worrying all the time that some hur-ricane's gonna drown people. Talk about getting high and getting by. *Coño*.

Getting high. Gant smiled. I hadn't thought of it.

Shit, what the hell else a guy do there all alone?

The life kind of appeals to me, muttered Gant.

That's jes' because ju worried ju too old to find jour dreams, *meng*.

They continued up the coast, past Lincoln City and

Cascade Head, past Oceanside, Cannon Beach, Tillamook and Brighton. The sun won its battle with the fog,
and the day turned warm. Tourists came out like lizards
into the northern light, scrambling for their places on the
road, scrambling for their places on the beach. The bor-
der of Washington State was like a guillotine for Gant,
a sharp line that was set to end one life and start another.
He was going to drop one child, if he could figure a way
to do it, and he was going to pick up another. At least
he was going to check out how exactly his blood had
mixed with the monster's.

He waited for the thought to summon her ghost, but
it didn't.

In Astoria, across the Columbia River, they stopped
to tank up. There were brick buildings here, and a picturesque residential section on a hillside. Near the four-
mile-long Astoria Bridge across to Point Ellice, one
hundred sixty-four steps led to an observation monument
which gave a view up the river to Altoona. Gant parked
his bike at the foot of the tall building and took the steps
three at a time, drawn to the top as if from up there he
might be able to see how to help Umberto surrender,
entirely certain now that he could no more let bank robbery and accidental manslaughter stand than he could let
a double murderer fly free.

When he got to the top, breathless, he felt as if he
were on top of the world. The river was glorious, clean
and sparkling and full of pleasure boats and barges. The
bridge seemed to float magically on its pontoons, and
from this great height, and in this stiff breeze, seemed
to sway a little bit, as if from the glad joy of the day.

Umberto appeared a moment later, less out of breath
than Gant, for he was running on younger, cleaner lungs.

The Japanese attacked this town, Gant said, reading a
plaque. They fired on Fort Stevens from a submarine in
1942. It's an historic place. Oldest American settlement
west of the Rockies.

It's pretty bitchin' up here, Umberto declared, reaching out with his fingers toward the distant river, as if he might actually be able to reach it, as if he were God himself and all this glorious fir country was his personal handiwork. Gant knew, at the sight of that innocent gesture, that he had to be straight about the call to Graciela.

What Gant did not know, however, was that although the Astoria police had given little thought to the FBI bulletin about Umberto—the boy was from Florida, after all, which was a distant peninsula so closely allied to Latin America as to be considered nearly a foreign country—Sam Patch's alert from Port Townsend had commanded the cops' attention. First of all, kidnapping a little girl was a grimmer crime than robbing a bank, asthmatic senator or no, and second, Audrey's imagined abduction had taken place in the Northwest, thereby besmirching the reputation of their part of the country, something for which Astoria's finest simply would not stand.

So it was that Gant's BMW, standing in the sun by the foot of the monument while Umberto's Triumph hid in the shade of a Winnebago nearby, piqued the interest of a state trooper on lunch break. He might have ignored it, if not for the Florida plates, as bikes were common up there in summer, but as it was, he ran the plates as he ate his sandwich, and when the results came back, he almost spit turkey.

Back atop the monument, Gant went for broke.

I need you to do something for me, he said.

Yeah?

I'm going on alone from here.

I figured that. I read the letter about ju kid.

Your kid.

Gant never actually heard the phrase before. Not out loud. The sound of it was like an airplane jet up close.

You did, huh. When?

In Coos Bay. While ju were making jour call. The envelope was sticking out of ju saddlebag.

Gant almost laughed.

While you were reading my mail, I was talking to Graciela.

What? Umberto blinked.

The cops have been sniffing about her like dogs. The FBI.

Gant wasn't surprised when the boy took a swing at him.

Fucker!

Gant grabbed his fist.

Nobody knows where we are, okay?

I trusted ju!

Like a father. I know. And I've cared for you like a son! I'm trying to help. Can't you see that? Sooner or later they're going to catch you on some lonely road somewhere, just you and some hick police cruiser, and they're going to shoot you down and rewrite history later. By the time they're finished, you will have strangled that senator with a dirty sock, laughing all the while, then danced naked on her kid's face. Don't you get it? They're not going to *let* you live the dreams you want! They're going to take them away from you just as surely as you took the money! Graciela's the key, Umberto. She can run interference for you. Through her, you can pick when and where and how you want to turn yourself in. With her help, you have a chance to do it safely, to not end up Swiss cheese, with nobody but me and her and maybe your parents crying over what you could have made of your life.

Umberto yanked his hand away, panting like a racehorse. Behind him, a three-masted schooner glided up the Columbia.

Ju had no business calling Graciela, *meng. Coño.* No way I'm giving up.

Listen to me, Gant implored. I've seen what happens to murderers. I've seen the way everything comes grinding down.

I'm no killer!

You robbed a bank and a woman died. It doesn't mat-

ter what you intended, what you remember, what was in
your plan. The woman died, she was rich and important,
and they're going to make you pay.

I'm outta here then, the boy flared. I'm outta the
United States.

Do you even have a passport? Think, Umberto! You
have a choice. You can't undo what you did, but you
can make it right!

Terrified, furious, thinking himself betrayed, the boy
dashed for the stairs and half ran, half stumbled down
the tower. When he reached the bottom, he took a deep
breath and composed himself, waiting to hear Gant's feet
on the steps behind him. When they didn't come, he
waited some more.

And some more.

They're going to make you pay . . .

Fuck ju then, he said, walking straight out of the
tower. Fuck ju and the bike ju rode in on.

The cop was standing at Gant's bike. Their eyes met.
Umberto, who didn't meet the description, walked on,
across the parking lot with the stolen money dangling
from his shoulder. He went around behind the Winnebago, slipped on his helmet, unlocked his steering,
pushed the Triumph silently across a patch of grass, and
pointed it down the hill. Out of sight and out of earshot,
he disengaged the clutch, sparking the engine to life with
no electrical whine and barely a puff of exhaust.

Gant stood frozen on the observation platform, thinking that damn it, he knew what it was to feel trapped!
He knew what it was to want to change your life, to
throw back the cards you'd been dealt and reach for new
ones. He remembered more than clearly his foster father's middle-class grind, the life of the cold-call sales-
man, door after door shut in his face. He remembered
riding with the old man sometimes, in his red, second-
hand Buick, and seeing him come back to the car with
tears in his eyes that might have been from rage and
might have been from frustration.

He remembered his third foster mother's tears too, quiet tears of housewifely servitude, of dreams cracked and broken. He remembered the way she miserably took refuge in the TV shows of the mid-sixties, living vicariously through episodes of *Hawaii Five-O, Bewitched, Mary Tyler Moore* because the man in her life beat her and the child welfare bureau didn't know. He remembered joining the army just to get the hell out of their house.

He would have been better off robbing a bank.

Why hadn't he said *that* to Umberto instead of calling him a murderer? Why hadn't he admitted that he'd killed a hell of a lot of people at war, most of them innocent, and he'd done it on purpose? Who was he to judge the boy's soul?

He had to tell him! He had to make it clear! He shot down the stairs, taking them two at a time, and burst out into the sunlight.

He ran to his bike, wanting to chase Umberto and fix things up.

Instead, he felt the cold barrel of an automatic pistol at the back of his head.

———

Without Gant, Umberto finds that everything has changed. Sights and sounds and smells that had been natural and exciting suddenly seem foreign and cold and wrong. He isn't prepared to cross the bridge to Washington State, which he associates with Gant's future, not his own, and with the end of the line. He figures maybe he should turn inland, head for Idaho and Wyoming, or maybe up to Montana. The whole United States seems suddenly to have shrunken down to map size. He feels confined, panicky, trapped.

He heads back down the coast, on the ocean side of the road now, and scouts for chicks on the beach. It's not Miami, and the girls aren't topless, but he spies a likely prospect lying alone on a towel, faceup, browning on the sand. She has long legs, muscled and tan, and wears a black bikini with the top strap undone. A paperback covers her face, and as he gets closer, shuffling through the sand, he sees that it's a romance novel, the cover showing a man, obviously rich, in profile, along with half a private airplane, a big diamond ring, the grille of a Jaguar, next to a blonde with a tear in her eye.

Umberto sits down silently in the sand beside her, avoiding a pile of kelp, shooing away the sand flies, looking alternately at the flight of pelicans and the mad rushes of sandpipers and the drops of sweat glistening on the back of the girl's thighs. Out beyond the surfline, an otter cracks an oyster on its chest and surfs the swell while eating.

He reaches out and touches the girl's arm.

Check out the animal, he says.

The girl slowly lifts her head, the book falls into the sand, and Umberto gasps. The skin on her face is stretched flat, a sheet of burns. Her eyelids are puffy with scar tissue on one side, both her brows are gone completely, her chin is a mass of stitch lines.

He jumps up.

The girl smiles, showing perfect teeth, but it's a horrible, twisted sight.

Coño, Umberto gasps.

The otters swim out there all the time, the girl tells him, thinking how handsome he is, and how much she loves otters, and how much she wants him to stay, how she'll do anything if he'll sit down again and talk with her, but how she knows he'll run. They all run.

Umberto's heart races. He feels terrible for her, but he can't handle this.

My bike, he mumbles. I jes' have to get something. . . .

He starts up the sand toward the road, but when he gets about ten feet away, he stops and turns to look at her. She's arched up to watch him, and her bikini top has fallen, revealing lovely breasts. He can see the desperate hurt in the one eye that still works like it should. He digs into his bag, wraps his fingers around a stack of bills and takes a step toward her.

She feels a surge of hope.

He tosses the money her way.

Here, he says hoarsely. Use it for surgery or something, huh? Money can change your life.

Then he's on his bike so fast he doesn't remember how he got there. The straps to his helmet flap in the breeze as he madly takes off, dodging cars and bicycles and pedestrians and trucks, until he reaches Columbia Beach, where he pulls over beside a coffee shop and takes his helmet off and puts his head into his hands and begins to cry.

He cries so long his face swells up, so hard his ribs hurt, so hard a waitresses from the coffee shop emerges to see what's wrong.

What's the matter, hon?

Umberto shakes his head. She wants to hug him. He looks to be the same age as her son, who works in a service station over in Salem and goes to school at night, studying to be an accountant.

The owner, an overweight, mustached Italian dressed in chef's white, comes out too.

Whaddyou got to be so sad for? he asks, stroking down evenly on both sides of his mustache and glancing at the tags. You young, you handsome, you got a beautiful motorcycle. You come all the way from Florida! You should feel lucky to take a vacation like that. Maybe you hungry? We make you a good omelette. Real feta cheese. Spinach. Mushrooms. Maybe you like a burger? I make you a big burger. No charge, okay? Just don't stay here crying. You driving customers away.

Ju got a pay phone? asks Umberto.

Around the back, the waitress tells him. Call and tell her you love her, whoever she is.

He runs around to the side of the restaurant. He punches Graciela's number into the phone, feeds quarters in until there are no more. It's Saturday. It's afternoon. He knows she's probably out shopping, but goddamnit he hopes she's not. He has to speak to her.

He *needs* to speak to her.

Hello?

One word from her and he is transported. He closes his eyes. His feet barely touch the ground. The way he's breathing, he's afraid for a minute she'll hang up before he can get a word out.

It's Umberto, he says.

The voice doesn't sound like his. Not to him, and not to her. It's changed somehow in the days since last they've spoken. It wavers where before it was steady. It sounds small where before it was big. And yet, somehow, he sounds more mature, because he speaks with the cadence of the road.

I'm pregnant, she says. I'm going to have your baby.

The receiver falls from his hands. He can see the ocean from here. The sand, the surf, the little bobbing heads of kelp. He stares at the line between sea and sky, between light and dark, and for a moment he is certain that the horizon has flipped over, just simply reversed, so that the ocean is on top of everything, and the sky is at his feet. He picks the phone up.

Que?

I'm pregnant. *Embarazada.* Maybe eight weeks.

Eight weeks, he repeats.

When are you coming home?

It's not so easy right now.

Do you miss me?

Yes.

I know what you did, Umberto. I know everything.

You don't know everything. You don't know what's inside me.

But I do. I understand how you wanted to be free. But now, I need you to surrender. For me. For our baby. I don't want to raise a child alone. I don't want to be a single mother. I have dreams, too.

You want to be in movies, he says faintly.

And what's wrong with that?

I saw you on the television. You were so beautiful.

Umberto?

I'm here.

Do you love me? I mean, really love me?

He's quiet a long time.

You weren't sure when you left, were you? she presses.

No.

And now?

Now I'm sure. I want to be with you so bad I can't stand to see another moon come up without you.

And it's not just because you're lonely?

You don't know. All I do is talk about you, Graciela.

To your friend Gant?

To Gant. He winces. Yes.

Then listen to him and give up, okay? For all of us. For the baby. This FBI man says they'll chase you and they'll kill you because of the senator. He doesn't want to see that happen. He wants to help you. I don't know why, but I think I trust him.

Everybody says I'm going to die.

Don't you dare! What will I tell our child? Your papa was a bank robber and he was too stubborn to turn himself in so they shot him dead?

This hurts Umberto so much he makes his decision then and there.

I'm in Columbia Beach.

Where is that?

Oregon.

Oregon! You rode that far?

I rode like the wind, Graciela. I flew. I'm on the coast, almost as far north as Washington. Come get me, okay? With the cop that you trust? I'm looking at a place called the Sandpiper Motel. I'm going to get a room there.

There's a long pause.

Umberto?

Yeah?

I love you too.

Smiling, the boy hangs up the phone. He rides his bike across the street. The manager who doesn't like bikers, tells him they have no rooms but is persuaded otherwise by a hundred-dollar bill.

Umberto turns on the TV and waits.

TWENTY

❧

What's this all about? Gant demanded, staring at the cop across the little metal table. Had they tied him to the bank robbery? Did they have him confused with the boy, or did they peg him for an accomplice, for having been in on the deed?

I think you know, the cop answered placidly.

I have no idea.

I kinda figured you'd say that. You better hope that she's alive, that's all I can say to you, 'cause if you've killed her, you're going to find yourself experiencing a new kind of Oregon hospitality.

Killed her? Wasn't the senator already dead? Had the newspapers run a false story in hopes of bringing the boy in? Was there some kind of conspiracy here?

What makes you think *I* killed her? Gant ventured. What makes you think I was even there when it happened?

If you did anything *else* to that little girl, the cop declared, ignoring the question, well then, I can't be responsible for your safety. No sir. I don't think anybody can.

Little girl?

I want a lawyer, said Gant.

There's a man coming down from up north to see you.

Save your wish list for him, 'cause frankly, I don't give a shit.

Outside, the sun gradually bowed out of the sky.

⋘◈⋙

The moon is full, but inside the *Merryweather* darkness is in absolute control. Hiram Bishop's ghost paces the decks, agitated beyond measure, the kelp strands that attend him barely able to cling on in the face of his fervor.

My God, she's going to die!

There arises in him a love which is just too much to bear. This just isn't right! How can there be a universe like this, devoid of checks and balances? Where is God? Why am I stuck here in this unspeakable limbo, fading in and out of woodwork, striding over cracking decks, too insubstantial and too inconsequential to even hold my own granddaughter, to even calm her quivering, stop her spasms, massage her cramps.

It's lack of water, that's what it is. Here, on a boat, on the Olympic Peninsula, one of the wettest regions on Earth, little Audrey is dying of dehydration. The irony doesn't escape Hiram, and as he watches her expand and contract like a tin roof in a sunshower, a scream of rage rises up in him, and with it comes an epiphany. He's in limbo in death because he created limbo in life, by the quiet, self-absorbed working of wood and designing of boats, the solitary way he slid off to fish on cold waters, alone with his nets and his thermos and the sights he saw and the raw feel of work. Not selfish, but self-absorbed. Like a dawn rising, he begins to understand, but right then Audrey takes a long, deep breath.

He cannot know that she has sighed with pleasure at the view she has from her balloon. She's up there, clinically delirious, floating in silence, free as a cloud, with all the world spread beneath below for her to see. There are giraffes and there are hippos where she is, and there are happy people dancing. There are whales, and there are dolphins too, turning their beady eyes skyward and slapping the sea with their tails as the shadow of her great vessel passes over. Audrey waves to them, of course, and they acknowledge her with gambols that make the patterns of Bach Brandenburgs on the water. She sees plenty, even though she has never registered the play of light as it can gloriously be, the finest hues of the rainbow or the diffuse suggestiveness of dusk, when moods are longest and anticipation most sweet.

She floats over a countryside that might be England, and the smell of castles rises up. This is a smell of mustiness, the same smell she has longed for since her Grandmother Ruth took her to Port Townsend's own castle, called Manresa, a residence constructed by a local tycoon for his queen. Why does she crave musty smells? Is it because Vivaldi's luscious Four Seasons were playing on the castle's stereo, and she loves the playful lilt of Vivaldi, which also makes her think of dolls?

She can see lakes below her, full of the only dinosaurs that survived the dust cloud of the great comet that was thought to have killed everything but mammals. These are hidden giants with bodies so big they could stay warm until the sun reappeared, hiding in the bottom of deep lakes like the one under her balloon, where hot water bubbles up from springs superheated by the liquid, bubbling molten center of the earth.

Beethoven's Pastorale!

She sees a long head with smiling eyes and a row of sharp little teeth.

Little teeth like her mother had.

Suddenly, she is looking up from Caroline's legs, having just emerged from that moist portal, uncomprehending, cold, frightened. Everything is so bright. Her mother isn't smiling. She appears exhausted.

Something crosses her face.

Goddamn you, Gant, Caroline says, and then her hand comes down, fast and hard, and there aboard the *Merryweather*, Audrey cries out loud, shedding tears and sweat beads she can ill afford, so dehydrated has her body become.

Hiram sees something different. Not the vision in Audrey's head but the wraith walking toward them. Caroline! How can she possibly have traveled all the way from the death chamber, how she can be free when he is so confined? Could it be she doesn't know her own fate?

You can't have her, Caroline, Hiram says slowly. She ignores him and gets closer to Audrey, drawn by the little girl's suffering and her closeness to death.

Hiram floats between them.

You can't harm her now, and you can't have her after she dies. Not again. Not ever. She's mine. I will always protect her.

Caroline raises a hand to her father and slaps him. Amazingly, Hiram's cheek stings.

He contemplates her for a moment, his outrage growing, the tedium and the frustration and the great sadness of having been in limbo so long bubbling up within him as death is bubbling up within his granddaughter.

You don't get it, do you? he says incredulously.

I get plenty, says Caroline. I get more than you'll ever get.

You poor, stupid, evil girl. Hiram shakes his head.

Get out of my way.

I'm not leaving. You are. Do you know why? Because you're in hell.

Caroline blinks. She feels a sharp pain down low.

What?

You can't be here, Hiram whispers. *You can't be here, because you're in hell.*

Mercifully, Audrey cannot see Caroline's beautiful eyes grow wide. Nor can she see Caroline's teeth start to fall out, see her flesh strip off, see the fire start.

Between her breasts.

Burning inward.

And upward.

Hiram covers his ears. He is, after all, her father, no matter what Caroline has become, and he can't bear to hear her screams. This goes on for a time, until all that is left is a wisp of Caroline's hair, which falls to the floor and becomes more and more insubstantial until it is no more than a dust mote burning a tiny hole in *Merryweather*'s plank.

To comfort himself, Hiram hugs Audrey tight.

There's so little left of the girl, he doubts she'll last the night.

————

You really better tell me where he is, Eagle Cooper insists. He's been patient, but he's in no mood for this game. He wants the collar, that's for sure, but he was ripped right out of Suzanne's sweet arms by Graciela's call, and he hasn't been too happy since.

The teenage girl shifts in her seat, clutching the armrests as the airplane hits a bump. They're over the Rockies. The sky is angry at the mountains' intrusion, still sore after all these years.

I'll tell you when we get there.

Cooper takes a deep breath. It's not Bureau policy to bring civilians along. If Nancy Fortier knew what was going on here, she'd have his job.

Is he in Portland?

Graciela shakes her head.

We're going to need a car then, right? In the middle of the night?

It's a big airport, she defends. We'll find something. You're a Fed. Deal with it.

He sighs and pushes his seat back, hard. The guy behind him keeps nudging him slowly forward with the pressure of his knees, as if he won't notice if it happens slowly. One more time and he's going to take out his piece and drill the bastard behind the ear.

Tell me about Umberto.

What do you want to know?

For starters, how he got lucky enough to find a girl like you?

This brings a small smile.

Umberto has always been a somebody, she answers. He had everything mapped out. He was going places.

Yeah. Straight to the penitentiary, Cooper thinks, suddenly hit by the full weight of this tragedy, suddenly envisioning this beautiful young woman twenty years down the line, no longer young but still determined, still faithful, stubbornly waiting, all alone, for Umberto Santana to get out of jail.

What was it like to be with him?

He's not dead! she flares. Don't talk about him in the past tense.

Sorry. How does he treat you?

Gently. She sighs. With romance and roses.

So how come he took off on you?

She shrugs.

This robbery, this mad ride across country, I know why he did it. It was his way of breaking out. He didn't want a life like his father has. He didn't want to join a gang and end up dead on some street corner. He couldn't afford to go to school, he isn't that much of a school person anyway, and he didn't want to work in a motorcycle shop forever either.

It was dumb, says Cooper.

It was desperate.

Together, as if on cue, they look out the window at the moon, which is huge, due to a peculiar refraction of light rays. Bigger than the jet engines, bigger than the wing. The way it looks, the avionics should be sounding a collision alarm about now.

He's a planner, Graciela continues, half to herself, half to Cooper. He thinks everything through, never doing anything chancy. He wouldn't buy lottery tickets, do you know that? He got mad at me for doing it. Told me I was wasting my money. Told me the odds were stacked too much against winning.

I guess he thought his odds were better.

You haven't caught him yet, have you? She smiles. And that woman who died, that was a freak thing, right? And it was doubly freak that she would be a senator, and that heavy-duty cops like you would get involved.

Look how she loves him! whispers Cooper's homunculus.

The little voice surprises him. It's been quiet for a while. Maybe because he's been doing everything right.

A flight attendant appears.

Extra spicy Virgin Mary, she says, handing the plastic cup over to Cooper.

She kneels down in the aisle next to Graciela.

I know you from somewhere. You're a model, right? Or an actress?

She cannot know how right she is. She cannot know that in just ten months Graciela will take a screen test and get a job working as an anchor for CNN, because the news producer who came into McDonald's will help her, not because he wants to sleep with her, although he wouldn't mind that either, but because he is a person who genuinely likes to help people.

You might have seen me on TV, Graciela admits, smiling. She's trying to sound ordinary and modest, like she gets this kind of thing all the time, but she doubts she's doing much of a job, the way she feels her face go flush.

That's so great, the flight attendant says. I want to do something like that sometime. And you're so young! Listen—she drops her voice confidentially—how about something to drink on me? Rum and coke, maybe? Or I could mix you a piña colada. They're canned, but they're pretty good.

No thanks. Graciela shakes her head.

You sure? We've still got a way to go. Might help you sleep.

I want to stay fresh, she says. I want to stay clear.

She doesn't talk about not wanting to poison her baby, she just orders a Mountain Dew. At that moment, Cooper knows she's pregnant, but he doesn't let on.

So where is Umberto? he pursues.

The Oregon coast. In a small town. He's waiting for us. What more do you need to know?

Waiting, huh? Cooper muses, his hand edging unconsciously toward his holster. He's filled out the FAA form. The captain knows he's armed. The crew knows where he's sitting. It was that or make a big show of taking his piece out and sticking it into his luggage right there at the check-in counter, something he doubts would have gone over well with the girl.

If you kill him, I kill you, Graciela says fiercely. Are we clear?

Cooper nods sadly and looks away, out the window, wondering how the world has come to be such a place that conversations like this can happen with such an innocent, pulsing, luminous moon as witness.

I'm not going to kill him. I'm going to help him. He has a raw deal waiting and I'm going to make sure it comes out differently than Rule expects.

Rule? The senator who died?

Her husband.

He wants Umberto dead, doesn't he?

He's not going to get Umberto dead. I'm going to make sure he just gets a few years. He's underage. That still has to count for something.

But Mr. Rule is rich.

Yes, and he is going to try to get the death penalty, Cooper answered, having no idea that after Stephan was successfully treated for post-traumatic stress disorder at a Miami hospital, Rule would donate an asthma research wing in his wife's name. But it won't work. There was no premeditation, Umberto is a first offender, and in fact never even knew the senator was present, much less ill. In the end, his anger will fade and he will use his money to establish an asthma foundation in his wife's name.

How do you know this? Graciela wants to know.

I know it because I have met Mr. Rule and I know that more than anything he wants to be a hero to his son.

Who do *you* want to be a hero to?

Cooper supposes the answer is Suzanne, which stuns him, because he's never had anyone to be a hero to before.

Nobody, he lies. I'm just helping because if I don't, nobody else will.

———

All night long, Umberto keeps the TV lit. He drinks two six-packs of beer, expensive stuff, the most expensive he could find, brewed by Trappist monks and sealed in bottles so huge a rich person's koi fish could live in one. He keeps two bottles open at all times, one in each hand, so that even in the mundane act of stupefying himself, his last willful act as a free man, he can feel opulent.

He can live large.

Gunsmoke is on the television. Old black-and-white scenes of an arid, unkind West. Stilted dialogue.

Reckon' I'll have to shoot you, then.

A criminal on the run. A killer.

A marshal on his trail.

Umberto keeps the windows open and the air conditioner off. A sea wind blows in, battering the curtain the way waves can batter a ship, making them flutter and snap, bringing him the sounds of people outside, coming and going, the hiss of tires on the coast highway, and, more distantly, the pounding of the surf. The drunker he gets, the less keenly he feels fear at every wash of headlights in the motel driveway. The drunker he gets, the more jumbled his thoughts become, his mind flitting from one to the other like a butterfly.

He thinks of his mother.

How is he going to face her?

Ha? The questions should be, How is she going to face him?

The senator had a little boy.

His mother is dead, but at least she isn't a whore.

On the television, the fugitive runs desperately through the bush. The marshal chases him, aloof and powerful, on horseback.

Like a god.

Umberto can't even watch. He turns away and thinks about his father. Will he be ashamed or proud?Umberto knows Pedro tried the gangland lifestyle. He knows his old man wasn't even been able to pull *that* off.

But Umberto has. Pulled it off and ran. Clean across the country. Had the ride of his life.

How about those twisties in Mississippi? How about blazing across the desert at speed? How about that tornado? He flew, goddamnit. He flew without wings! He found a cure for gravity! Those were some times he had with Gant. The champagne in New Mexico, the trucker, the fortune-teller, the ghosts.

Before this ride he didn't even know if there were ghosts.

He wonders if he is going to have to face the senator's little boy in court. A dim memory of the boy's face floats by like a cloud, and Umberto reaches out and holds on to it for a moment. He wonders whether the kid will be able to understand that Umberto hadn't meant to hurt anybody, that he hadn't known the senator had asthma, or that the sight of an empty gun would make her gasp to death.

He turns his head into the yellow chenille bedspread, and the little cotton berries press into his cheek as he cries.

Graciela!

How could he have left her?

He thinks of her beautiful face, her thick black hair, her smooth legs, her small nipples, her fingers, her lips.

She is the mother of his baby.

His child! It is going to be a boy, and he is going to name it Mercury. He doesn't know where this information comes from, but he trusts it.

Shots ring out. Umberto jerks upward in the bed.

On horseback, with eyes of steel, the TV marshal stares down at the groveling fugitive, who is dressed in rags, who has a hole in his chest, whose blood runs out onto the desert sand, whose life ebbs away.

He is going to be a father, and he is going to go to jail.

He suffers through a private vision of hell, of him reaching through the bars, taking a little child's hand in his, telling the kid things will be okay. Telling the kid he loves him.

His eyes pour salt water, and the motel bed takes it all.

TWENTY-ONE

❧

Despite her best efforts, Graciela has fallen asleep in the
front seat of the car they had to wait four hours to rent.
They are westbound, on Route 26, in the middle of the
Tillamook State Forest, and it is nearly dawn. She is in
the middle of dream sex with Umberto, feeling his head
between her hands, the weight of it, the texture of his
hair, when she is awakened by the sound of laughter.
She blinks and wipes her eyes, taking a moment to remember where she is.

Cooper is howling with laughter. He is hitting the
steering wheel, he's having such a good time.

What's so funny? Graciela demands, figuring maybe
it's the six cups of coffee he drank at the airport.

Breathe deep. He giggles.

She does, and smells sweet smoke.

Pot? she asks, still half asleep.

You got it, he laughs. We're driving through a marijuana fire.

Cooper cannot know the consternation this fire is
causing a local grower, who has hidden his crop in the
middle of the state forest and who has started the con-
flagration himself, by dropping a joint while making a
nighttime inspection of his secret enterprise. The smoke

cloud has turned the moonlit Oregon sky chocolate brown.

Cooper tries to control himself, but the ridiculousness of it overcomes him and he bursts out laughing again. Graciela, who hasn't really laughed since Umberto disappeared, begins to snicker too, and pretty soon the two of them are cackling together on the night road to the coast.

Umberto snores not far away, the motel TV shedding snow.

Route 26 ends just north of Cannon Beach, and they turn north. It's still dark, but there is a trickle of light to the east. The laughing has become an embarrassed silence. The game is over, the hunt is done, they are about to find the boy. Graciela prays he doesn't have a gun. Cooper does too. He can't imagine he would shoot very well in this light, with traces of marijuana still wafting about in his brain. The only thing worse than having to take aim at the boy would be getting shot himself, all alone up here, so far from home, without backup, in the company of a teenage girl.

When finally they spot the Sandpiper Motel, Graciela identifies Umberto's motorcycle, that big, black, cruise missile of a Triumph, parked right in front of room 14.

What about this fellow Gant? Cooper asks quietly.

What about him?

Do you think he's in the room too?

Umberto didn't mention anything about that.

Cooper is thinking that maybe this shadowy figure, this Gant, has masterminded the whole thing. He's thinking maybe this is some kind of a trap. He's suddenly very nervous. He suspects everyone. He is, after all, a policeman.

I'm going in, Graciela declares.

No way. Cooper shakes his head.

But that was our deal, Graciela protests. I lead you to him, you let me go in first and bring him out.

Not a chance, repeats Cooper. He's thinking double

cross. He's thinking hostage situation. He's thinking of an incredulous, furious look on Special Agent in Charge Nancy Fortier's face.

Umberto!

Graciela screams, warning the boy.

Hey! Cooper cries. Be quiet!

Inside, through a fog of misery and booze, Umberto claws his way to consciousness. The bag of money is on the floor, across the room. He stands up, cocks an ear, coughs once, tries to still his swirling head.

Outside, Graciela kicks off her shoes.

For an instant, Cooper has the absurd thought that she's much smaller than he thought, and then she's running, bolting like a deer, covering the parking lot in graceful strides—those powerful thighs!—and bounding up the steps to Umberto's room.

Open the door! she commands.

The door swings open, and she is in his arms. She doesn't care that the room looks like a hurricane hit it— little does she know about the boy and spirals of wind— and she doesn't care that he is unshaven, hung over, and reeking of beer.

Wow, he says, taking her into his arms. Ju really came.

She holds him to her like he's her own beating heart, like if she lets him slip for one tiny contraction, life as she knows it will end. He inhales her, takes in the ozone of the airplane, the puzzling smell of marijuana in her hair, her smooth dark skin, her tidy skirt. He drops to his knees in the holding, putting his mouth to her belly, down low, where his seed has taken root, and he kisses her there, over and over and over again.

You're so stupid, she whispers in his ear.

Ju are so beautiful, he whispers back.

Your gun was a fake one, tell me it was.

It was real but it was empty. I'd never shoot anybody, he murmurs. I didn't mean for anyone to die.

This is how Cooper finds them when he bursts in,

Glock at the ready. They don't even notice him. They don't care about nine-millimeter bullets and badges and cuffs. Cooper himself is transfixed. Love can do that. Even to a cop. His homunculus breaks in.

Put the gun down, you idiot. He's not going anywhere.

Umberto rises to his feet. Cooper makes a quick search for a weapon. The boy is naked, so there's no worry there. He kicks the bedsheets aside, checks the drawers, then the money bag. The sight of all that cash dries his mouth.

Time to get dressed, he says. He hovers, ready for anything, while the boy slips into his underwear, his socks, trousers and shoes. Graciela buttons his shirt for him, a white oxford, formal for this time of year, formal for this hour of the morning. Cooper clicks the cuffs on, and Umberto looks at him for the first time. There's so much in those eyes, the cop finds he has to look away.

I got the right to remain silent, right? 'Cause ju will use shit against me in a court of law?

Right, Cooper affirms.

Thanks for not shooting me, *meng*.

Thanks for not shooting *me*.

See how easy? coos Cooper's homunculus.

So I'm going to prison, right?

You'll do time, says Cooper, but you'll behave yourself and you'll get out quickly enough to raise your son.

Graciela rocks back like Cooper has hit her.

Ju told him? Umberto asks.

She shakes her head.

Right then, Cooper knows that he is going to marry Suzanne. He has a vision of their wedding, of making love to her in the back of that old Rolls-Royce, both of them still in their wedding clothes, before they can even make it to the hotel. He smiles as he picks up the telephone and calls the local police. He identifies himself clearly and speaks like a king. In the moments before the sirens shatter the dawn, Graciela dropkicks the money bag, over and over again, as if it were a rat in her kitchen. When she's too exhausted to continue, Cooper hangs his badge from his breast pocket for all to see, takes Umberto by the elbow and Graciela by the hand, and goes outside.

Gentlemen, says Cooper, when the cops pull in. Thank you for coming.

I had one hell of a ride, Umberto says as they hustle him off. Ju wouldn't believe the shit I saw.

He's still so young he thinks the cops care.

What about Gant? Graciela calls after him, thinking that the man needs thanking.

He was my friend, Umberto calls back.

Gant, echoes one of the cops, pricking up his ears. Did you say Gant?

TWENTY-TWO

❧

At the police station, as clean and white and antiseptic a building as existed in the field of law enforcement, Special Agent Eagle Cooper informed his office of the bust and made arrangements for the transfer of the prisoner back to Miami. Graciela sat quietly in a corner, feeling colder and colder and more alone, while Umberto was fingerprinted and his personal effects put in a little wire bin. The money was taken from the motorcycle bag, counted by a team of men—to reduce temptation—and laid out on a conference table. A total of $18,000 was found missing.

It's time to talk, Cooper told Umberto. I need details.

Not yet, the boy replied. There's something I need from ju first.

Cooper took a deep breath. The kid should be thanking him. The kid should be bending over backward to help.

Yeah? What?

Get these cops to free Mercury Gant. He didn't do nothin'.

He's being held on charges of kidnapping and murder, Cooper replied.

Ten days ago. Yeah, I heard. It's bullshit. He was with me. We rode across country together.

He didn't mention riding with anyone, broke in the cop who had arrested Gant.

He wouldn't, you get that? He's not a mentioning kind of guy. But I got motel receipts, *meng*.

You keep receipts? the cop asked dubiously.

I taught him to do that, Graciela piped up. In case he had to take something back. A lot of times he changes his mind about shoes.

Another cop brought Umberto's wallet out of the property locker and Cooper went through it right there. A few minutes later they faxed a photo of Gant to the swank hotel in Santa Fe where Umberto claimed they were staying right about the time Audrey Bishop disappeared. The manager said he clearly remembered the pair checking in. On motorcycles.

All right, said Cooper, as the cop went for Gant, now let's talk about Vicky Rule.

I'm sorry about her, Umberto said right away.

Did you see her?

Yeah. I saw her. I didn't know she was dying, though. I thought she was just mad at her kid.

Don't talk to him, Umberto, Gant boomed, walking in.

He looked older. There were lines under his eyes and he hadn't shaved at all.

Ju don't look so good, *meng*.

I didn't shave, he said. Something different every day, remember?

Then shave tomorrow, okay?

Gant gripped the boy's hand in two of his own.

Okay.

It's good to see ju, *meng*.

It's good to see you too. And listen. I've got something to tell you.

Ju always got something to tell me.

Gant smiled at that, feeling the same tears brimming in his eyes that he saw in the boy's.

Yeah, well listen to me this time. This thing you did,

the bank and all? It was wrong and it was bad. But I gotta tell you, it wasn't half so bad as going to war. It wasn't half so bad as things I did in uniform, even if that poor lady did die. I just wanted you to know that.

Umberto nodded, turning to hide his face. When he turned back, he was smiling.

I'm gonna be a dad. Ju believe that shit?

I believe it, said Gant. I always believe wonderful news. There's too little of it in this world.

It's a boy, said Umberto.

How do you know that? Graciela broke in.

I just know. And Mercury? I'm gonna name him after ju.

Aw, don't do that to the poor kid.

Are you kidding? Mercury's the greatest name I know.

They all stood looking at each other, in silence, until Eagle Cooper cleared his throat.

Take care of him, Gant said, kissing Graciela's cheek.

I hope you find your daughter, she said.

Me too, added Umberto. So take my bike, okay? I won't be needing it for a while, and it's twice as fast as that shitheap ju riding. Take it and don't argue for once, okay, *meng*? For saving my life? For helping me fly without wings?

Gant looked at Umberto Santana one last time, then gave him a quick hug.

You and me, he whispered into the boy's ear, we're really the same.

TWENTY-THREE

❦

He rides north on the Triumph, across the Astoria Bridge, in the heat of the day. The time for smoke and fog has passed, and the sun is impossibly strong. Seeing the Columbia River shimmer like glass, Gant remembers Caroline standing naked beside the statue of the winged messenger in her crystal gallery, the reclining mermaid looking on. As he rides into Knappton, Washington, his heart becomes positively poisoned with worry. What has become of his little girl? How could she have gone missing before he even had a chance to see her?

This desperation is new to him, containing a power previously reserved only for issues of his financial future and nightmares of the elderly destitution he might face, alone, if his various business ventures had failed. He knows instinctively that this new vulnerability is a banner of the new Gant. He has been transformed, through the course of his life, from orphan to adolescent to soldier to loner, and now, through the fire of a cross-country trek, to caretaker. It is a transition that feels right to him, but one which burdens him with dread for Audrey.

He powers up through South Bend and Cosmopolis, and at Aberdeen, at the tail of Gray's Harbor, he turns east toward Puget Sound. He has lived five years without Audrey. How would he have lived differently if he had known she was alive? What risks would he have skipped? What responsibilities might he have assumed? What choices would he have made differently?

Goddamnit, how much of Caroline might there be in his daughter?

Speaking of Caroline, how come her ghost hasn't shown up again?

He picks up U.S. 101 just west of Olympia and hurries past Lilliwaup, Eldon, and, later, Quilcene. He can't believe how strong Umberto's bike is, how smoothly and effortlessly it devours the tarmac and blurs the trees into walls of green. In his mind's eye, he can see the headlight as he saw it, day after day, in the desert, in the mountains, in the rain and fog and even in the air, through the sideview mirrors of his trusty old BMW. He can even see Umberto's tall form bent over the handlebars, his aerodynamic helmet cutting through the wind.

Yet the views he's being treated to are too compelling for him to dwell on the past for long. This is God's country, just as surely as Gant's right hand is the one on the throttle, and the farther north he goes, the more pristine and sparsely settled it becomes. At Discovery Bay, where Audrey touched the whale, he makes a slight jog eastward and heads up the Chimacum road straight into Port Townsend. Victorian mansions of early sea captains and madams line the promenade, and small craft made of wood ply Admiralty Inlet, right off Water Street, in the heart of town.

He parks in front of the sign he's been looking for—the sign that says Bishop's Shoes.

———

This fellow Gant is not our man, Sam Patch tells Ruth reluctantly. He was in the Southwest the day Audrey disappeared.

I've been thinking about that. The whole thing didn't really make sense. He's her father, after all. He only had to ask for her.

It's not good news, Ruth, Sam continues. He was our only lead.

Ruth begins to cry.

I'm never going to see her again, am I, Sam?

Sam doesn't know what to say. This is why he prefers to clean his pistols. This is why he loves the clear, emotionless world of the bull's-eye and the barrel. He can't lie to her. It's been over a week. The chances of finding Audrey have dwindled past unlikely to frankly slim, and there's not a damn thing he can do about it.

She's in the FBI missing child directory now. We just have to wait.

The string of brass bells from India tinkles as the front door opens and a handsome man, a fit man, a man with silver eyes, steps in. Sam surveys him. There is a soldier there, although middle age is creeping in. There's an erectness of bearing, but it's tempered by compassion and gentility.

They stare at each other, Gant and Ruth do. She recognizes Audrey's silver eyes, and he recognizes Caroline's hazel ones. Suddenly, despite his odd coat, he vaults straight over the counter like a gymnast, and right there, amid the Birkenstocks, rain boots, Docksiders and espadrilles, takes Ruth in his arms.

Mercury! She breathes, moving her hands all over his back as if she'll find some answer there.

He strokes her gray hair, which in recent days has turned whiter. She cries and she gasps.

Sam backs uncomfortably out of the store.

A mile and a half down the road, the ghost of Hiram Bishop feels a shock of electricity go through him.

Is there any news of her? Gant asks.

That's the first thing he says. Before he even says hello.

None. Ruth sniffles. The police say things don't look good.

Take me to where you last saw her.

Now?

Yes. Right away.

His intensity commands her.

She locks up the store.

She drives him down the road.

She pulls up in front of the supermarket.

Gant gets out. He smells the sour cloud from the mill. Funny. He hadn't noticed it before. The wind must have shifted. He looks across the street.

What's that? he asks, pointing.

Just a commercial marina.

She's in there, he says.

He doesn't know how he knows, but he does. Some old voice is telling him. It is hoarse and it is tired and it is faint, but he can hear it.

Don't be silly, says Ruth. She couldn't have gotten across the street. Look at the traffic.

She's in there, he insists.

But she couldn't have crossed the street.

Somehow, she did.

But folks looked there.

They didn't look hard enough, says Gant.

He heads toward the dry docks.

Keep going, says Hiram, whose voice is getting stronger as Gant closes in.

He shivers as he enters the marina. There are men working around the place, wheeling a sailboat in on a rolling frame. They pay no attention to him. They are concentrating on the path of the tow tractor.

Mercury? Ruth calls. Where are you going?

Just a little bit farther

Gant reaches the *Merryweather*. He stands looking at the remains of the old boat, stunned by the perfect angle of the smokestacks, amazed at all the finish work just above the waterline, where the teak of the deck meets the planking. And the portholes! Who would have thought of a shape like that?

How beautiful, he murmurs. He suddenly has a vision, a vision he will one day fulfill, of bringing this boat back to her former glory, of making a living up here on this beautiful peninsula, taking photographers out, and whale watchers and fisherman and lovers. Just Gant and his gorgeous old boat, cruising.

With his daughter.

Board her, says the voice.

Gant scales the ladder. Things are pretty decrepit up top. There are holes in the decking, and the door to the grand cabin creaks back and forth on its hinges.

Hooooooooop.

Haaaaaaaaa.

Mercury? What are you doing up there? Ruth calls from down below.

Come inside.

Gant makes his way into the salon.

Farther, urges Hiram. *Find the galley.*

The first piece of Audrey that Mercury sees is a pale white hand. It droops off the bench so limp and lifeless that Gant feels a stab in his heart. He rushes to her. Hiram moves aside, not because he has to but out of respect. Gant scoops her up in his arms. She's exquisite. A little doll with a scarecrow body and Caroline's beautiful face.

Audrey, Gant whispers.

Hmmm. She stretches.

She's alive! Gant's heart leaps like a marlin. He sees how parched she is, and how shrunken. He presses his lips to her brow.

Wake up, honey. Daddy's here.

Her eyelids flutter, then open, and she stares at him.

You have my eyes, she says.

Hiram's ghost feels his chains of kelp drop away. As he begins to float upward, he gazes down and blows Ruth a kiss.